ANNA LOMBARD

ANNA LOMBARD

Cross, Victoria

www.General-Books.net

Publication Data:

Title: Anna Lombard
Author: Cross, Victoria
Publisher: New York : Kensington

How We Made This Book for You
We made this book exclusively for you using patented Print on Demand technology.
First we scanned the original rare book using a robot which automatically flipped and photographed each page.
We automated the typing, proof reading and design of this book using Optical Character Recognition (OCR) software on the scanned copy. That let us keep your cost as low as possible.
If a book is very old, worn and the type is faded, this can result in typos or missing text. This is also why our books don't have illustrations; the OCR software can't distinguish between an illustration and a smudge.
We understand how annoying typos, missing text or illustrations, foot notes in the text or an index that doesn't work, can be. That's why we provide a free digital copy of most books exactly as they were originally published. Simply go to our website (www.general-books.net) to check availability. And we provide a free trial membership in our book club so you can get free copies of other editions or related books.
OCR is not a perfect solution but we feel it's more important to make books available for a low price than not at all. So we warn readers on our website and in the descriptions we provide to book sellers that our books don't have illustrations and may have typos or missing text. We also provide excerpts from each book to book sellers and on our website so you can preview the quality of the book before buying it.
If you would prefer that we manually type, proof read and design your book so that it's perfect, simply contact us for the cost. We would be happy to do as much work as you would be like to pay for.

ANNA LOMBARD

DEDICATED TO

"Verona's summer hath not such a flower."

PREFACE.

r I HAVE been challenged by certain papers to state my intentions in writing " Anna Lombard." This is my reply: I endeavored to draw in Gerald Ethridge a character whose actions should be in accordance with the principle? laid down by Christ, one that would display, not in word but in his actual life, that gentleness, humility, patience, charity, and self-sacrifice that our Redeemer himself en joined. It is a sad commentary on our religion of to-day that a presumably Christian journal The Daily Chronicle should hold this Christ-like conduct up to ridicule and contempt, stigmatize it as " horrid absurdity," and declare! that for such qualities a man ought to be turned out of thei service. I challenge The Daily Chronicle and all who follow its opinion to find one act which does not reflect Christ's own teaching, committed by Gerald Ethridge. He forgives the sinner, raises the fallen, comforts the weak. He works and suffers to reclaim the pagan and al" most lost soul of Anna Lombard. Fearlessly, and with the Gospel of Christ in my hand, I offer this example ol his teaching to the great Christian public for its verdict, confident that I shall be justified by it.

VICTORIA CROSS.

ANNA LOMBAKD.

ANNA LOMBARD.

CHAPTER I.

A FLOOD of glaring yellow light fell from the chandeliers overhead, a sheen of light seemed to be flung back from the polished, slippery, glittering floor which mirrored a thousand lights above and a hundred lesser lights fixed to the walls, dazzling hi white and gold. There was so much light, so much glitter, that it seemed to hurt the eyes coming directly from the soft, dark night outside. It seemed to wound mine as I stepped through the long window open to the marble piazza where I had been sitting, silent, by a pillar, alone with the gorgeous Eastern night.

The music, too, was stirring and martial rather than soothing. It was the splendid band of the Irish Grenadiers, and just then they were playing for all they were worth. It seemed as if some one had bet them they could not make a noise, and they had bet that they could. From end to end the room was one blaze of color, the scarlet and gold of countless uniforms standing out prominently in the general scheme. There were comparatively few present in plain civilian dress and no undress uniforms were to be found, for it was an occasion such as might not be known again for two or three years, or more, in that part of the country. It was the ball given by the commissioner of Kalatu in honor of the viceroy, on the latter passing through that station.

I stood leaning against the pillar of the window by which I entered the room, watching idly the brilliant, swaying crowd before me, and wondering how much real joy, pleasure, and gayety there was in the room in proportion to the affected amount of all these.

For myself, I felt singularly mentally weary and disheartened, yet I was generally considered a much-to-be- nvied person, one of Fortune's particular favorites. I was foung not yet thirty, though sometimes, possibly the result of much severe study, my brain and inner being seemed singularly old I had, some five years before, come idut head of the list in the Indian Civil Service examination, and had been granted the coveted position of assistant commissioner; my pay was good, my position excellent, my work light, and, indeed, far beneath the capacity my severe education had endowed me with; girls smiled upon me, mammas were not unkind, and " lucky fellow that Ethridge " was a comment frequently on the lips of my companions. And yet, in spite of all this, how empty life seemed to that lucky Ethridge himself! As a boy, always given rather to dreams, speculations, and ideas, how fair that same life looked to me; in my cold, hard, chaste youth of study and work, how much there had seemed to be done in it, to be gained, to be enjoyed! When my work is done! I had so often thought, and now, behold! my work was done, and I was free to do, to have, to gain, and to enjoy, and suddenly there seemed nothing particular in it all. No such wonderful joy to be enjoyed, and no such marvelous thing to be gained. This arena, that had looked so fair and dazzling while I was still shut behind its gates, seemed rather circumscribed and empty now that I was actually inside, and I, as it were, seemed merely walking aimlessly about in it and kicking up the sand which was to have been the witness of such great achievements, according to my former vague ideas.

After a minute or two I was conscious of some one standing close beside me, and I turned slightly, to see a young lieutenant in the uniform of the Grenadiers.

"Beastly thin that girl is! Just look at her shoulder-bones!" was his first remark addressed to me without any preface.

My eyes idly followed his, and I noticed the girl passing us, rather a pretty, graceful debutante, thin with the thinness of extreme youth and immaturity. Her shoulders rose white and smooth from her white gown of conventional, one might say viceregal lowness for at balls given to the viceroy, gowns are cut lower than usual in honor of the occasion but certainly beneath their delicate surface two little bones stood out rather too prominently. I looked at them absently, thinking it was the quality of the heart that beat beneath them that would exercise and influence me most in my judgment of their owner.

"She is very young," I returned. " In a year or two she will probably be fat enough to please you."

' Thanks; then she will be passee, don't you know. Confound it, these English girls are all thin when they're young and when they're fat they're old. There's no get-ting one just made to suit a fellow."

"And what about the girls; are the men made to suit them?" I inquired, turning to look at him more fully.

He had a square, white face, with pale blue, expression-, less eyes, a weak, receding chin and forehead, a weaker mouth, and a slight lisp in his voice. In his hand he" swung an eye-glass, which he lifted only occasionally when an unusually striking girl went by. He laughed good-humoredly a fatuous, conceited laugh.

"Aw, ah I don't really know, upon my word; but they seem devilish glad to get us, don't you know, when they have a chance."

I did not answer. The conversation did not interest me; but where was I to find any better? I glanced along tho line of vacuous faces by the wall to right and left of me. What was the use of moving? I should only hear some? thing like this from the next man beside whom I should find myself.

There was a few moments' silence. Then my companion glanced suddenly at his card and affected to start witlj sudden recollection and contrition.

"By Jove! I had forgotten that poor Miss Scemler. She is waiting for me all this time. Promised her thi dance, you know d d scrawny girl, too, but then she'd be so awfully disappointed, you know. See you again," and he mingled with the line of idlers passing round the room, in his search for the doubtless tremulously eager and expectant Miss Scemlar.

Hardly a moment or two later another acquaintance came up to me. This time it was a handsome young fellow with a dark, eager face and high color.

"Well, Gerald, old man, what makes you look so awfully blue? Come and have a pick-me-up, a bitter or something is just what you want. Come along to the bar. You ought to be there, too. We're talking the race, you know. There's a fellow there has got all the tips. Now'a the time to lay your money. He says Lemon won't be in it; they say now Parchment is; but you'd better hear it from him. Come along."

I stood still by the pillar and looked at his animated face with a slight smile.

' Thanks. I don't think I'll come. I do feel rather blue to-night."

"Why," he returned, rather blankly, "I think it an awfully jolly ball. I have been having a first-rate time."

"What have you been doing?" I asked, with a faint stirring of interest. Perhaps he could show me how to have a good time too.

"I have been in the bar all the time. The champagne is going just like water. All free, you know, and good stuff too. He's a jolly old com. He doesn't do things by halves."

The interest died out again.

"Don't let me keep you. You may lose some of the valuable tips," I said. " I'll stay here. I don't care for the races or the champagne either."

"You are such a queer fellow," he replied, eyeing me askance. " What do you care for, I wonder? But you'd better come."

With that he passed on, and I was again left alone. A short, stout, elderly gentleman scudded up to me next. He was a great talker, and it was a treat for him to find some unoccupied person apparently able to listen to him.

"Good-evening, my boy. I see you're enjoying yourself with the rest of the young folks."

"Good-evening, colonel," I replied.

"I've discovered all about that Brentwood affair tonight," he went on, coming nearer to me and speaking confidentially. " It's a scandal, a shame; it's clear that Brentwood accepted a contract for the lumma road and never meant to build it, never meant to, I say; the service is rotten, rotten through and through, and if the Government don't take some steps about it well I don't claim any particular brilliance of intellect; I don't suppose my brain is more acute or my vision clearer than the ordinary man's"

Here he seemed to pause, as if he would like some interruption, and so I gratified him with a murmured:

"I don't know about that, colonel."

When he proceeded, happily:

"And, therefore, what I can see others can see. If I know these things are going on, why, others know it. Now, I am proud of my country, I am proud of"

I am afraid I lost what else furnished him with a cause of pride, for my attention wandered. Somehow I did not seem to care if the service were rotten or if Brentwood had contracted to build fifty roads and then backed out of it. My former interlocutor was right; I was queer, I suppose, since none of these vital matters interested me.

I really had an engagement for the coming dance, so when I had listened respectfully to the whole speech, and the colonel stopped to take breath for a moment, I said:

"You must excuse me, colonel; I have to look for my partner for this waltz."

"Very good, my boy, very good," he replied, genially, having at last, as he hoped, impressed some one with a sense of Brentwood's enormities. " I don't grudge you the dance or the girl. I like to see boys enjoy them." selves."

With which comforting assurance in my ears I started listlessly to find my partner.

That young lady I soon discovered sitting on afauteuil

"I thought you had forgotten our dance!" she exclaimed the moment I came up, and she looked at me with an arch expression that told me very clearly she thought such a thing would be an utter impossibility.

She was slight and round, very well-dressed, with a pretty face, frivolous expression, and a mouth that was always laughing. I assured her that the dance was what 1 had been waiting for all the evening, and we started together. She talked the whole time. She told me how the last man she danced with had held her so tightly the flowers at her breast had all been crushed and broken; wasn't he a wretch? Not but what she liked to be held tightly, she exclaimed, as, involuntarily my arm round her loosened, but not, of course, so as to crush her flowers: but they were all dead now, and it didn't matter. A hateful girl, too, had trodden on her train; they trains were a bore of course in dancing, but didn't I think they made you look more graceful yes, well, she thought so too, and was glad I thought so; and, fancy, that ugly little Miss Johnson was going to marry Captain Grant of the Eleventh, and wasn't it wonderful what he could see in her, and didn't I think she was ugly? Not know her by sight? why, of course I must know her. She sat three pews behind me and in the left aisle at church, and when the con gregation turned to the east to say the Creed I could certainly see her.

While this was being poured into my ear, I had to keej my eyes well on the alert to guard against possible collision, as the room was very crowded, and just as we passed a corner my gaze fell suddenly on a figure in white silk sitting alone on a fauteuil. I don't know why, but something in the figure caught and held my eye; perhaps it was only, in the first place, that it was alone and therefore possibly disassociated with all this crowd, with which I myself felt so out of tune.

"Do you know the name of that girl in white we have just passed?" I asked my companion, breaking in, I anr afraid, rather abruptly upon more confidences.

"That?" she replied, looking back over my shoulder " Why, you must know her, surely; she's the general daughter Anna Lombard."

"Anna Lombard," I repeated. " It's a curious nama, It sounds somehow to me medieval, a Middle Age sort of name."

"Oh, Anna's not middle-aged," returned inconsequent ly my rather flighty companion. " She was twenty-ono yesterday, and just out from England, where she was kept at study and things regular lessons, you know. Don't you think it a shame to keep a girl studying so long? It's made her so serious. She says it made her serious, made her feel and think a lot, and see things in life, I mean more than most people I don't know how to express it exactly but you feel she's different from other people. Of course, sometimes she laughs and is just as gay as the rest of us, but she can be serious, oh, just too dreadful for anything, and she says there's a great deal in life, and you can get a great deal out of it if you choose, and oh! funny things like that. I don't see much in life not much that's nice, I mean excepting dancing and ices. Could you get me an ice now, do you think, Mr. Ethridge? I really should like one. Take me out on the terrace and then bring me one, will you?" v I took her out on the terrace, found her a chair and then dutifully brought her the ice and sat beside her. The glory of the night had not changed since I sat there alone, only, as it were, deepened and grown richer; the purple sky above was throbbing, beating, palpitating with the light of stars and planets, and a low, large, mellow moon was sinking towards the horizon, reddening as it sunk. What a night for the registration or the consummation of vows! One of those true voluptuous nights when the soft, hot air itself seems to breathe of the passions.

It was a night on which, as the Frenchman said, all women wish to be loved. I glanced at the girl beside me and wondered if she were moved by it, but I thought not; she sat sipping her ice cheerfully and diligently for ice, like virtue, does not last long in the tropics and watching sharply the groups and couples that passed across the lawn and through the trees before us.

"I'm engaged for the next dance, so you'd better take me back to the room," she said, as she set down the empty lass at last, with a sigh, on the stone. " And I'll introduce you to Anna, if you like," she added, good-naturedly, J and you'll see what you think of her. Some men seem to like her awfully, and others can't get on with her a bit."

She rose and shook out the folds of her immaculate silk and muslin, and we went back to the ball-room.

The figure in white was still seated, calm and motionless, on the fauteuil, and remained so as we approached. I looked at her hard and critically as we came up. She had a tall, strong, beautiful figure and a face that was like an English summer day. Her hair was fair and clustered thickly round her head in its own curls and waves. It was parted in the middle, and was so thick that it rose on each side of the parting as hair is made to do in sculptured heads, and it had the same waving creases in it, a few short, tiny locks came down on the soft, white forehead, and at the back it fell in a doubled-up plait on her neck; her eyes were blue, like pieces cut from a summer's sky, and her skin like the wild rose in the English hedgerow first opening after a summer shower.

Such was Anna Lombard as I first saw her at the age of twenty-one.

"Anna," said the girl with me, as we stopped beside the fauteuil? "Mr. Ethridge wants me to introduce him to you. Mr. Ethridge Miss Lombard."

The girl addressed looked up and smiled, and I was surprised at the effect of the smile on the face; the red lips parted and showed, slightly, perfect white teeth between, and the eyes flashed and seemed to deepen in color and light up with curious fire.

"I am delighted to make your acquaintance," she said in the conventional manner, and moved just very slightly to one side of the fauteuil, which was large, to indicate I might sit down by her, which 1 did.

"Now you can amuse yourselves," said Anna's friend, lightly, as her partner made his way up to her to claim her. " Good-by," and she whirled away at the first bar of the new waltz.

It is difficult to say what we talked of or what it was lent "such an irresistible charm to that conversation, but looking back, I think it was partly the great interest and animation with which the girl both talked and listened. Her lace was brilliant, with her deep blue eyes darkening and flashing, and her milky, stainless teeth sparkling through her crimson lips as she laughed. Everything was new and Iresh to her in this wonderful India of ours, and life itself was just dawning in all its beauty before her mental vision. Ber childhood had been passed in the hardest study and closest intellectual training in a dull, fog-laden old town urn the Cornish coast. There, she told me, she had walked on the sea-beaten sands repeating her lessons in the classics to the wild, wet winds that were busy blowing the color jnto her exquisite skin, while her restless, impatient mind had been wandering far off in the sunny lands and speculating on those strange passions and emotions she was learning of through the lettered pages. And now, suddenly transported to the vivid glowing East, taken from that quiet solitude of study and placed in a whirlpool of human life and gayety in these gorgeous surroundings of Nature for nowhere on earth is there a more dazzling or brilliant arena for life to play itself out than in India she was ike an amazed, delighted, and clever child watching the curtain rise for the first time on the splendor of a pantomime.

We sat and talked through two entire dances, then as the strains of a particularly seductive waltz reached us I asked her if she would not give it to me, and she assented, with I fancied the slightest possible flush. She con- fessed to me later that though she had been carefully taught and made to practice dancing at home, this was her first " real ball." My heart beat as I put my arm round her and guided her among the dancers. I can not say or divine exactly the attractiveness of her manner; but there was a sort of appealing timidity in it that, united with such an obviously clever and gifted mind and such a sweet face and form, had in it a keen flattery.

I held her close to me, and with a perfect unity of step and motion we glided round the room in the great circle of other dancers. The warmth of the slight white arm on my shoulder and the white breast against my own, the sight of the fair, animated face, and a swift glance now and then from those passionate, blue eyes, seemed working on me like a subtle charm. I felt happy, contented; India was no longer a gorgeous but barren desert, life was not full of disappointment after all, and this ball was the greatest, the best, the most interesting function I had ever attended.

How sweet she was, this girl; what a soft, gentle voice; what smiling, caressing eyes, and what a low, slim waist that my arm encircled, and that seemed to yield so readily as if seeking and desiring protection! When the music ceased we found ourselves in the outer ring of dancers and iust beside the open windows. By a mutual impulse we both passed outside on to the low stone terrace into the soft heat which yet held the freshness of grass and flowers in it of the outer air. It was the same night, the same terrace as it had been when I was there an hour ago, only my companion was changed, and what a change that makes! Anna sunk even into the same chair the other girl had sat, and that was still there, but how different everything seemed now from when that hard, frivolous, worldly little doll occupied it. My heart beat more quickly than usual; and where, an hour ago, I had been silent and quite indifferent how I might appear to my companion, now my whole energy woke up in an effort and desire to please. Perhaps I succeeded, for smiles, blushes, and laughter swept by turns over the radiant, expressive face raised to mine in the subdued light of the veranda. She did not talk very much, seeming rather to wish to listen; but everything she did say was full of brightness and wit and a sympathetic intelligence that only comes from a really jlever brain. With all her knowledge for I drew by my. persistence from her reluctant lips the confession of one atudy after another wich which she was familiar she seemed full of diffidence of herself, and fixed her large eyes upon me, as she asked me questions, with the deference of an inquiring child. For the first time in my life I felt repaid for my hard youth given over to learning; yes, more repaid for those years of toil than when my name appeared heading the examination list. For the first time in my life the knowledge I had acquired seemed inexpressibly dear and valuable to me. She was listening, she was interested, she wanted to know and to hear things that I could tell her things that Lieutenant Jones and Captain Scrubbins could not have told her. She liked me, I was sure of it; she was thinking that I knew something, and she cared for these things that I cared for, far more than the last details of the pigeon-shooting match, the latest score of the Gymkhana, the newest development of the growing scandal round the major's wife, in all of which Jones and Scrub-bins could easily have surpassed me. These thoughts rushed through my brain as I leaned over her, smiling and exerting myself to the utmost to please her, and the time flew by and we neither of us heeded what was being played. or what dances danced in the room behind us till suddenly " Home, Sweet Home," in the guise of a waltz, reached us, and we realized suddenly the evening our evening! was over. We both looked at each other with a quick glance, and both knew that we wanted this dance with each other. How little stiffness, how little formality there seems to be from the first when two people meet who are going to feel a great passion one for the other, even before the passion can be said to be lighted, and certainly is not recognized.

Nature's own hand seems to slip loose some bandage which is usually before our eyes, and we act with a certain tenderness, earnestness, and simplicity that is foreign to our usual life and other relations.

As we heard the first sounds of the waltz, Anna looked t me and then slipped that soft, slender, white arm through mine with a little, happy smile, and I, with a sudden sense of happiness and delight in life that I had never known, pressed it close, and we joined the moving circle within. As we danced, and when, at the corners of the room, her weight was thrown on me slightly and I caught, a breath from her lips that reminded me of the scent oi the tea-rose, and the same faint tea-rose scent came from the laces on her breast, this feeling of happiness merged into an ecstasy. It seemed I had never known life before, and, in fact, I had never known love, not even any of its base counterfeits. The soft waist yielded the more pressed it, and filled me with an infinitely tender impulse toward her, the gentle arm against my shoulder seemed oi delicious weight. I met her soft, half-wondering, innocenf-eyes with their pleased smile, and I knew I was really alivo at last.

The waltz ended somewhat abruptly. It was three m the morning and the musicians were. tired.

"Would you go and try and find my father?" Ann asked me. " He does not dance, and I am afraid he maj be getting tired waiting for me somewhere."

Just as she spoke, General Lombard came toward us. We knew each other well, though his daughter, only having just come out, I had not seen before to-night.

He greeted me pleasantly, and when I asked if I mighl call on the following day he assented with a smile. Their in a half-dream-like state of feeling I escorted them tc their carriage, and a murmured " Good-night" and glance from two beautiful, passionate eyes out of the darkness of the carriage closed the evening for me.

That night I had a curious and horrible dream horrible because it was filled with that nameless, causeless, baseless horror and fear that only visits us in dreams. Whatever may happen in our waking life, we never feel that same peculiar dread which seems reserved for our brains to know only in sleep. I felt I was standing in a garden, in the center of which a large and beautiful white rosebud was unfolding itself before me, as I stood and watched it with an increasing sense of delight. It was the only flower in the garden and dominated the whole scene. At last the final and most lightly closed petals were opening and spreading, and in an ecstasy I leaned forward to see the heart disclosed, when suddenly, instead of a heart, a great rent was revealed a jagged, cruel chasm in the beauty of the flower and I fell back shuddering, a prey to that j groundless, reasonless fear of dreams. I awoke abruptly, feeling cold in the sultry tropic night, and turned and tossed uneasily, and fell asleep to dream the same dream again. When I awoke the second time I had a confused feeling, such as troubles the half-wakened brain in the darkness of night, that my dream was connected with Anna. Then I d-d iny own foolishness, and went to sleep for the third time, and then into blank silence and rest. The next morning, waking late, with the brilliant sunlight rushing like water through all the cracks of the closed jilmils, I felt in excellent spirits, dressed quickly, and descended to the dining-room of my bungalow in the best of humors. My plans for that day and many days to follow were distinctly laid. I would go to Anna, be with her, talk with her, ride with her, and then and then and the rest seemed one bright flame of light and happiness.

How strange it was, I thought; how life seemed to have quickened in me; how all the senses seemed tuning themselves to the enjoyment of existence; how the compound seemed to smile before me, the scent from the thousand opening flowers to delight me; the blood seemed spinning gayly along through my veins; I wanted to laugh, hum, or whistle out of mere light-heartedness, and what was it all? Surely some electricity had passed out of that soft, fail form I had held in my arms last night and kindled a fresh life in me. I sat down at the breakfast-table and glanced at the pile of letters waiting my attention, but deferred opening them and giving my thoughts over to business for a few moments longer. After I had sipped my coffee and mused another ten minutes, I laid my hand on a long, official-looking letter, and rather absent-mindedly broke it open and unfolded it.

I read the letter through to its last word it was curt enough for that matter then I crushed it down on th table under my hand.

"D n! D n everything!"

The two native servants, mute bronze statues, though they understood no other word of English, understood that, one of four letters. They both started violently. The kitmargar removed my unfinished cup of coffee tenderly, and inquired, softly: ' The sahib has had bad news?"

"Yes' I groaned, and then added, "Pack everything have everything ready. We leave for Burmah by the night train."

"Protector of the poor!" exclaimed the man, clasping his hands. " The sahib is transferred?"

: Yes. To Lihuli, Burmah. You wish to accompany me"

The man hesitated, and great tears filled his large, brown eyes and then rolled down his cheeks. They are hys-tericalj these natives, and my news had startled him.

"That is in my heart. I wish to. But my wives ar sick. Yet if I stay I have no money for them."

I knitted my brows. My own case dictated more sym pathy for his wives than I should otherwise have felt.

"Allah forbid that I should take them from you, or that you should want. Stay till they are well, and I will seo you get the same pay as now. When they are recovered you can follow me, with them, if you wish. Now go. I want to be alone."

For all answer the man flung himself at my feet and clasped them and kissed them and wept over them. All of which is extremely embarrassing to an Englishman, and makes him feel somehow that he is not so fine a thing aa he generally takes himself to be. Then they withdrew, and I was alone in the room full of gold light, reflected from the desert through thejilmils, alone with that letter, my bad news, and my feelings. I stared at the open paper, feeling doubtless as many a prisoner may have felt when shown his death-warrant. How curious it was, a flimsy sheet of paper, with a few scrawly words the handwriting was execrable, I remember could deal such a blow of deadly pain.

Since a few moments ago, the whole situation was changed for me: my hopes of last night, that pleasant vista of days spent here, that yielding to the intoxication of passion for Anna, that teaching and arousing of her dormant soul, and that drinking at last of the one cup that this life holds worth draining all this that had floated before me, not as certainties, indeed, but as delicious possibilities, was stamped out, and a hideous reality rose in its place. I was transferred to Lihuli, a lonely, desolate station in Burmah, at once, and for five years. Lihuli, or the place of swamps! I read the letter through again.

"This means separation from Anna, and separation means loss."

This is what 1 thought as I laid it down, and the resentment against it was so great that a hundred means of rejecting it rose in my brain. " Go to her; carry her away by the storm of your passion, and take her with jou." Then came the thought, "Take her with you! Where? n To the place of swamps; to a place where there is always some epidemic raging sometimes it is called the black cholera, sometimes the plague, sometimes smah-pox; where there is a never-varying accompaniment of malarial fever and dysentery; where the air, night and day, is tainted and suffocating; where the evening, that brings coolness elsewhere, brings but a sickly white, miasma-tainted mist from the swamps and clouds of mosquitoes; where the face of a white woman is never seen; where there are no bands, no dinners, no dances; and where there is nothing but desert, disease, death, and duty. How could I take her there? And if I could, could I keep her there? And I shuddered. " Then make her wait for you," was the next angry, turbulent thought that came rolling along in the tide of anger and resentment that came surging through my brain. " What! On one evening's acquaintance, ask for a girl's love and faithful waiting for five years, and such a girl as Anna!" Conceited fool though passion will make a man, still it had not blinded me so far as that. I sat on like a statue, thinking hard, and a thousand mad plans, all equally impossible, for evading my duty came before me and were dismissed.

As far as I myself was concerned, I felt no hesitation. I would have gone to her and spoken freely, gladly oh, how gladly if I had allowed myself to be swayed by my own impulses, though I had known her but a few hours. It is not in the nature of things that a great passion, or even that embryo which is to become a great passion, should admit of hesitation. These feelings sweep over the human being resistlessly. They do not permit him to argue or reason with them; they dictate. And, moreover, they carry with them a conviction to his mind which renders argument unnecessary. Lesser emotions, I admit, allow of reasoning this way and that, and weighing and considering; and doubtless more than half the men in the world have long periods of oscillation before they say those revocable words I would have said so willingly now, with- mt a tremor; but this vacillation only proves that the voman they are so considering is not the one of all this life for them, and she will never be the object of the intensest paasion they are capable of. The case is much the same as that of a man waiting in the street to meet some friend of vhose appearance long absence or other causes have made him not quite sure. How anxiously he scans each one of the passers-by, and fifty times imagines he sees a resemblance about which he debates in his mind is that he or is it not? And only hesitates thus because each of these is not the man. When the friend appears, his glance lights on him, he recognizes him. That is the man; there is no question, no doubt, no hesitation. And he walks up to him with outstretched hand. Similarly my mind instinctively and unconsciously had been waiting, as the mind of every man not occupied with passion is practically waiting, for the woman to pass by me in the way of life that was-he fulfillment of the indefinite standard in my thoughts. Others who were not such women might come and go, and, moved by resemblances, I might have hesitated and looked and hesitated again; but Anna had stepped up to me in tfie stream of human traffic that goes up and down the Way, and my mind had instantly recognized her, and my hand was outstretched, and there was no hesitation and no doubt.

Doubtless, if more time had been allowed me, I should have used it, out of a sense of the fitness of things, decorum, and, above all, deference to the girl herself; but even then it would have been the shortest time I could have set. Indeed, I knew that the impulse to caress her, to clasp her in my arms and know her to be my own would be a difficult one to hold down by the throat for long. So that the prospect of being forced to speak at once would not have been terrifying in the least to me, if only and I groaned out loud. Circumstances seemed so willfully and needlessly to have arrayed themselves against me. Had I been ordered to a hill station, one with even a moderately good climate and where white life was not wholly excluded, I might have had courage enough to ask her to occupy a large, cool, rose-covered bungalow, situated somewhere where the breezes came, and to continue her gay, brilliant life of dances and dinners and idle amusements as the wife of an assistant commissioner instead of the daughter of a general; but I could not take a girl, straight from England, to share with me a fever- and cholera-haunted swamp, even if she would come. Somehow 1 did not feel wholy certain that she would not come, and her smiling eyes, as they had looked at me last night, swam before me. I lifted my head and glanced involuntarily down the breakfast-table to where, at the end, a large and brilliant mirror in my sideboard gave me back a reflection of myself. It recurred to me suddenly, then, that I was usually considered good-looking, and my heart gave a beat of pleasure. I had never thought of nor valued the fact before; but just as last night, for the first time, I had felt thankful for my little store of learning, so now for the first time I recalled with genuine pleasure the general verdict of my friends, (t is, perhaps, rather to the credit of the human being in general that he or she thinks invariably little of any personal gift until the question arises of pleasing some other by it. I looked again at the glass. Yes, the features of that face looking back at me were straight and perfectly regular, the skin pale and clear, the eyes large, and eyebrows and hair as black as an Asiatic's; and I remembered delightedly that fair people always incline naturally to and admire those who are dark, and vice-versd. Nature's craving to return to the type which is neither extreme in all cases has mixed that inviolable instinct with men's and women's desire. Then the next instant that little rush of vain egotism and self-contentment had passed. Though she consented a hundred times I could not take her to that horror of desolation and disease that I was ordered to. It was quite, quite impossible, and I put my head down in my hands, ashamed that for an instant it had seemed so possible.

At the end of an hour and a half I rose, put on my solar topee, and walked out of my compound toward the Lombards' bungalow to make the promised call only now it was a farewell one. When I reached the house, the servants told me the Miss Sahib had had breakfast one hour ago and had gone out, but only into the compound, and if I would wish to wait in the drawing-room they would take my card to her. I gave the man a rupee and told him to go within himself, and that I would seek the Miss Sahib in the compound. With an intelligent smile of perfect com- prehension and a salaam of profoundest gratitude the man withdraw into the cool darkness of the hall again, and I redescended into the wilderness of blooming beauty and glaring light of the compound.

I threaded my way quietly through the tangle of blossom-laden and flowering trees, glancing on every side as I parted them, not knowing at what minute I might come upon her. The morning was unusually hot, the sun seemed to have a peculiar intensity and its fiery beams to be distilling the utmost of their perfume from the flowers. As I advanced farther into the compound I became con. scious of a damper, cooler air and of a mossy woodland scent; the gurgle of water reached me, and then at the next step forward I stood motionless and spellbound: the girl herself was before me and unconscious of my presence asleep. In the thick, cool shade thrown by a luxuriant' Jy tangled cluster of bamboo-trees stood a low, broad, stone couch covered with thick, square velvet-and-satin cushions a Turkish divan, in fact in the open; and one prepared, evidently, with skill and care, for all round the stone base was hollowed out a groove filled to the rim with water, thus forming an impassable trench to the innumerable tree ants of enormous size, that were crawling in black ribbons over the mossy ground. And on this couch, fully extended, with arm above her head, lay the girl tranquilly asleep. Noiselessly, hardly breathing, I stepped closer andl looked down upon her. She was wearing a loose garment of white cambric that was unfastened at the neck and showed the whole of the beautiful, solid, white throat at it base, but which, of its own will apparently, closed itself completely over the softly rising and falling bosom; the head was thrown back, and her face, fresh as a flower, was upturned; the cheeks were like the petals of the wild rose, the mouth deep crimson like a pomegranate bud, and hei light hair, ruffled and loosened, fell in glistening waves over the arm beneath, white and bare for the kindly sleeve was loose and wide and had fallen back from it almost to the shoulder. So might have Aurora herself, wearied with tending the flowers, been found sleeping in the Ely-sian fields. I stood entranced, letting my eyes travel reverently over the sleeping form. The cambric was delicate and transparent almost as a cobweb, but its multitudinous folds veiled all but the beautiful outlines;

the hem of the garment seemed lost in the flounces of lace, or perhaps these came from some other under one, and from these issued two bare white insteps, the rest of the feet being cased in little indoor shoes. Beyond those delicate white feet was quite a long space of the divan, covered with a velvet cloth of cashmere work, and o this, mechanically, I took my seat. I had no thought of waking her. Awake, she would become Miss Lombard and I, Mr. Ethridge, conventional words would be spoken in conventional tones; it must be so, and what words could give any idea of the rushing tide of regret and sorrow and disappointment that was rolling through my brain at leaving her. No, this silence, this perfect harmony of beauty suited best our farewells. A deep, unbroken silence lay over all the compound, a heat that seemed of deadly weight fell from the brazen sky, and the transparent air seemed to quiver in it. But here in the deep shade of the feathery bamboo there was coolness and perfect peace. A large tank of water, reflecting the branches overhead till it looked like liquid emerald, stood bedded in the moss close by, and the tiny trickle and gurgle of water flowing from it round the couch seemed to intensify the sense of surrounding coolness. What a scene it was! One possible only, perhaps, in India, where the stream of Saxon civilization, with all its richness, comfort and wealth, flows abruptly into the wonders of native Indian beauty, into that store of gorgeous coloring, of blossoms without name, of scents without definition, of skies and gardens past belief. Beyond the compound lay a sea of radiant color, a wild confusion of pomegranate crimson and rose-pink and syringa white, that seemed swaying under the dazzling effulgence of golden light. Over it hovered lazily from flower to flower great butterflies large as one's two hands put together and blue as though they were fallen fragments of the sky itself; and now and then a crimson-headed paroquet or golden oriole would fly silently across from bamboo to palm. Nearer me, the cool green shadow, the flowing water, the white stone couch, the sleeping girl. Could Milton have seen anywhere a fairer vision for his Eden, Theocritus toave dreamed lovelier things for his idyls, or the ancients have imagined more for their Elysian fields?

But such surroundings are every-day and commonplace in India and the birthright of every Briton. My eyes wandered everywhere and then came back to rest upon the sleeping girl. How calmly and deeply she slept! How unconscious of the excited heart beating so near her! So this was to be the end of a passion but just lighted, the end to that new life which had rushed through my veins when I held her in the dance. A passing away in silence while she slept. And yet I did not think it would be the end. I had a dim prescience that this tranquil, sleeping form was bound up inextricably with my future; but I also felt that never again should I behold her as she now was, in the fresh, pure, unsullied morning of her youth and virginity. It is strange how these vague, dim thoughts pass through our brains, as if sometimes our future were vaguely reflected in some dark and misty mirror, and being only stray, idle fancies, as we think, we take no notice of them. It is only afterward, sometimes, a startling remembrance rebounds upon us from the past and we recollect what we have thought.

A great sadness seized upon me and pervaded me, and for a moment the temptation came over me to awaken her by kisses on those ivory feet so near me, awaken her and make her listen to me. Surely this enchanting scene, this languorous Nature that seemed everywhere bestowing her caresses, breathing into everything her rich fervor of life would favor me. How could I not tell that this sensitive, impressionable girl, wakened suddenly by a passionate kiss in the garden where all was glowing, sense-inflaming beauty, would not be inclined toward me? My heart beat violently; for an instant I swayed and had almost clasped that smooth instep. Then I stayed myself, and the grim realities rose before me. What had I to suggest? And again the reasoning of the morning passed through my brain. Five years of waiting for me here waiting, for her; she ardent, impetuous, just roused to a sense of the joy of life, and eager, impatient to stretch out her hands to its glittering toys; or five years' banishment with me to a notoriously dangerous and desolate spot in the Burinah swamps! No! I could not be such a selfish fool as to offer either. The decision was the same as I had come to before, and must be the same if I thought of it a hundred times. I sat on there in silence, steeped in a dull sense of pain, and she, wearied and fatigued by the long hours of last night, slept on without a movement or a murmur.

My Aurora with the wonderfully smooth, round, delicately tinted cheeks, and the long, black lashes curling upward go that I thought each moment the lids were just opening! Well, I would leave her, but it should not be in absolute silence, and I took out my pocket-book and tore two or ttiree leaves from it, and covered them closely with words. First I gave her the text of the command, verbatim, as I had received it. Then I described Lihuli as I knew it, and then I merely added my farewells. When I had finished it I drew off the amethyst signet ring I always wore, and adding a line to beg her to keep it as a trifling souvenir of me, I rolled the paper round and thrust it through the circle. Then I rose, and leaning over the couch, drew Hown a flexible spray of bamboo and bent it over in an arch, fastening the end to a niche in the stone side of her resting-place; from this arch I suspended the ring and the little scroll by a tendril. It hung just over her bosom, and she could not rise without first breaking or detaching the bamboo and seeing the ring. Then I looked down upon her with an immense tenderness and reverence though that was nothing to the tenderness I was to feel jater fixing that fresh, pure face in my heart, and then moved away softly as I had come. It was time. As I retraced my steps through the blazing compound I heard the wheels of the general's carriage on the gravel. A few moments more and she would be awake, or be awakened. Those minutes of silent calm and beauty, that glimpse into the Elysian fields was a thing of the past. My face was turned to the practical, every-day life and duties of a civil commissioner.

CHAPTER if.

WHEN my train drew into Lihuli it was evening, and a refreshing softness filled the heavjr, magnolia-scented air. No other European was going- to alight at this station, and I saw my solitary carriage waiting fof me beyond the platform. It was a golden evening; everything seemed gold, and not a glaring, but a soft, melting gow. The sky, the air, the motionless palms, eveh the broad road down which my carriage rolled for a short, tawny moss grew all over it, and caught and. gave back the brilliant amber light. We had driven for about fifteen minutes when the first bungalow came into view. It was a low, white stone, flat-roofed building, from the side view almost buried in banana-trees; then, as we drove on, I saw it faced on to the road with a great, broad, inviting veranda full of long cane chairs.

"Club-house gymkhana, sahib," volunteered the driver, slackening his pace, and I saw four or five men, clad in what looked like sleeping-suits, troop through the window on to the veranda. They waved their hands and set up a feeble cheer as they caught sight of me. They all had the same blanched, pinched-looking faces, wan eyes and dry white lips. I stopped the carriage, and they came halfway down the steps to meet me as 1 got out.

"Very glad to welcome you to Lihuli," one of them eaid. " Train must have come in early or we'd have met it."

They all looked so sickly and listless, like men one sees hanging round the balconies of public hospitals or convalescent homes, that the idea of their doing anything so far requiring an effort as meeting their new deputy commissioner seemed rather a joke than anything else. I merely laughed and suffered them to guide me up to the veranda, where there was an informal and hazy introduction.

"That's Jones, of the railway survey, and Knight of the telegraph here; and this is Doctor Kennings you'll probably have a close acquaintance with him pretty soon and Hunter, engineer, and these two kids Seymour and Robertson. Sit down and we'll have some pegs. What do you take?"

They pulled up a small table, and giving me the most prominent chair, they drew their own round me and proceeded to pump me for news.

"It's a perfect Godsend to see a new face," remarked Knight, after we had been talking pretty briskly for some minutes.

"We've had no com since poor old Burke went crazy and shot himself."

I saw one of the other fellows kick the speaker furtively under the little bamboo table.

"Burke was the last man the com, I suppose?" I queried. " What sent him mad?"

"Oh, I suppose the the heat, and being alone, you jnow," stammered Knight, confused by the kick on his thins and looking guilty. " But the bungalow has been renovated, and, in fact, the room where where it happened has been pulled down, and he left a note saying he was glad to go, and the change to the cooler climate of h would do him good. He seemed quite content."

"You d d fool!" muttered his vis-a-vis, glaring at him over the glasses of long straws. " What do you want to tell him all that for the first night?"

I laughed.

"I'm not afraid of ghosts," I said lightly; " and so far, it seems as cool here as one could reasonably expect below."

"Oh, yes, it will be all right until it rains," chimed in Hunter; " and a man's all right here if he can only adapt toimself. You must settle down, take a wife, and live regularly. Burke never did. He was always fretting for some girl in England."

"Take a wife!" I echoed in surprise.

"Yes, a Burmese wife. Oh, don't look so contemptuous. You'll come to it. They most of them do, and it eaves time and trouble to settle down at once. Now, tomorrow morning you will have an assortment brought to you. Your choice as the American stories advertise for one hundred rupees down, and the remainder in installments later. She will then be contracted to you for five fears; that's your appointment here, isn't it? Yes, very good. Then you'll have some one at the head of your Fable and to look after your house for you; they're first-rate little housekeepers, though they don't look it. Then you'll enjoy legitimate matrimony for five years, and when your time's up you pay the bill and say good-by, and there's no trouble."

The other men listened in listless indifference, and one or two nodded in confirmation of their companion's statement when he had finished. I myself knew enough of the customs of Burmah to know that he was not chaffing or jesting. I had heard of these Anglo-Burmese marriages before, and how the Burmah girl, at the end of the white man's term, goes back to the nouse of her parents, sometimes with two or three children of mixed blood, and is in no way looked down upon by her own people for the same, and is probably eventually married to one of her own caste.

I suppressed a yawn.

"My own company, study, and books will be more tt my taste," I answered.

Hunter looked at me pityingly.

"This is a country," he said, impressively, " in which a man can live, but he can not live alone. But you can try it, of course as Burke and others have."

Then there was a pause, and it seemed as if a chill had come into the lambent, yellow air. Then, as a welcome distraction, the doctor suggested we should go inside and dine, and we all rose with alacrity.

The dining-room was a large, lofty, airy room, and they seemed to possess excellent wines, soda-water, and spirits-at least that kind that can be kept in bottles and well' hung punjcajts swung briskly the whole time.

We sat long over our coffee and smoked and gossiped, and my new presence seemed to make them all quite cheerful. It was late, and the moon had risen before they put me into my carriage again, and with cordial good-nighta watched me drive off to my own bungalow down the steamj road that looked misty in the moonlight, and where the wheels moved without sound over the spongy yellow moss.

The next morning, as soon as it was light, I was awakened by the sound of subdued but incessant and eager chattering, apparently just beneath my window. I got up from the charpoy, disentangled myself from my mosquito cur tains, pushed open the jilmils of the nearest window, and looked out. What a scene it was to meet the eyes especially eyes like mine, not yet satiated with, nor even accustomed to, the splendors of the East! The sun had not yet risen, only a golden glow intensifying every instant near the horizon in an otherwise pearly sky heralded ite approach. The compound stretching beneath my windov and all round the house was one mass of roses of every tint and shape and size; toward the gate of the compound and all round the walls were clumps of the broad-leaved banana-tree swaying in the slight breeze of the dawn, and two or three trees of Bougainvillea bursting through, from between them, stood pouring their torrents of magenta blossoms to the ground; there is no other way to express it, for the parasite grown to a tree yet can not forget its nature, but trails its branches to the ground, and for yards round the tree-roots the earth has a carpet of its pinkish violet flowers. Beyond the walls and broad-leaved banana-trees stretched miles of golden sand, like a calm, golden sea, broken here and there by green islands of cocoanut palm, that moved languidly against the pale-growing azun of the sky. One glance took in all this beauty, and my curiosity as to the voices returned. I looked through the network of giant convolvulus that completely covered one side of the house, and peering between the great violet and white cups of the flowers, I saw beneath, seated in a circle in a small open space of turf, an old native woman and five other evidently younger women round her. I could only partially see them, but they appeared to be in festive attire, and suddenly the warning at the club last night came back to me. These were, no doubt, the threatenec " wives." With mingled disgust and amusement I with. drew from the window and commenced my toilet, the chat. tering and jabbering continuing unabated the whole time, sometimes rising to a shrill clamor, and then sinking to almost whispers. I went down to my dining-room, where breakfast was waiting for me, and which I had perfectly undisturbed, then the servant withdrew and I lapsed into thought, swinging absently on my chair and staring up to the roof, which was high enough from the floor for the bate to come in and hang there in quiet comfort.

Suddenly the lattice door was pushed open, and the old woman I had seen in the compound entered, followed by the five little women, all holding one another's hands, and grinning the whole width of their little, painted mouthy They were all dressed in very tight, narrow petticoats so narrow that they produced the effect of a bolster-case or one wide trouser-leg these were of different gay-colored silks, and reached just to the little ankles of the wearei, which were loaded with blue china bangles. Above, they each wore a silk zouave, heavily embroidered, which, while it covered each breast, left the space between them exposed; their throats were quite bare and peculiarly round, smooth, and boneless; their arms were bare except for countless glass and china bangles, and they all wore flowers stuck in their straight, oily, black hair and behind their ears. The old woman flung herself flat on the floor before me, with her forehead pressed to the ground, and the fiv little creatures went down on their hands and knees, duck' ing their flower-decked heads, and subjecting the absurdly tight, silk petticoat to a terrible strain over the broadest part of their small persons. After her obeisance, the old woman sat up and addressed me in a flow of excellent Hindustani. She had heard that the sahib, who was her father and mother and the protector of the poor, had come to shed the light of his most glorious countenance, which was like the sun rising in majesty upon Lihuli, and she had hastened her aged footsteps to minister to the wants of the sahib, and she brought him five flowers of the morning, and he was to stretch forth his kingly hand and indicate which would best suit him for a wife. When she paused, the five little girls also sat up and eyed me somewhat anxiously. Some chalk or white paste had been rubbed over their faces to simulate the Aryan complexion, and a round, pink spot painted in the middle of the cheek. Their faces were Mongolian in type, more like the Chinese face than any other, but the mouths were soft and pretty. Their diminutiveness was the most striking thing about them. They seemed like little children.

"How old are they?" I asked the woman.

"Eleven, twelve, and thirteen," she answered, sharply, looking at me suspiciously. " Surely the sahib doesn't think that too old?"

"Old! Good God! no; they're not old enough," I returned speaking, of course, always in her vernacular.

The old woman looked relieved, and pulling forward the biggest one by the arm, she brought her close up to me.

' See here," she proceeded, " she's plump and good-sized."

With this she pinched the girl's bosom, and dug her fingers into her neck precisely as poulterers pinch the breasts of their fowls for customers.

After that, she went into various details pertaining to the girl with a degree of frankness that makes it impossible to repeat them. I sat back in my chair, surveying the scene with amazement at the strange commingling of ideas these little, half-formed things, and wifehood, motherhood, and the modest Anglo-Indian Government that will not have the word prostitution printed in the newspapers, and yet countenances such things as these. For all this was perfectly legal, and the girls probably all came from Burmah families of some standing.

"Here, Nanee," exclaimed the old woman to another of them perhaps the prettiest of them all " go up and make yourself amiable to the gentleman."

At this Nanee approached in little, bare, velvet feet, and nestled close to my side, one tiny hand, soft as satin, absurdly flexible at the wrist, and seemingly perfectly boneless, she placed on my knee, and looking up straight at me, she lisped, softly, "Ashik karti," or " I love you," to show me she too could speak Hindustani.

I looked down on her with a smile. The idea of love seemed to me ludicrous. What could I do with this little atom of doll-like, child-like life? But I smiled upon her as one does on a pretty child asking for a kiss.

"Now, which will the sahib, who is lord of all the virtues, decide upon Nanee or Lalee?" asked the old woman, in a business-like tone.

I saw it was time to negative the matter at once, and I said, decidedly:

"I am not in want of a wife, and I have no intention of taking one."

The old woman fell back, sitting on her heels, and stared at me blankly.

"B"ut, sahib, protector of the poor, you are here for five years; no white woman at all in Lihuli, no woman allowed in bazaar! What will you do?"

Five years! So she knew the exact length of my appointment, probably the amount of my salary and private income to an anna. They know everything, these people. I looked up and saw, standing just inside my door, patiently waiting till the market should be concluded, a clerk with a long strip of paper and a bundle of reed pens in his hands. His duty was to make out the agreement between us, and give me a receipt for any money paid on account.

"I don't know," I said, abruptly. " When I want a wife I will send for one. I don't want one now. I have spoken."

"Let the sahib think once more. He may look from one end of Lihuli to the other and he will not find such buds from the garden of Paradise as these again."

I glanced at the buds of Paradise and saw that their little faces had grown sad and wistful as they heard my decision.

"They are beautiful beyond comparison," I said to reassure them, and perhaps save them from the old woman's wrath; " but I have no need them. If I had, there are none I could wish better."

"Well," muttered the old woman, somewhat appeased, while the buds looked considerably happier, "I am but a poor woman, and the sahib is the lord of gold and silver."

I understood this, and it was an appeal to which I could respond. I put my hand into my pocket and drew out a handful of rupees. These I dropped into her outstretched hands, and she fell on her face again and declared I was more her father and mother than ever, and otherwise very nearly related to her.

Then I got up and filled each of the little, soft, brown hands of the buds with rupees, and their tiny fingers could hardly close over the large coins.

"Now go," I said, and clasping hands as before, they all wriggled in an uneven line to and through the door, followed by the clerk.

Then I threw myself into a chair and laughed, yet it was rather a sad laugh and ended soon, leaving me staring thoughtfully imto the sheen of gold sunlight beyond the lattice door. I felt sorry for them, and after a time this impersonal sorrow merged into sorrow for myself. The old woman's words, "Five years! What will the sahib do?" rang in my ears. It is a curious fact how, if we are in an unpleasant position, another person's sympathy or pity seems to stamp it into our minds and bring out sharply its most disagreeable points. She saw the position more clearly than I did. She had seen my predecessor come and go. She knew, probably, more of the way in which heat and silence can work on the white man's brain than I did. My thoughts were decidedly unpleasant as I stared up into the great arch above me. There was no ceiling-cloth stretched across. The eye could go up far among the great timbers and cross-beams and watch the black, mummy-like bats clinging there in rows, head downward, with their claws sheathed till the night-time.

It was ten when I ordered the carriage and drove down to the city to see the native quarter and find my office. Lihuli is a place with a very large but straggling population, and without those grand buildings, tombs, temples, and mosques one stumbles over at every turn in the native cities of India. Nothing but piles of irregular, badly built, badly kept mud, plaster, and stone houses leaning against one another, one on the top of the other, as if an earthquake had shaken them together, met my eyes on the left of the broad road I was traversing. And this was the town. On the other side of it lay a wide, flowing stream doubtless but a dry, stony bed for many months in the year and between the river and the town rose a high, stone wall which intervened to prevent the miserable little, mud houses slipping into the stream and being whirled away to the great swamps of the plain. Eunning through the town there was one respectable street, and in this 1 found the court-house and my office a two-storied building in stone adjoining. The lower story one could enter from the street; but to arrive at the second, one had to pass through the ground-floor out into the square yard beyond, where great white oxen, reposing on their fore-knees, gazed at one steadily through the blinding glare of the sun, and by picking one's way carefully through piles of green fodder and pools of slime, one reached the airy, frail wooden staircase that ran up to the balcony of the second story. The house was a corner one, and the balcony at the side here overhung a narrow, native court. The buildings were not high, and the sun fell richly into it. Glancing across, I saw a little, grated window opposite, low down and white with the dust of the road. Two native women sat behind the bars, and I caught the glint of a red and blue glass bracelet as a tiny brown hand clasped one of the rails. It was fairly cool and shaded in the balcony, because an awning of English manufacture stretched over it made it so. Beneath, in the dust, sat the sellers of sweets arid cakes, cross-legged, calling out their wares in a crooning, droning voice. I passed on and turned the corner of the balcony, coming round to the front of the office, where the long windows opened into it. Some white pigeons had their cote on the gray wall of the court-house adjoining, and they whirled round the balcony, their snow-white wings flashing in the gold sunlight against the blue sky. I watched them for an instant, and they seemed looking at me wonderingly. " Poor Burke!" I thought, " perhaps these birds were favorites of his, and are asking themselves if I am he come back to them." I shuddered and turned into the office. It was all so neat and in such perfect order. It seemed as if he had just stepped out of it except that the dust lay thick on everything. The jilmils of the windows were closed, and all was black darkness to me stepping from the yellow glare outside. I started as a shuffling on the matting came to my ears and the light of a pair of eyes to mine, looking out of the shadow. The next minute I distinguished the figure of a native clerk bearing a bunch of keys.

"Why, where did you spring from?" I exclaimed, or a near equivalent to that in Hindustani.

"Behold, heaven born, there is an inner staircase," replied the clerk, bowing, and then I noticed that a second little staircase just outside the office door led below.

I took over the keys and went to work dry work for the most part reading letters, filing and answering them, and writing judgments on cases I had not tried; and hot work, for there was no punkah, and ordering one put up for tomorrow did not make it any cooler to-day. The sweat gathered on my face and poured persistently off my nose, blotting and blurring everything I wrote in the most pathetic, approved, tear-stained way. It was pathetic, I thought; a few tears would not probably have cost me as much.

By five in the afternoon I was free, and shutting up the dusty, airless room I strolled out on the balcony and found compensation.

The Burmah air was round me, dazzling, yellow air, like liquid gold, and heavy with those strange smells of smoke and rose and incense and spices. Above, the Burmah sky of silver blue; below, the broad Burmah road, with its countless forms in white and blue and yellow passing up and down, and its bullock-carts with their heavy, large white bullocks moving slowly in from the teak forests that lie toward the west. I leaned on the rail of the balcony and looked down, realizing how truly the East was in my blood. It seemed my home, its air my native air. "With all its miseries and its sins I loved it and I knew that I did. The wish of my childhood, boyhood, and youth had been accomplished. I had come to the East, and did not think I should ever want to return. It holds one with too many hands. I leaned on one elbow gazing down on the careless, light-hearted stream of Orientals passing below people whose brains are like the brains of a genius, whose daily life is the life of a child, and whose passions are the passions of a beast. A feeling of contentment stole over me, borne on the heated, languid, spice-laden air. Had I only had beside me that yielding form and those speaking eyes I should have been happy, far too happy; and this is doubtless what the gods thought when they arranged things differently.

I went down presently by the little, rickety outside staircase and through the court-yard, where the bullocks were still wallowing in the blue mud, and through the lower story of the building, which was the office of a native and full of dusky native clerks, perched on high stools in their straight white garments, with their long, black, braided hair falling down to the floor. The place was dark, with closed windows and jilmils; but the rolling eyes of the clerks as they turned on me, passing through their midst, almost lighted it with their gleaming whites and jetty pupils. And so at last out into the now cooling, brilliant air and to iny carriage. A thought came to me. I was not hungry; my lonely dinner in my empty bungalow did not invite me. I would leave it till later and go now and see the notorious swamps, the blue, miasma-laden, death-dealing swamps of Lihuli. I would go now while I was fresh and strong, before the place had thinned and weakened my stock of clean blood. I found out from the native coachman that we should have to drive down to the river where, at certain places, there were landing-stages and boats the common boats mostly used for merchandise, for the river higher up was fair and broad, a good highway for traffic. Here it became but a poor and sluggish stream that lower down, below the town, found difficulty in struggling through the wide morasses in its path.

Accordingly, through the balmy, red-gold air we drove down to the river-side, and found, by chance, an old Bur-man sitting on his heels beside a still older boat, damp and sticky yet from its recent load of half-rotten fruit. He was smoking peacefully, watching with dull, unseeing eyes the pinkish ripples of the stream tumbling along in their muddy bed.

The coachman threw his whip at him, by way of attracting his attention; and this, catching him full in the middle of his blue-brown, naked back, sufficed to arouse him from his reverie, and while I stood on the little quay the following colloquy, as far as it can be approached in English, took place:

"Hi, there, you son of an owl, this heaven-born person of distinction wishes to descend the river. For how many annas shall his nobly proportioned body confer honor on your stinking old tub of a boat?"

"I am the servant of the heaven-born. or fifteen annas we will descend even to the swamps."

"And return, thou base-born?"

"I said not return."

"For fifteen annas thou shalt go and return and see that this king among men returns unharmed, or thou wilt sway in the wind as a leaf of the peepul-tree."

"It is well. I am but a poor man and the sahib's will is my will."

At the end of this I disposed of my " nobly proportioned body " in the old fruit-scented craft, and we pushed off from the bank by the aid of the long pole the old Burman used punting fashion. My sais got off the box, and, sitting on his heels beneath the noses of the horses, watched me go down stream, supremely satisfied with the coachman's bargaining. Easily the boat rocked its way down the river like a drunken man, pleased with himself and all the world, rolling homeward; pushed by the old Burmau now from one bank, now from the other, it kept its middle course down stream, and the rank grass and long weeds at the sides stretched out their snares in vain. I sunk into a reverie that the warm stillness of the air and the ripple and the lap of the water aided, and it quite startled me when the punter ceased his work suddenly and waved his arms round his head and then toward the landscape in general, with a shrill cry to attract my attention. I sat up, raised my eyes, and looked about me.

The swamps were round me, stretching on every side of me as far as vision could reach, except in the west, where the great teak forests rose in dark masses against the glowing sky; and desolate, tainted, deadly as they were, they yet possessed a peculiar beauty of their own that same wonderful beauty that rises before one's eyes everywhere in the East and is the consolation for all its trials. They lay around me, a wonderful plain of varied color, here the light amber and pale green of lichen and moss growing on fallen timber, there a patch of vivid scarlet from some nameless flowers springing out of the rotting vegetation, there a long, dark, green band of rushes tipped with gold in the flood of the evening sun; and over them all, faint and indefinable, hung a pale blue mist, a shifting veil of blue vapor.

The river had widened out and shallowed, and great tussocks of coarse moss rose out of its straggling bed. Against one of these the boat jarred and finally rested. The old man laid down his pole and squatted on his heels. I gazed long and curiously about me, away over the masses of sodden moss, over the little, fiat, gleaming pools turning blood red in the evening light, away over streaming patches of decaying vegetation and forming carbon, away into the pale, poisonous mist on every side. It was quite silent but for the sing-sing of the mosquitoes round us. Far off on the edge of a gleaming flat of water, motionless as an ibis carved on an Egyptian wall, stood a long-shanked bird. I could see his profile, all long beak and tufted crest, defined against the amber distance. He was the only sign of life; all around and between him and me stretched decay, poison, and death. I sat for a long time in contemplation, as the light sunk lower and lower over the dismal swamp, and the old Burmah began to get uneasy and move about in the boat. At last he raised his arms over his head to attract my attention, and I nodded to him that he might return if he wished. Slowly we pushed and punted back up stream, between the rank and muddy banks, and before we reached the landing-stage, darkness had swept over the face of the swamp; it had veiled itself in the night quickly and deftly as a woman draws her veil across her face with one turn of her hand. It was quite dark when I regained my bungalow, and I eat my solitary dinner by the light of one solitary lamp set in the center of the table, which threw owing to its abominable shade, manufactured in Birmingham a dazzling circle of light just round its foot on the white table-cloth, leaving the whole of the rest of the large and lofty room in complete obscurity. I heard the bats whiz in and out and repair to their haunts in the far-away ceiling undisturbed, and the lizards and spiders scurrying and clinking about in the shadowy, far-off corners; they doubtless gave the construction of that Birmingham lamp their unqualified approval. As the sole society of these companions is not very interesting, and I was too tired to seek the club, 1 went off to bed early.

Three weeks passed, and by the end of that time I felt myself settled into an old resident. I found I had court work to do, and this rather amused me. Needing an interpreter by my side all through the court business irritated me. I like to hear a native's evidence straight from his lips, and by the coupling of particular looks and glances and motions of the face with certain words, I can tell pretty well which lie he is telling. Therefore, in most of my leisure hours I studied the Burmese language, and each day, after dinner, the bats, lizards, and spiders listened from their corners to a high-class conversation in the vernacular. I hired an old Munshi to teach me and to talk to me, and often he would bring two or three friends with him. Then, all crouching on their heels in a circle round my chair, they would all talk to me, in turn, by my special request, otherwise they would have all talked together.

In addition to this study, which was my form of amusement, I had found time in that three weeks to paint a portrait of Anna.

I hardly needed a portrait on canvas, since a very clear and, I hoped, indelible one was stamped in my brain; but one never knows about these things. The human brain is one of the crankiest creations, and a good stiff attack of fever will sometimes wipe away and make a blank of its dearest impressions. So I committed her face to canvas, in view of contingencies; and it was pleasant to see it smiling out upon me from the hot gloom of my dining-room, when I came back sick and weary from a crowded courtroom, with my retina weary of photographing infinities of black visages. I really found little time for going to the club, and the members did not see me there very often; but some of the men would sometimes bring their Burmese wives with them, and there was quite a family gathering on my veranda. It was unnecessary generally to bring out extra chairs for the women, as they were so small they could slip in beside their husbands into the same chair without his being cramped; but usually they preferred to sit cross-legged at his feet. Some of them were excellent musicians, and occasionally brought their pear-shaped guitars and sung native melodies in perfect time and tune; but for the most part they liked to sit idle, smoking their huge white Burmese cheroots, that are at least four times the size of our cigars, and which, sticking out from their little mouths, stretched quite round to hold them, do anything but improve their appearance,

One evening they followed me into my sitting-room, and spying Anna's portrait, which I had stood upon a table by itself, they crowded over it with eager curiosity. Lihuli is not an advanced Burmese community. There was no white woman there then, and perhaps had not been for years perhaps not in the lives of these little creatures and the fair, bright countenance looked to their dusky, peering eyes as a thing unseen and unknown. But it was the hair that struck them most. They could not understand that fair, clustering mass, full of waves and golden lights. They gazed at it in awestruck silence, and then I heard them murmur to one another:

"Peri hai," " It is a fairy."

"No," I said, rather sadly, " it's not a fairy. It's a living woman, who will love and be loved and have children some day, just like yourselves."

It is only by such images that one can convey the idea of womanhood to the native mind.

"But look at the hair," they said, pointing out their soft, dark ringers at it, and then turning to one another and examining one another's heads.

This was all they knew of hair, this mass of coarse, heavy, straight threads, each of uniform length, that, when dressed and oiled, lay in a black, solid lump against their heads, or when undone fell in uneven, unwaving lines to the floor.

"That is English hair, and she is an English woman," I said; but as I followed them out on to the veranda, I heard them muttering to themselves, "Sachbat ne bolta hai, Peri hai," "He is not speaking the truth; it is a fairy," and they looked dubiously on my veracity ever after.

During this time I had several letters from Anna, and they were characteristic ones, which delighted me. All the social news of the station, and what she had been doing in that way herself, crammed into the first few sentences and put as shortly as possible; and all the rest of the sheet filled up with some idea or theory of hers, or else a continuation of some argument or theory started in mine. Her first letter, too, had filled me with more hope than I had had since I had left her. It seemed full of a sorrow at my departure that she did not like exactly to express, but yet managed to indicate very clearly, he thanked me for the ring, and said that she wore it on the middle finger of her right hand, and wound up her letter with:

"Why didn t you wake me?"

Altogether, so far, life in Burmah did not seem absolutely insupportable to me, and I grew deeply interested in my judicial work. I made headway in the language and watched everything, noted everything, and stored up all the native lore and knowledge of native life with which to surprise and please Anna in that far distance when we were to meet again. She was deeply interested in all that I told her of my Burmese friends, and every incident that was unusual or striking of my crowded court-room made the back-bone of a diverting story for her. One instance, however, I forbore to mention, though it was a great deal more to my credit than some others. On a certain Monday morning, when there had been an unusual number of cases, and I was wearied out in the heavy atmosphere before the lunch hour arrived, a case came before me of abduction, of which the facts elicited, at length, from a mist of lies, were as follows:

A low-caste Hindu woman had married a low-caste Bur-man, and their daughter, a low-caste hybrid, had been married and left a widow before she was eleven years old. Her husband's mother thereupon used her, according, indeed, to Hindu custom, as a household drudge, and endeavored to add to the cheerfulness of her existence by frequent blows and a scarcity of nourishment. The Burmese father, of the mild, gentle Burmese disposition, unable to bear the pitiful tale of his daughter's woes, summoned up courage, with several of his friends, to effect a forcible abduction of the girl, and had rescued her from the old woman's clutches. Hence the suit, and now the whole four stood before me. The court-room was not very large, with four high, narrow windows facing one another, two on each side. These had bars without and shades within to keep out even that much of the pitiless sunlight; the door had a square of open-work grating in it, to let sure current move, if possible, the stifling air; the back of the court-room was crowded with narrow wooden benches, black and polished from the continued contact of oily, naked arms, legs, and bodies. In the forepart was my chair, a little raised, with a puntcali swinging over it, and on this particular morning there were ranged before me the old, witch-like mother-in-law, the prosecutrix, the gentle old Burman, the accused, his wife, and their daughter Lulloo, a very beautiful, half-developed woman of eleven. She had very little to say; she stood with her great eyes under magnificent arching brows fixed upon me the whole time, and her dirty white, ragged cotton tunic turned down from her back and shoulders. They were horribly scarred and cut, while her left breast was swollen, and had a large circular red patch on it. Now, it is difficult to make a black skin red, and when a patch shows up dusky crimson on it, it means blood badly extravasated underneath. I knew what a cruel blow must have been given to cause that mark, and I was not much inclined to patience with the old woman when she explained to me at great length that the girl was her son's property and her property, and could not, under any circumstances, go back to live with her own people. All this was perfectly correct as far as Hindu India went; but the law was different in Burmah; moreover, a right to a person's custody is forfeited by excessive cruelty under any law.

"The girl is lazy, and will not work unless she's beaten," screamed the old woman.

"Is that true, Lulloo?" I asked, curious to have this beautiful, silent, helpless creature speak.

"No, it is not true," she answered, calmly. " I have worked from dawn till dark for a handful of rice and two dates. Let the sahib take me for a servant in his house and see how I will work. Let me be only meteranni in the house of the huzoor."

I smiled, and shook my head.,

"I have no use for women in my house," I answered. " Do you wish to return to your father?"

The girl looked down and fingered a dried and faded circle of clematis on her wrist, and then said, in a low voice:

"Yes, if I may not go to the house of the sahib."

I signaled for the old Burman to approach.

"Take your daughter and keep her. The court gives you the right to her."

The girl, instead of joyfully throwing herself into her father's arms, as I anticipated, flung herself at my feet, kissing and crying over them. The old woman, as soon as she fairly understood the sentence, began screaming and vociferating.

"Take her away," I said, peremptorily; and two stout Burmans, ushers of my court, dragged and hustled her out between them.

We could still hear her shrill clamor outside, through the thick stone walls. Lulloo was still weeping at my feet, and a stray ray of light from the window fell across her bare shoulders and showed up the hideous weals and cuts upon them. I lifted her up.

"Don't you understand, child?" I said. " You won't be beaten or starved any more. Go away now with your father."

The girl ceased sobbing, and turned away to her father, muttering to herself, "I am not a child. I am a woman and a widow." Then she went away with her parents to the back of the court and other cases came crowding on, through all that long, hot afternoon, and I thought no more about her.

The next morning, strolling out into my compound to breathe a little cool air before the sun had fairly struggled over the edge of the plain, I saw something white in the centre of one of the big banana leaves of a prominent tree which grew close to the main path of the compound by the gate. I walked up to it and found a note, rolled up and stuck through a hole in the leaf. The writing was that of the professional bazaar letter-writer, and then, signed at the bottom in large, unsteady, straggling characters, was the word " Lulloo." I laughed and read the note. When a native is in love, he or she may not be very constant or faithful, and what he feels may not be the highest class of emotion, but at least he is very earnest for the time being, and his language is always remarkably explicit. He loses, in fact, no time whatever in coming to the point. The present note was no exception to this rule.

Lulloo, having apparently lost her heart to me the previous day in the court-house, wished to draw my attention to that fact in the most emphatic manner. I read and reread it several times for it was in Hindustani, both substance and character, and therefore good practice, for one can not be too well versed in this sort of literature. Then I tore it in the tiniest fragments and gave them to the now stirring morning breeze and went inside to breakfast. A week passed, and I saw nothing of Lulloo; but the notes continued, and I found one each morning stuck in the banana leaf. Some reproached me for not having answered the former ones, and some merely begged me to give her some sign of my favor. At the end of the week the notes ceased, and I thought my absolutely ignoring them had had the desired effect. That evening, however, just as I was leaving the court, Lulloo sprung up, apparently from nowhere, and stood in front of me. I was quite astonished at the change in the child since I had last seen her, with matted hair, thin cheeks and ragged, dirty clothes in the court-room. Now she was clean, plump, and radiant, with a brand-new bolster-case petticoat of green silk and a white muslin zouave.

"Sahib! sahib!" she said, joyfully. " Look at me!"

"Where did you get all these fine clothes?" I asked, smiling.

"I buy them. They are all mine. I make much money now by my profession."

"What is it?" I pursued, watching the sun strike the purple lights in her hair.

"Snake-charming. All snakes know me. I can charm them all. They never hurt Lulloo. Would the sahib like to see my snakes?" she added, insinuatingly, coming a little nearer me and throwing back her head at an angle, where her curled lips and arching brows looked most beautiful. " Shall I come this evening with my snakes and show the sahib?" she repeated.

Native like, there was not a word about the notes nor any allusion now to those deeper feelings that had been breathed in them. What is it that sometimes sways us to grant, sometimes to refuse, a request that we ourselves have no personal interest in? I see now that I should have refused this one; but weakness, I suppose, took hold of me and I consented.

"Very good, Lulloo, come up at eight o'clock this evening and bring your snakes. I shall have some friends coming. You shall show all you do," and then I got into my carriage and drove away.

Lulloo, the instant her request was granted, had disappeared. I had invited four of the fellows to come and dine with me that evening, and it struck me the snake-charming would be a good thing to amuse them with afterward, and I myself would not be sorry to see the thing done genuinely and watch it at close range.

So eight o'clock that evening found myself, the doctor, Knight, Hunter, and Jones seated in a semicircle facing the veranda, smoking, sipping iced brandies, and waiting for Lulloo. With customary unpunctuality our watches marked the quarter-past before Lulloo came on to the veranda and appeared before us, followed by an old, wizened Btirman who was carrying a wooden box bound with brass that seemed to sway with a movement of its own as he carried it. I saw the men glance at one another with surprise, as the girl, with her easy steps and Bacchus-like face, came into the light. She might have served perfectly for the model of any of those beautiful antiques of the youthful Bacchus. She salaamed composedly to us all, and then sat down, crouching on her heels, opened a small, square door in the hutch-like box and gave a shrill whistle. Almost instantly the circular space around her was alive with snakes of all sizes and colors; they came tumbling through the small opening, one over the other, and went writhing, wriggling, and gliding in all directions over the matting.

"I say," whispered Knight, in my ear, moving uneasily in his chair. " This is too bad. It's like a fellow having D. T. without deserving it, you know."

"Perhaps you do deserve it," I retorted for Knight was a consumer of many pegs. " Now, I don't mind watching them in the least."

Lulloo was catching up her snakes one by one and squeezing their throats till their mouths opened, so that we could all see that they were fully fanged. There were more snakes there than I knew the names of, but I recognized two fair-sized rattlers and a small python. She lifted the python with some little exertion of strength for he was fat and heavy and tied him round her waist as a girdle. Then she took the two rattlers by their necks, one in each hand, and knocked their heads together. They spit and hissed violently. Then she laid one down and slapped the other with her free hand, moving with incredible swiftness to avoid the darting tongue. Then, when the poor beast was worked up into a thorough loss of his temper, she brought out of her zouave a little square tablet of wood, and put it before his jaws. He struck at it viciously, and we plainly saw, when she drew it away, the yellow drops of venom his poison-fangs had left on it.

"I say, I don't half like this," muttered Jones. " It's just playing with death. Suppose the brute catches her hand instead of the board, she'd be dead in half an hour."

"He who harbors love in his heart is in more danger than if he held a hundred snakes in his bosom," crooned Lulloo, as if she had understood or divined what he was saying, and she threw an eloquent glance in my direction that made all the men laugh and nudge one another.

"I say, you've been going it with this girl must have. You'll get into trouble," remarked the doctor; and Knight added:

"Seems awfully stuck on him. I imagine we're expected to leave early."

I felt myself flush up with annoyance, but said nothing, and the clematis-crowned head in front of us bent low over the snakes as the girl twined the reptiles round her neck, letting a bunch of squirming heads hang down like a pendant or locket between her firm, round breasts.

She had knocked both the rattlers about and let them each strike at the wood tablet several times. " Now they are tired," she said. " See!" and indeed both snakes lay in a heap on the matting, apparently quite exhausted.

"You cruel little beast!" said Knight, in Hindustani, chaffingly shaking his finger at her.

The girl laughed, and picking up one of the dormant rattlers by the middle of tne body, flung it full in his face. I have seldom seen a man so abjectly frightened. He turned livid and sprung to his feet, the snake slipped down between his legs and wriggled back toward its mistress.

I frowned angrily at Lulloo.

"How dare you, you rude, ill-bred little girl! I am sorry I had you to my house."

The effect of my words on Lulloo was remarkable. She stared at me with wide-open eyes for a moment, sitting back on her heels. Then she burst out crying and flung herself forward, clasping my feet and murmuring incoherent words of contrition.

Knight sat down again with a forced smile, but he had not altogether recovered his composure. It is not pleasant to have a full-sized rattler flung suddenly in your face, even though it is exhausted.

The other men looked on, amused. Lulloo's attitude to me interested them a good deal more, practically, than her snake-charming. I drew my feet away, and said:

"You should apologize to my friend, not to me."

Lulloo looked up and gazed resentfully at Knight out of her great, star-like, tear-filled eyes, then glanced back at me and finally crept toward Knight, clasped his feet, muttered some apology, and drawing from the bosom of her zouave a tiny, long vial of attar of roses, dropped some of it on them. The idea of well-blacked and polished London-manufactured boots being anointed with attar of roses amused the men; they leaned back in their long chairs and laughed at the scene till the cane creaked. Knight, looking uncomfortable, tucked his feet under his chair, and Jones leaned forward, spreading out his handkerchief.

"Here, little girl, put some on this."

Lulloo again looked questioningly at me. It was plain she would obey me to any limit; but she had no particular liking for my friends. They were laughing at her and making fun of her, and a native, like an animal, does not forgive this.

I nodded gravely, and she accordingly dropped some of the priceless stuff on the outspread handkerchief. Jones covered his face with it.

"Phew! that's nice. I say, how these snakes smell! Have you noticed it? They are worse than a tank full of muggers. Come on, you fellows. I think we had better be going."

"Have you anything else to show us?" I asked Lulloo.

"See me as the snake girl," she said; and picking up the smaller snakes, she twisted them together into a wreath and put them on her head; they hissed a little, but did not attempt to untwine; the next larger in size she knotted into a collaret and slipped round her throat; the large python formed her waist belt, smaller snakes her anklets, and smaller ones yet wriggled in twisting rings along her arms from shoulders to wrists. Then she stood upright before us, looking like some wonderful little Indian god, her whole body a mass of writhing, twisting snakes, and her perfect, Bacchus-like face looking out at us from under her garland of hissing, moving heads and darting, forked tongues. She stood still for a second, then gave a shrill whistle, and as by magic all the snakes dropped from her; rapidly untwining and uncoiling, they glided down over her face, breasts, and body, and in a moment they were all writhing about the floor at her feet again. She sat down and began unceremoniously packing them back in their box.

"Come and have come pegs before you go," I suggested, and took the men over to the sideboard.

They drank them with much appreciation, especially Knight, who declared he had an uncanny feeling yet in his face where the rattler had hit him; and then, with a good deal of laughter and chaff upon my having refused legitimate Burmese marriage ties and then succumbed to the wiles of a snake-charmer, they departed, and I walked back to the veranda where Lulloo was sitting.

She ordered the old Burman to pick up the box and retire, which he did, and then she and I were left alone. She seemed in no way disposed to hurry, but came closer to me and looked up in my face with parted lips and half-shut eyes.

"Well," I said, putting my hand in my pocket, " how much is it to be?"

"Let there be no price. Am I not the slave of the sahib? But let me stay this one night in the house of the sahib."

Then I saw my folly in accepting the snake entertainment at all.

"I have told you before, Lulloo, it can not be," I returned, drawing from my pocket enough to amply repay her, and trying to force the money into her hand. " G home, my child, and find happiness among your own per-pie. I am here but for a time. If I loved you to-day, I must break your heart to-morrow. Go to your own people and forget me."

Lulloo let the money fall and scatter on the floor as she slipped to her knees and clasped mine, putting both arms round them and commencing to sob pitifully.

"I ask but to remain this night. Am I, then, so distasteful to the sahib?"

Now, to argue with a native is worse than useless; it does nothing but confirm him in his own view. I bent over her and took hold of her shoulders to raise her up.

The skin underneath the thin muslin was soft like satin, and the warmth and electricity of it ran into my palms. But I think the only feeling stirred in me was a rush of wild longing for Anna, and as I raised my head, my eves went straight over to the picture of her, fair and smiling, looking out at me from the darkness. I raised her up and almost carried her to the high lattice door, put her outside in silence, and closed and locked the door between us. She stared at me for a minute through the yellow lattice woodwork, and then fled away into the darkness with one sobbing cry, "Sahib! sahib!" It came back to me over the magnolia jungle of the compound in a faint wail and then there was stillness. I went inside and upstairs and threw myself on my bed, but I could not sleep. I felt nervous, excited, supremely dissatisfied with myself, without exactly knowing why, and troubled about the girl and her genuine distress. I tossed about till morning, and got up with shaking muscles and aching head. I went round to the club after breakfast and found there my four companions of last night finishing their coffee and perusing some aged papers. They looked up as I entered and eyed me all over with a sort of sympathetic curiosity that I found very obnoxious.

"You look very tired this morning," observed the doctor; and at this remark a sly smile went round the circle.

"Yes; I got no sleep at all," I returned, yawning and dropping into a chair.

This statement was the signal for a fire of covert and idiotic chaff and innuendo. I listened to it all in silence, balancing a paper-cutter in my fingers and looking through the window. Then, when they had quite exhausted their stock of wit and were quiet, I said, crossly:

"If you think that girl stayed at my place all night, you're mistaken. She left five minutes after you did."

There was silence in the room.

Something in my look, voice, or manner convinced them, I suppose, that I was speaking the truth, for the doctor, after laying down his paper on his knee and looking at me over it in silence for quite two minutes, said, slowly:

"Ethridge, you'll come to a bad end. You're intemperate, and intemperance in India, no constitution can stand."

"What on earth are you driving at now?" I asked, more crossly still, for I did feel excessively irritable, and, so to speak, unnerved that morning. I wheeled my chair round on its hind legs and stared at him sulkily. " I'm not intemperate."

"Yes, you are," persisted the doctor, stolidly; " you are intemperately virtuous, and it won't do. You won't even have the consolation of that girl of yours weeping over your grave. She won't coine down to Burtnah to do it. You drive things to extremes, and one can't stand extremes here. You are extremely moderate, and it won't pay. You should be moderately moderate. The moderate man is the only one who lives here. Moderately bad, moderately good, drinks moderately, eats moderately and is moderately virtuous. A man is made, apparently, for alternate vice and virtue; and this alternation suits his health better than a strict adherence to either. That theory has been threshed out in a novel called ' The Woman Who Didn't." I would advise you to read it."

"I think you are talking a d d lot of rot," I said, angrily, and got up and walked out of the club-house. But in my heart I knew the doctor was right with limitations. I went as usual to the court-house and then back at noon to my bungalow. I had no heart for billiards or cards or any of the club diversions. I had hardly got inside my compound gates when a wild figure ran toward me, tearing its yellow tunic, and throwing handfuls of dust against its breast.

"My child, sahib! my child, my only child! Give me back my child!" and then, as it groveled in the dust at my feet, I recognized Jhuldoo, the old Burman, father of Lulloo.

"I haven't got your child," I said, wearily for my head was aching, my eyes swollen, and life in general was a burden.

"No, sahib, she is dead, dead, hanged in the old stable by the bridge that spans the river; and Jhnldoo is childless, childless!" and ne rocked himself backward and forward, sitting in the narrow path-way that ran up to the house.

I stood motionless, paralyzed by his words, and felt myself grow cold in the blighting heat of the full noontide sun. Lulloo dead! Hanged! Hanged herself, doubtless, after her flight from me into the darkness. And so had added one more to the terrible list of Hindu suicides! I stood still, trying to realize it. The banana-tree drooped over us, and the figure in the dust went on swaying and rocking itself and moaning like a wounded animal.

"What did the sahib do that she should end her life in the stable by the bridge that spans the river? "What did the sahib do?" he moaned over and over again, yet without daring to demand or even waiting or seeming to expect an answer.

"I don't know," I said, mechanically, at last. " Come up to the veranda, Jhuldoo. I can not stand here. Come up and tell me about her."

I walked forward with a sick, sinking heart, and Jhuldoo got up and shambled after me. When we reached the shade of the veranda he sunk down and recommenced his crooning and weeping. I dropped into a chair and gazed blankly into the sunlight. Dead! choked! hanged! with a rope round that pretty, soft, round throat, and that beautiful child's face swollen and livid and distorted. Poor, pretty, little child! What an end! And I had brought her to it!

"The sahib could have gone to the city; he could have gone to the bazaar; he could have had a hundred wives; he need not have taken Jhuldoo's only child. Jhuldoo is a poor man! poor man! poor man!"

The " poor man! poor man! poor man!" rose to a piercing wail and went through the compound and distracted me.

"Jhuldoo," said I, passionately, "I have done nothing to your daughter nothing. I am not responsible for her death. She came here and begged me to use her as my toy and my plaything for an hour or so, and I would not. I bid her go back to you. She was here in my house last evening when I and my friends were here, and showed her snake-charming. She left here at the hour of ten, unharmed. I know nothing more of her than that. I give you the white man's truth."

The old Burman lifted his head and scanned my face with his heavy, reddened eyes. "How should I not believe the sahib?" he said, at length; " I know that his word is truth. Nevertheless, she has hanged herself in the stable by the bridge that spans the river, and Jhuldoo is childless and a poor man, a poor man!" He rocked and sobbed again, and I sat still, feeling very cold and sick-hearted. " It was an evil day when she first saw the sahib's face in the court-house. Yet do I not blame the sahib. He discouraged her, as I well know. Yet it is hard to remain a widow at eleven."

Then he wept afresh.

Much has been said about the avarice and greed of the native; but, whether my experience of them has been siu-gularly happy or not, 1 do not know, I have always found them rather indifferent to money certainly when any of their deeper emotions have been stirred. Now, when I offered the old Burman money that being, it seemed to me, the only thing I could do, not in any way as consolation for his daughter's loss, but simply to aid in the expenses of her funeral he put it aside and would not look at it. Although I think he was convinced that I had given him an absolutely truthful version of the matter, he still hated me for the loss I had unwittingly brought upon him, and he would not touch my money, and when he rose to leave, he shook the dust of my veranda from his clothes and shoes with something very like a curse. 1 watched him shamble away down the sandy path of the compound a queer, bent, twisted figure with his bluish-black skin contrasting oddly with the crude yellow of his ragged garments and then, with a hot mist in my eyes, I turned into my empty bungalow. It seemed very quiet, awfully quiet, and something crackled under my feet as I passed from the veranda. I turned to look what it was, and saw a little, dried, and withered garland of white clematis.

After this incident, life grew a good deal more intolerable to me. The thought of her death depressed and haunted me, and I felt a sort of distaste to black faces, which, considering they were all round me they and nothing else was bad. I felt an aversion for the court-house; some other of these narrow-petticoated maidens might hang herself on my account and her father come and sit on my doorstep and reproach me. The weather grew steadily hotter and hotter as we neared the rainy season, and Anna's letters grew less and less frequent. I was evidently, and quite naturally, slipping out of her existence, slipping out of her thoughts and memory. I had gone down to Burmah that is, I was virtually dead and buried and was now fast being forgotten. And I had only been here not quite one year. At the end of five I looked forward with dismay, and I began to feel more and more sympathy with Burke, who had blown his brains out in that tepid stillness of the bungalow, which was beginning to weigh more and more upon me each night. The time seemed to pass slower and slower, so that sometimes I caught myself wondering if it meant to stop altogether and keep me anchored forever and ever in Lihuli. A day seemed to stretch and stretch out its long, hot, elastic hours; and a week, to look back upon when it had passed, seemed like a year. " Take a wife and settle down." Yes, that was doubtless one way to kill the oppressive silence and keep a rational head on one's shoulders. Knight had done so, and certainly seemed comfortable enough. He was growing portly, and but for a little trouble with his liver kept his health wonderfully.

When I went round to see him in the evening, I used to find him generally smoking peacefully in his dining-room with his wife and family crawling about on the floor around his chair. He had three little round, fat, toddling bundles of babies, the youngest of whom was as white as its father.

"But, Knight, what will you do with all these when your term is up and you have to leave?" I asked him one evening when I came upon the scene of happy domesticity.

"Oh, well, she " with an airy wave of his hand " will go back to her own people, you know, with the kids."

"But what about that little one it's a gin, isn't it? and as white as we are. You won't want her to go into the bazaar, surely, and lead a dog's life among these blacks your own daughter, with your blood in her veins. It's horrible!"

"You're quite right, perfectly right, my dear fellow. It is a horrible thought, and that's why I never encourage it. I never think about disagreeable things. What's the use?"

I gazed at him fat, rubicund, cheerful, and comfortable as he leaned back in his chair; then at the pretty, childlike being who sat on her heels under the table, weaving a garland of clematis and crooning to herself; and then at the three little creatures tumbling round her, that he had seen fit, for his own amusement, to bring into the world and to such a miserable heritage.

"How different people are," I murmured, more to myself than to him. " To me, all love any sort of tie of that kind means responsibility."

"Does it?" returned Knight, sleepily. " To me it only means amusement." There was silence for a minute or two, then he added, "I'm afraid you will go off your head, like Burke, with all your responsibilities and serious notions. I suppose that's why you didn't have anything to do with the little snake girl?"

"Principally," I answered. " Suppose I had consented, and at the end of my term what then?"

Knight raised his eyebrows.

"Why, you would have been dead sick and tired of her probably long before that."

"And what about her feelings?"

"You've no need to think about them."

"That depends on how you are made."

"Exactly. And you are made all wrong for your own comfort."

Which was true in the main.

I stayed and had their after-dinner coffee with them, a cup of which the little Burmese hostess brought to my side and then sung us a song in her soft, lisping voice to her oblong guitar, while the babies rolled about contentedly on the matting. Burmese babies never cry. They only laugh and croon and sprawl about and grow fat. It was a soft, heavy night; hot, so that we dripped where we sat in the thinnest of duck suits; but beautiful with the fireflies whirling in burning circles through the dark, the air laden with the scent of the white swamp lilies, and a great, mellow, red-gold moon climbing slowly up over the misty green of the rice-fields.

As I walked homeward I noticed a pale, tearful ring round it, and I thought: " The rains are at hand."

Next day the heat beat on the walls of the bungalow and came up from the cracked, thirsty earth like the glare of a furnace. Calling round early at the club for possible letters which I did not find I learned that three of the members were very ill with fever and the doctor himself down with dysentery. I went on to the court-house, and the only incident of the burning, weary hours was that one of the native witnesses for the prosecution in a case was seized with heat apoplexy and dropped dead on the floor in the course of his testimony. This simplified the case for the defense, and I drove home early. Entering the bungalow felt like walking into a lime-kiln, and eating was an impossibility. After a pretense of taking some dinner I went out, involuntarily seeking for cooler, fresher air out- side. But there was little difference, except that outside one had to forego the slight relief the punkali gave. There was no breeze, not the faintest breath stirred the crystal, gilt air. The sky was calm; there was silence everywhere silence and suffocating heat. The trees seemed holding themselves rigid; not a leaf even trembled on them; there was no hum of insects, no rustle of a lizard even in the parched and withered grass. The earth seemed waiting, tensely expectant, and there was a universal hush as it awaited the coming of the rains.

I strolled along very slowly, for each movement meant a fresh burst of drenching sweat pouring down one's skin, and the quiet of expectancy all round one got into my own blood and made me move silently and breathe lightly, so as not to disturb the omnipresent stillness. The sky above me was pale, pure, transparent, and gleaming like the inside of an oyster-shell. The air seemed like liquid gold to look at, and like a best Whitney blanket to breathe. The tawny moss beneath iny feet was so dry it cracked with a little, hoarse whisper as I trod on it. I went on with my head down, thinking of Anna, and noticing in a vague way how the heat was increasing in intensity each moment, just as if I were walking steadily toward a furnace. At last, even movement, however slow, seemed overburdening fatigue. I stopped and looked up and round me. The sky had changed a little. I was to witness the thunder and lightning that would usher in the rains. Now, a thunder-storm with black clouds and night-like sky, with forks of lightning rending and splitting the dark curtain that seems drawn between earth and heaven, is an ordinary sight, one common to all men's experience, and that is impressive enough. But here was a roseate sky, luminous and transparent as a rose-leaf held before a flame, of itself exceedingly beautiful and clear, save for one enormous cloud that, rising almost from the earth, so low it seemed, towered into the sky and overspread all the center, white as the purest snow, delicate, soft, and filmy; while all round, to the west and east and north and south, the glorious bell of the sky hung unruffled and glowing with a few shining silver planets showing white in the translucent green and gold, and rose near the horizon.

I stood gazing up at the gigantic mass of white vapor, piled up like tossed and drifted snow, and apparently hang- ing so close over me that it almost seemed by stretching my hands upward I could bury them in its soft, fleecy masses. Then, as I watched it, it suddenly changed to gold; light seemed poured forth from it and through it, until the whole was one dazzling, burnished, blinding mass of gold, towering to the centre of the perfect evening sky. Then suddenly from behind it there came a terrific crash, a splitting, rending roar of thunder like the bursting of a thousand cannon at my side; and the lightning great, savage, silver forks of it was thrown out from behind the glowing, golden mass, as if by an unseen hand, plowing up furiously the pearl and rose of the tranquil sky. If ever one could believe one was witnessing the wrath of the immortal gods, if ever it might seem to a poor ordinary mortal that he was warned to stand aside while the flashing car of Zeus swept upward through the sky, that moment of blinding glory was the time. I flung myself backward on the baked and glowing moss, and leaning upon my elbow, I gazed upward and let my brain interpret the scene in any fanciful way it would. Onward and upward swept that magnificent cloud of gold. Only for a few seconds had the charioteer of Zeus allowed the wheels of the chariot to graze, as it were, the surface of the earth, but for that moment earth's face had been transfigured. Everything had caught a golden flame, reflecting the celestial fire. Onward now through the clear blue expanse rolled the cloud, and to my eyes it almost assumed the form of a chariot. It seemed really as if Zeus himself was sitting within, his majesty veiled by that whirling nimbus of gold above it; as if the lightning, which kept falling from it in splitting, jagged rays on every side, were bolts scattered by his hand; and the long, low, threatening roll of thunder, that passed resounding through the listening air, was the thunder of his wheels. I lay and watched and waited. There was no other sound: a tense, breathless, expectant silence was all round me; there was nothing to be seen above but the measureless, glorious track of infinite blue and the tender green and lambent rose and gold of the west. In this direction the cloud was traveling rapidly, shedding its forked lightning all the way, farther and farther, higher and higher; and the long, low rumbling of the chariot-wheels grew fainter and fainter. At last, the light in the west grew of an almost intolerable brightness, and before my straining eyes it seemed to open suddenly with light, and into an effulgence that was more than vision could bear passed the chariot of cloud. It was gone; nothing but a brazen shield of purest light hung in the west. Was it the outside of golden gates that had opened to the coming of Zeus and swung to behind the Immortal One? There was no lightning now. I listened. There was not the faintest echo of thunder. Not a sound. The sky was once more exquisitely serene, and Nature was waiting silent as before. As yet not one drop of rain had fallen. I rose and walked slowly homeward. I was convinced the rains would come in a few hours. What had I witnessed just the inaugural thunder-storm or a sign from the gods to the parched and patient air? I laughed a little, but in a hushed way; the awful silence that seemed hanging everywhere like a suspended curtain in the pellucid air, it seemed profanity to break. Well, if it were but a thunder-storm it was certainly unique and most beautiful.

Wearied out with the intense heat and utterly exhausted, I went to bed early that night, leaving every slat in the closed jilmils turned open, and the punkah swinging over me with its musical squeak. Before I went to sleep I noticed the extraordinary amount of animal life that had taken up quarters with me. Hundreds of the white, transparent lizards that for want of knowledge of the biological name I call glass bodies, since every organ in their sinuous little bodies is visible through their transparent skin, scampered above over my walls and ceiling, devouring the green-and-gold flies that marched in, in perfect armies through every crevice and crack; dozens of solemn, heavy-bodied spiders, too, came waddling in from the garden and verandas and advanced, clicking their long legs on the matting; long ribbons of black tree ants journeyed steadily over the floor in the direction of my bath-room, while during the process of undressing I came across no less than six snakes of a harmless kind incased in my slippers, nightshirt, and other suitable places. I was too weary to attempt a useless war against my thousands of small invaders. Doubtless a message of the approaching death from the skies had been conveyed to them also, and they sought asylum with me. So beyond picking up, by means of a tumbler and a bit of paper, a portly and venomous-looking scorpion, that was making its way up to my bed, and throwing him through the window, I made no attempt to defend myself, but flung myself on the charpoy and was mercifully soon asleep. It may have been midnight or later at any rate, it was pitch dark when 1 was again awakened. The punkah had ceased. The heat was so intense that I sprung up, involuntarily fancying for the moment some one was trying to smother me with pillow or blanket. But no. It was only the intolerable pressure of the thick, suffocating air. All round me there was a roar in the air like the roar of a flood, and the noise of the rain beating on the roof was like shrapnel firing. I sat up for a moment trying to get my breath. There seemed no air to breathe. It had all become, apparently, pea soup. Then I was startled by the drip, drip of water falling with a tinkle into the matting, and I suddenly put out my hand and found my sheets and pillow were sodden wet. I struck a light and put it to the candle. The wick flared up and showed me my room. Room! Great heavens! It was more like an unfinished aquarium. The roof was leaking in a dozen or more places, one being directly over my bed, and the animal inmates were scurrying about in the greatest alarm on discovering the frail nature of their shelter. Snakes wriggled uneasily over the floor, the ants came trooping back from the bath-room, the spiders raced desperately up the curtains, and the lizards ran backward and forward over the dripping ceiling, sneezing. I got up, kicked aside the snakes, and put on my boots. Then I dragged my bed across the floor to a part of the room above which the ceiling appeared to be dry. The heat was inconceivable; the exertion of moving the bed made the sweat pour from me, and I sat down gasping with that awful sense of there being nothing to breathe nothing such as we are accustomed to think of only this horrible thick mixture that makes one feel one is sinking in quicksand. In that moment, as I sat dripping with perspiration, with limbs that seemed of cotton wool, and with mouth hanging open, gasping, I thought of the unhappy fish I had seen, when with anglers, lying straining and heaving on the dry rocks and I was glad I had never fished. When I Lad recovered a little, I walked round the room rescuing my most precious possessions books, papers, and clothes from the persistent drip, drip that was coming now from every part of the ceiling. As soon as I had done this I noticed the rain was leaking through the dry corner of the ceiling and iny bed was again being dripped upon. I moved it again to shelter and lay down on it. I dozed after a little while, with the roar of the rain in my ears, and I woke again with water warm, tepid water splashing on my face. I rose again and dragged my bed after me, but only gained a few minutes' respite; the roof seemed giving way all over, and the few weary hours that remained of darkness I spent chasing my bed round the room and puddling after it in dripping, steaming pajamas. At the first light I put on a holland suit and went downstairs. The staircase had been transformed into a dashing waterfall. The rain had poured into the veranda rooms upstairs, and rushed out again on to the landings in the house, and from there found its way in a whirling, eddying torrent down the staircase. I picked my way down it, and entered my dining-room, to feel the carpet under my feet give like a sponge and go squelch, squelch at each step. On the table I saw no signs of my fine white damask cloth that usually adorned it. All over, for one-half inch deep, lay a mass of struggling, dying ants and fallen ants' wings. Every cup and saucer was full of them, and the bread and butter invisible beneath piles of filmy wings. These creatures, indued with wings for a short time at this season and driven in by the rain outside, enter the room in flying swarms. Their wings drop from them, they shed them everywhere table, floor, sideboard alike are covered while their struggling bodies fall, either to die at once, or crawl away reduced to their ordinary means of locomotion again. I sighed, gazing at this repulsive breakfast-table, and then looked through the verandas. Long, bright, diagonal lines from the sky to earth everywhere, so close and merged together that they made a wall between vision and landscape, and a white mist, thick as smoke, rising upward from the steaming, thirsty, drinking earth.

I called my servant and breakfasted as well as I could upon ants' bodies and wings flavored with coffee, and ants spread upon bread-and-butter, and then ordered my carriage and drove down to the office, with the rain lashing the top of the buggy and the running water in the road over the axles of the dragging wheels.

It rained for one whole month without intermission, and no one can tell what I suffered during that space of time.

Every road became first a running stream and then a sort of quicksand, in which foot or horse's hoof or carriage-wheel sunk hopelessly, so that exercise without became an impossibility, and one was confined to the lifeless, sultry air within the silent bungalow. Existence became a cruel blank; and it so happened that then, when I would have prized them so unspeakably, all my letters failed me, and day after day passed and post after post came in, and not a line came to me from that dear outer world, where people were living, any more than news comes to the inmates of the grassy graves. And on the last night of the month, I came home, as I remember, from a vain attempt at a walk in the torrents of lukewarm rain, that fell persistently in long straight lines from sky to earth, deadening every thing, shutting out sight of everything but itself, shutting out sound of everything but itself. The court-house had been closed a week, owing to the amount of prevailing sickness, so that that exercising ground, as it were, for the thoughts, speech, and feelings, had been shut up. I had not spoken one word beyond orders to my servants for the last fortnight. The club was closed, nearly all the members were sick or had managed, on one pretext or other, to get away for a little leave. I entered my bungalow that evening, knowing there was nowhere to go, nothing to do, no one to see, no one to speak to. I was completely alone in this blank, tepid silence, shut in upon myself on every side by walls of falling rain. I went through the rooms, desperately looking at all the books; I had read them all, and the newspapers all exhausted long ago. Oh, how I longed for a letter; how priceless one would have been to me then; it would have seemed like a hand stretched out to me from the real, living world that was somewhere far off, away in the distance. Where was I? I seemed out of the world. Dead, buried, and forgotten. I stood still in the center of my dining-room, staring blankly before me, and listening to the eternal low wish, wish of the water falling on the long-since sodden earth.

"Poor Burke! poor Burke!" I thought. " These were just such moments as he had."

Then I thought I saw Burke himself advance from one of the dark corners, and he seemed to beckon to me and say:

"Come on, come on; one little shot in the temple does it, and, after all, you are buried, and you may as well be dead."

Then I sat down and hid my face on the table with a smothered groan. I am going mad, I thought I certainly am. Oh, God! save me from that! Deliver me from this place! Then I sat still and listened to the rain again. It was very quiet, with no sound at all but this and the dull response of the long, rank grass to it. Just exactly as it must sound to the corpses in the grave-yard, I thought to myself. Then I wondered why solitude should have such a terrible, disorganizing and demoralizing effect on the human brain, and I found myself murmuring over and over again:

"They had to destroy Millbank and the solitary confinement system; they pulled it down for the same reason. All the prisoners went mad, yes, they went mad! and they were only confined a fortnight at a time."

And the rain fell outside unceasingly and the hours crept by silently.

That night I took a large dose of chloral, pouring it put with an unsparing hand. I would run the risk of sleeping forever rather than remain awake that night.

The next morning there were really letters for me several letters and though they were all in long envelopes and looked horribly business-like, I seized upon them as a drowning man upon a life-belt. They were life-belts to me, drowning in this dead sea of solitude and silence, lifebelts flung, as it were, from that huge, comfortable liner, the world, full of lights and life and companionship, standing far off from me. How I tore open the tough blue envelopes! I was till really then alive, a human being to be reckoned with. Positively, last night it seemed as if six feet of good church-yard soil was pressing above my breast. I commenced to read the letters through, and half an hour later I was walking round the room with two or three sheets of blue paper clutched in my hand and telling myself " it was impossible," " incredible," the chloral of the night before had affected my brain, and I was going cranky like Burke. For one letter informed me curtly but those words seemed to me the sweetest that had ever been written that " various changes necessitated my immediate recall to Kalatu," and the other with equal brevity that, by the will of my late cousin, deceased, I was the master of an estate worth nearly two hundred thousand pounds. The liner had indeed thrown out not only lifebelts but a life-line and was rapidly hauling me on board! And I felt exactly that sensation. When I grew a little calmer and had read the letters again and assured myself that the words were really written there in good black ink, I took up my own pen and wrote off at once to Anna. Not one second would 1 delay now that I was free to speak. Her phrase in her very first letter, "Why didn't you wake me?" came before my eyes and encouraged me, and I wrote all that she should have heard then. I told her my own news, and wound up by saying I should start for Kalatu at once, and that she was not to answer me till my arrival there, when I would, the very first evening, come to see her. Then I began to walk up and down my room, trying not to feel too glad about it all. Had I been a Greek, I should have certainly seen in this unexpected and unusual good fortune the forewarning of some dire calamity for no mortal is allowed to be equally happy with the gods for long but I was only a happy-go-lucky, unsuper-stitious Briton, and I did not feel the least uneasiness.

The next few days my departure from Lihuli, rain-soaked and steaming, wrapped in a white mist; the long, hot journey north; the arrival and the first sight of Kalatu's palms and sparkling, sapphire line of sea beyond the desert is all lost in a bright haze of pleasure; the clearest point being when, tired and dusty and travel-stained, I was back in my old room in the old bungalow on the Kutcherry road, with Anna's housetops just visible across the palms of the intervening compounds.

I changed my clothes hastily, a perfect fever of joy, hope, expectation, and nervous pleasure throbbing in my eins. Then I came down the steps of the bungalow in the glow of the evening and flung myself into the carriage and drove to the Lombards. As 1 entered the compound the sky flamed up with orange and saffron light, the broad meidan on every side rolled away like a sea of fire. As the wheels ground on the sandy path Anna herself stepped out on the low stone terrace. My eyes rushed over her in a second. She was the same, untouched and unaltered. There was the same exquisite freshness of the morning in her face. She came forward with a soft, sparkling smile, and the light in her hair. I sprung from the carriage, which drove rapidly to the back of the bungalow and up the few steps. We stood on the terrace alone, in the orange sunset, with only great, warm, vital, whispering, indulgent Nature round us. I took her outstretched hands, very slim and white and half lost in the filmy laces of the sleeve, and so drew her closer to me. I was burning, overflowing with the force of my joy, relief, and suppressed passion. Perhaps the electric force of all these passed through my clasp into her, and, for the moment, dominated her; her figure inclined docilely toward me, and she came one little step nearer. My eyes were fixed on her and blazing with the fires within. She raised hers to them and, for an instant, it seemed to me there was something unutterably sad in the depths of those passionate, dark blue eyes; but perhaps it was only seriousness as she felt a crisis in her life approaching. The light caught the almost feathery tips of the wonderfully long lashes and made the face indescribably soft and touching.

The next instant, reading her permission in that first language of the world the looks I had bent forward and kissed the soft, sweet lips.

Within the next hour the whole station knew that we were engaged.

CHAPTER IIL

THE next morning I woke up, I suppose, perhaps the happiest man in India. The bearer, bringing in the morning coffee, found me with my arms crossed behind my head gazing out through the open jilmils to the compound full of the cool glory of an Indian dawn. Anna belonged to me, the one woman between the ends of the earth that I wanted, that was necessary to me; and not that I wanted this hour or day, in a careless gust of animal passion, but the being, the personality that I should want all my life, without whom existence had been empty before and would be empty again, but with whom it was full, complete, rounded out, padded stuffed, as it were with contentment. Lucky Ethridge! The title seemed justified at last. It was curious how completely Anna fulfilled every detail of my ideal of girlhood. Ideal! It is a hackneyed word, but it must stand. It represents that which every mind, consciously or unconsciously, possesses, and mine had been stored away in the recesses of my brain almost unknown to myself and yet sufficiently alive to turn me away from all women I had met until I saw Anna. I looked back through all those long rows of women I had known till now, and there was not one that I had felt the faintest impulse to take with me as my traveling companion down the road of life. I recollected some very beautiful how beautiful they had been! What faces rose before me, with their delicately penciled eyebrows, perfectly modeled noses, and rounded chins to match those of statues. And now, Anna was hardly beautiful at all. She was wonderfully fresh, like the dawn in spring, but all that perfection of feature was wanting. Yet those beautiful faces had been like empty masks hung in a bazaar for me. There had been selfish hardness behind some, stupidity behind others, a sordid commonplaceness of thought and mind, or empty frivolity. And beyond all to me cleverness was a necessity. Then there had been clever women how clever and brilliant! but in this I had never found Anna's superior or equal. Never had I known in man or woman any brain like this, so clever, so logical, so gifted, so full of force of intellect, which seems to make itself felt in even the simplest words and actions of the one who possesses it. And then the other clever, great minds I had known, they had all been coupled with intolerable defects, of which hardness of heart and a cruelty in the moral nature were the most common. Anna's hardness and keenness existed in her brain and intellect alone; it left a heart, the softest, tenderest, most compassionate possible. Then yet there was another class of women women with beautiful faces and soft, lovable natures, sweet voices and tender ways like Anna's, and passionate, sympathetic hearts like hers, and to these I had been drawn most of all; but, then, on a little acquaintance, how they wearied one! There was nothing more than this. There was no brain to be a companion to one's own; there was no comprehension of one's deepest thought, nothing to meet one's own idea, and the sweet, mild glances from the beautiful eyes at last wearied one and disappointed one and left one unsatisfied. There was no mentality to rush forward in a passionate ecstasy to meot one's own through these gates to the soul. They were beautiful gates, it is true, but less to a soul than a desert. And Anna seemed to stand before me this morning arrayed in my mental vision just as I would have her. There was the glory of the morning, of sweet life and youth and color to charm and lead captive my senses and give to all my mental adoration of her that last touch of ecstasy that physical passion alone has the power to bestow; there was the tender, loving heart, on which a dying, bleeding soul might rest and forget its wounds, and think that death was sleep; and there was the bright, sparkling intellect, ready and eager to understand, to respond, the one gift that makes man in this brief life equal to the gods.

Yes. To me she was perfect. She was all that I wanted, all that I had ever wanted, and she was mine. I got up and dressed.

That evening I did not go to dinner, but called afterward and found the Lombards and some friends all seated outside on the stone veranda. I joined them and was accorded with a smile the chair next Anna. We all chatted together for some time, and then the general suggested somebody should sing.

"Don't let us go inside," said Anna, gently. " It is so much cooler here."

"Well, Ethridge plays the guitar," he returned. " You'll find a guitar just inside the dining-room," he added, turning to me. " Fetch it and start some of these young people."

I went obediently and fetched the guitar, resumed my seat, tuned the instrument, and then announced I would accompany any one who would sing. But no one hastened to accept the offer. Then the general made an individual appeal to each in turn. Most of them made excuses, and the young man next Anna drawled out that he did not know anything to sing. When it came to Anna she said:

"I will sing you a little Greek song, if you like. I don't seem to remember anything else, just at this minute."

There was general acclaim at this, and everybody declared that a Greek song was what they had been most wishing for, and, indeed, almost expecting; and I thought, as I nervously pulled up the string a little higher, "Good heavens! what sort of an accompaniment will that want?"

Anna, as if divining my fears, leaned toward me and hummed the tune in my ear. It was a very quaint but simple one, and I caught it and managed to follow her. Then she sung Anacreon's famous ode to the dove.

The tune changed in the second verse and had a most catching ring and swing in it, as the soft, expressive voice sent out the words on the still, pearly air.

Most of the men present, with myself, understood the expressive words, and it brought back curious, misty recol-. lections of college days, which somehow seem so far oil when we have once gone out from port on life's ocean; and for the women it was an amusement to hear the quaint-sounding old language and the curious, swinging tune. When she ceased there was much applause and gratitude. Only the young man next her drawled out with a most contemptuous sneer:

"Fancy having your head so full of Greek that you can't sing anything else!"

The tone was so inconceivably rude that I sprung up in my chair with a retort on my lips. But Anna was clever and her brain sharp as steel, in spite of her rose-like softness of looks, and she could quite well take care of herself when she chose. She had turned in her chair and answered, with an exact imitation of his tone:

"Fancy having nothing in your head, so that you can't sing at all."

And there was a general laugh that was decidedly with Anna.

For two days for this reason memorable days in my life I was happy, supremely content and satisfied. Work was light to me, hours flew by on their gilded wings like moments, and the blood in my veins seemed a mixture of fire and wine, rather than the ordinary legitimate British material. But the evening of the last of these two days brought with it a chill of apprehension. It was a something very light and slight, such as the first little cold whisper of the wind flying in front of a still distant storm. I was walking home alone through the sultry, gorgeous tropic night from a long evening spent almost alone with Anna on the veranda and in that paradise of whispering palms and bending grasses and sleeping flowers, the Lombards' compound. I had been persuading her to fix the hour, the day, fo our marriage; and the soft, distressed, yet determined resistance I had met with had at first astounded and lastly frightened me. Her head had been on my shoulder, her arms round me, our breasts pressed close till the hearts beat one against the other. Yet a chasm was opening between u, because our desires were not the same.

"No, Gerald, I really don't wish it."

And I did wish it, and there was the great abyss between us.

Then I pressed for reasons. I asked questions. Did she love me?

Yes, she loved me with all the strength of her nature and what a wild, passionate nature that was I alone knew, and was to know still more profoundly later. Were there any family reasons for delaying our marriage? Had her father any thing to do with her answer? No. None. Nothing. It was simply her own wish.

Then how could she love me so much and not wish to marry me?

She couldn't tell. A year ago she would have consented at once; but 1 had delayed for a year, and now she wanted to delay a littlej she could not tell how long.

Would she really have accepted me before I went to Burmah? I had asked, and oh! the agony of my heart as she had answered:

"I would have married you that same day, had you wished it. I felt, after our first meeting that first night, that you were the being in the whole world I was to love with all my soul. My whole nature went out to you and accepted you. I felt my heart opening to your smiles as a flower uncloses itself to the touch of the sun. Your arms held me in the dance, and to those arms I would have trusted myself forever. I can not explain to you why, except that love and trust and confidence in you were borne in upon my mind."

"And when I went away without speaking you were disappointed?"

My voice was uncertain; a hot mist was forcing itself over my eyes.

"Yes."

Her answer was so frank, so certain, so unwavering.

Then I broke out into wild protestations, my reasons for my action, my love for her, my unselfish motives, all my thought had been for her. To which she listened quietly and as quietly replied;

"I know. You have told me. I understand. But in acting as you did, you ran the risk."

"But you say you still love me?"

"I do! I do!"

And her lips were pressed to mine with a passion that went through and through me in waves of fire.

"And no one has come between us in the interval?"'

"Could I love two men at the same time?"

I laughed.

"Well, what is it? What is it? You are the soul of truth. Tell me why, just your reasons, and I swear I will be patient."

"I have told you. It is just a wish of mine to delay a little as you did."

"But I had my reasons."

"You did not tell them to me."

And so at last I had come away from her, confused, perplexed, puzzled, distressed beyond words and frightened. Yes, for as a slight symptom will tell to a physician, surely and without hope, the approach of a loathsome and relentless disease, so to my brain this strange phase of her feeling foretold something, though I could not discern what, of menace to the future.

And as I walked onward, reviewing all that had been said by us both, I grew cold and chill in the sultry air. When I reached my bungalow I opened a bottle of champagne and drank half of it, and then flung myself into a long, cane chair for a smoke and I began to see things more lightly and philosophically. It was certainly very extraordinary, and all that Anna had said that evening had been most contradictory, but there might be some very simple explanation of it all. She might have some secret girlish motive for wishing to postpone the marriage, that she was too shy to confide to me. The main point, that she loved me, that her heart was mine, entirely mine, seemed to be absolutely self-evident. She really loved me; no man, I think, could mistake those thousand little evidences she gave me in every tone and action; and, therefore, loving me, she could certainly love no other. Would not any man have reasoned as I did that night?

Then it flashed upon me that she might have become ywasi-entangled in some engagement with some man she ttid not love. That would account for all, including her denial of love for any one else. (And here an error had crept imperceptibly into my caiculations, for she had not given me any such denial.) The following day I would make inquiries. I would try to find out whether, in my absence, talk had connected Anna with any one in the station. There could hardly be anything existent in the way of an engagement, love-affair, or merest flirtation, that the station would not know of. Then I would try to straighten matters out for her; and if I once knew the point, perhaps some point of honor with her, I could help her with some counsel or consolation. Having thought all this out to my satisfaction during the smoking of seven cigarettes, I turned into bed much comforted. The next morning I immediately began my investigations with the greatest care and caution and delicacy. But evening came and found me with precisely the opposite result of my inquiries from that which I had expected. In fact, my own previous opinion of Anna had been completely ratified. Every one agreed that there was no individual in the station that Anna favored more than another. And the announcement of my engagement to her had come partly as a surprise, but more as an explanation of her exceeding seriousness of conduct and coolness of manner to every one else. She distributed her dances evenly, seldom dancing more than once with the same person. If she allowed Lieutenant Tomkins to ride with her one morning, she accorded that same privilege to Lieutenant Simkins the next. In short, the whole time I had been absent she had been noted for her gentle though cold indifference to all the officers and civilians in the station. To some extent pleased with all this, I fell back on the idea that Anna had some purely personal and fanciful reason for delaying our wedding; and I came to the conclusion that it would be best, whatever it cost myself, to humor her and be as patient as I could, to allw the subject to remain untouched upon for a week or two, and then press my petition again. In the meantime I devoted my energies to devising all sorts of entertainments. My principal object in this was to delight and amuse Anna and find excuses for having her perpetually with me. But also, undoubtedly, the station expected great things of me. The news of the fortune I had inherited spread all over the neighborhood and confirmed everybody in their envious refrain of " lucky Ethridge." Now, as a young assistant com-

missioner with no income but my paj, I had been generously entertained by every married woman in the station, when I could give little return for hospitality beyond general amiability; and now that I was installed in a big bungalow of rny own, with a surplus of ready money, I was only too willing to pay off my social debts. The more I was thrown in Anna's society and the more we talked together, the more her remarkable character and intellect shone out before me. I felt somehow a vague sensation that she was not entirely suited and fitted to this humdrum nineteenth century, that her character and her mind belonged rather to seme more stirring time, when personal courage was at a premium and excitement was every-day food for every one. It was not that she was not perfectly calm and irreproachable in every way, in conduct, looks, and words. She had a peculiarly graceful and fascinating manner, and every one in the station agreed she was charming. It was only when we were alone, riding cr driving, and had escaped from the beaten tracks of conversation, that she said things and expressed opinions that gave me a faint, peculiar sense of her extreme independence and of something wonderfully strong in her character something large, larger than the nature of mrst women, something also extremely courageous, that called for an heroic age to find its natural exercise. Among the other things I had studied, the history of the Middle Ages had always possessed a great fascination for me; and now I was suddenly drawn again toward it by the name of the girl I loved, and by the peculiar timbre of her nature that seemed familiar to me and came to me as an echo from the past. I began to read again in my odd moments of leisure between government and social work and really the latter is nearly as hard as the former! the volumes of medieval history I had brought out with me; and night after night, when it was too hot to sleep, I sat turning over the pages of the musty old tomes that chronicled the events of those musty old times. One night I came suddenly upon the biography of Catherine Sforza, and read it through from beginning to end. At the end of the old quarto volume was a full-page portrait of this notorious and evil woman. And I looked at it for a long time with peculiar interest. It was a fine engraving and represented the Sforza in a moment of triumph, just after she bad completed to her satisfaction the manufacture of one of her deadly poisons. She was represented in her laboratory, and having just removed her glass mask, she looked out at you from the print with a peculiar arresting gaze. There was something curiously familiar in the expression, in the look about the luminous eyes of force great mental force and power; and all at once, in a flash, it came to me whence arose that feeling of recogni-tion.

"Anna could look like that, I am sure she could," I thought. I sat for a long time with the open page before me, and a strange fancy came to me that I would like to see her, just so, in this attitude, dress, and environment, and see whether, in reality, the resemblance was fulfilled. But what excuse could I give if I told her this? And everything in the picture was so unlike the surroundings one has in modern India that I certainly never should see her thus. Then another thought flashed upon me: "Get up some tableaux vivants!" What could be more orthodox, more commonplace than that? What would please the station more, and all the empty-headed young girls and foolish old women in it more than this an entertainment where they could dress as extravagantly and as unsuited to their years or their faces as they pleased, and wear their hair down? Great idea! If I knew the station well in which I lived, nothing could be more popular, more universally acceptable. I shut the book and went to bed. And the Sforza with her flaming red hair stood at the foot of the cjiarpoy all night, holding her glass mask and looking at me with those strange, compelling eyes.

The next morning I invited four of the youngest, gayest, and most friendly married women to luncheon with me and unfolded my scheme to them, begging them to be my managing committee.

As I anticipated, it was hailed with cries of delight.

' Mr. Ethridge, yon are just too lovely for anything!" exclaimed Mrs. Sinclair, who possessed fine hair all her own.

"It must be the greatest fun in the world, only those things cost so," remarked Mrs. Wilson, the wife of a lieutenant, with a sigh.

I explained that I proposed to make a general fund of two thousand rupees, from which any of the committee might draw all they wanted. Costumes, curtains, lights, wigs, every source of expense I would provide for with the greatest pleasure. Every one of my committee was to have absolute carte blanche. This delighted them beyond everything.

"I would so like to be Joan of Arc an'd wear my hair down," recommenced Mrs. Sinclair, putting up her hand to it.

"We must choose the pictures to-day," announced Mrs. Muggridge, decisively, who also had tine hair, but could not exactly have been wearing it down for forty years at least.

"What have you chosen for Miss Lombard?" demanded Mrs. Tillotson, who was young and keen of mental vision.

I knew that perfect frankness with women, who always see through you whether you are frank with them or not, was the only safe policy, and luncheon being over, I rose and got down the heavy quarto volume, found the place and opened it there, in silence, before them.

"That dreadful woman!" exclaimed Mrs. Sinclair. " Why, Mr. Ethridge, that's not a bit like Anna!"

"How very strange!" murmured Mrs. Muggridge. " Now, I was going to suggest Gretchen sitting at the spinning-wheel. That fair hair of Anna's, you know, in two plaits, and then her coloring, so Saxon, almost German, one might say."

"Gretchen is not in the least the type of humanity that Anna is," I returned, " and I can not imagine her spinning."

"But, good gracious! you don't imagine Anna is like this type of woman?" asked Mrs. Wilson, in a shocked tone.

"No, I don't," I said at once with energy. " Only there is a certain link between them. I don't quite know what, but I think it is the link of courage and intense mentality."

The three women looked at me with that deferential blankness of expression one meets so often in society when one is not in the least understood. Mrs. Tillotson bent over the picture in silence for a minute, then she nodded approvingly.

"What do you think?" I asked her.

"She will do it," she returned, laconically.

And so, without further opposition, that was decided upon for Anna. The rest of the afternoon was spent in arranging the general plan of the entertainment and choosing pictures for the four on the committee. I had a whole library of great volumes, and in gratitude for their cordial support, I diligently searched away in them till pictures for each one of them had been found that supremely satisfied them. Mrs. Sinclair was furnished with a most striking Joan of Arc, bound to a stake, with hair to an indefinite extent streaming round her, as one sees in the advertisements of Edwards's Harlene. Mrs. Muggridge was easily persuaded that she alone could do justice to her favorite Gretchen. A certain stoutness of figure was not wholly unsuited to the florid style of German maidenhood, and her hair was certainly light and would lend itself to two plaits. Mrs. Wilson, who was the wife of the lieutenant on two hundred and fifty rupees per mensem, reveled in the picture of the " Queen of Sheba," loaded with the most astounding silks and jewels. Mrs. Tillotson, tiny, slight, dainty, small-footed and agile, fluttered the pages of innumerable volumes contemptuously, then, opening a book of French travel, she hit upon the picture " A Paris Gamin." This young gentleman, in ragged coat, shirt, and trousers, with a shock of untidy hair and fun-loving eyes, was depicted in the act of throwing a somersault, and was practically standing on his hands, head downward, with his bare feet in the air. She would be that or nothing, she declared. The remainder of the committee was shocked.

"And you couldn't do it, my dear. You couldn't maintain that attitude," urged the kind and maternal Mrs. Muggridge.

"It will have to be a short tableau," coolly returned little Mrs. Tillotson, " a snap-shot, as it were," and she gazed lovingly at the gamin's high-poised feet the most striking thing in the picture.

What a chance to display those little feet of hers the only ones in the station that could wear a No. 2 shoe! She had no hair to boast of, so that the downward hanging shock head did not trouble her. And finally she had her way. At five o'clock they left me, burning to carry the news to the station, and I sat down to write to a Bombay firm the order for the material I wanted for the Sforza's gown, and to others for the accessories such as glass masks, mortars, etc. things which can not be found in the highly respectable shops at Kalatu. That same evening I had my bearer carry the volume, containing the picture, to the Lombards. I showed Anna the picture and told her my ideas. She looked long at the picture, then she said:

"Catherine Sforza was a cruel and a wicked woman. I do not want to poison any one, and should never be at all likely to do it."

"No, I know!" I exclaimed, eagerly. " Oh, Anna! you have the teuderest heart in the world. You have nothing in common with this woman, nothing except the force of character, the courage, the strength of brain she must have had to live the life she did.

Her crimes were the crimes of her century. Her great mental force threw itself into crime, because crime was the order of her time; and you have that same force, which you would throw into great and heroic deeds if they were to be done."

"I don't know, I'm sure," returned Anna. " But I'll try to fulfill your expectations as to looking like this picture, though I really do think you might have found some more orthodox person for me."

"I do not think that would have been nearly so suitable, you see," I returned, laughing.

For the next fortnight I hardly knew my own house. The committee took possession of it, and my sedate Mohammedan servants, I believe, gained the impression that I was inaugurating a seraglio. It was not altogether comfortable to be so invaded, but I was amply repaid by the freedom it gave me of Anna's society. It was very delightful, coming back from my work at five, to find Anna and Mrs. Tillotson sitting on a carpenter's bench in my front drawing-room, with cups of tea, supplied from my pantry and kitchen, in their hands, chatting together, and watching the work that was going forward in the back drawing-room, namely, of transforming the wide-pillared arch between the two rooms into a colossal picture-frame, and with the floor all round them, and every chair and table covered with silk scarves, gilt crowns, jewels, antique prints, and wood shavings. Then Anna would look up and say:

"Oh, Gerald! we've been waiting for you to advise us about this!"

And I would sit down by them, and then Mrs. Tillotson would go off! x fetch something, and Anna and I would be left alone on the carpenter's bench, in the disordered room, with only the native workmen at the other end of it hanging up gilt moldings.

But if I had looked forward to seeing Anna pose and repose before me, I was disappointed. " Somehow," she said, looking hard at the picture, "I can work myself up to looking like this once; but if I rehearse it I shall lose he spirit of it, and I sha'n't be able to do it. You had better give me all the things and tell me what has got to be done, and I'll try to do it when the time comes."

I told her I was having the dress made exactly as it was in the picture; but the darsi would want to fit her some: ime, and that I had sent to Bombay for a box of powder Jor her hair.

"Catherine had red hair, hadn't she? How are you joing to make mine red?"

I looked at her sunny, yellow hair, running into flaxen or gold in its different creases.

"If you put this bright red powder all over it thickly, it will be the Sforza's hair. Do you see how it clusters and waves in the picture? With the red powder yours will be the very thing."

"I don't see why you should be so anxious to see me in such a horrid character," she said, discontentedly, staring at the print and knitting her delicate, marked eyebrows. " That woman murdered dozens of people. Now, I couldn't murder anybody."

"Yes, you could, my Anna, only with a good motive, I know; but if you had that, you would not hesitate, I am sure of it."

She was staring at me with wide eyes.

"Gerald! How can you say such dreadful things? Why, I can't bear to kill anything. 1 won't let the meteranni kill the spiders in my bedroom, though I hate them. I wouldn't kill anybody to save my own life even in self-defense."

"No," I said, gently, "I know all that; but to save another you would me, for instance."

She looked at me, laughed, and colored.

"What nonsense we are talking! Here comes Ethel back again, Now, be sensible."

Ethel Tillotson reappeared, bringing in her train two angry-looking girls. They were the two prettiest girls in the station a Miss Johnson, tall and lithe, with dusky hair and skin and midnight eyes, and Miss Jeffries, short and round and fat, with Saxon hair and skin, and eyes like great, flat turquoises under a brow of snow.

"Now," said Mrs. Tillotson to Anna, " you are to be a Solomon and settle this matter. Here are two May Queens! What are we to do about it?"

Anna looked at both the girls quietly flushed, wrathful, and confused at finding me there, whom they evidently had not expected.

"You should be the May Queen of England," she said, calmly, to the Saxon girl without the least hesitation, while Miss Johnson opened her eyes and glared at her wrath-fully. "And you," she added, turning to the other, " will make a magnificent Rosiere the Rose Queen of France. Won't that do? The pictures are almost identical, only you will each be types of the two different countries, and the pink of the roses will suit you much better than English May."

The girl bent over the picture of the " Rose Queen of France," and her wrath disappeared.

"How clever you are, Anna!" she said, with a gay smile over her shoulder as she went away with the engraving.

"Well done, Solly," said Mrs. Tillotson, patting her head. " Now you've just got to leave Mr. Ethridge and come and show me how to fix this chair so that it won't be seen by the audience. I must have it to lean upon when I am standing on my head."

Anna rose with a bright parting smile at me, and Mrs. Tillotson carried her off behind the scenes.

Now, as every one knows, there is nothing so efficacious as private theatricals for bringing out the innate selfishness, conceit, and smallness of human nature, and I fully experienced this through the next fortnight; but among all the pettiness, the malice and uukindness, the fret and fussing of all these women, Anna stood out alone as unmoved and unspoiled by it. She said very little about her own part, and took all the chaff and remonstrances aboufc the "horrid woman" she was to personate, and her " hideous red hair " in good part.

"Gerald wishes it," was all she said in answer to jests, questions, and mockery.

She helped prettier girls than herself to dress their hair and choose their garments to the most advantage. She lent generously from her own wardrobe and jewel-case. She smoothed out quarrels, and turned the venomous remarks of one woman to another aside as often as she could; and praised, consoled, complimented, and softened the temper of them all. And in those days I grew to know her and love her better than ever. There was no meanness, no small cruelty, no hardness in her character. It was like some of our Indian stuffs, woven true, both sides, upper and under alike, and velvety all through.

At last the eventful evening came, and I, who had not once seen her stand for the picture, was full of wonder and curiosity as to how far she would catch the spirit of it. From early afternoon my whole house had been in a turmoil, like a bee-hive in which there is an internal revolution. But by eight o'clock, when the curtains were to be drawn aside from the first picture, everything seemed to be in perfect order. The audience were all seated, and, as far as they could judge, perfect peace and calm reigned behind those heavy maroon curtains. I, who had seen the back of these for the past two weeks, doubted the last proposition; but appearances were admirably maintained. The front drawing-room was an enormous room, and now, cleared entirely of furniture, it accommodated a large number of chairs. All the station had been invited and quite three-fourths of it had come.

I hardly noticed the other pictures. Anna's was the sixth on the list, and I waited for that one with my heart beating and my eyes hardly seeing the others as they passed before me. When the curtains were drawn aside for the sixth tableau, they revealed Anna standing alone in the center of the stage. There was little to distract attention from her. The whole picture was that one figure, the wonderful pose and expression of the face. She stood at her full height, but leaning a little forward toward the audience. In one hand she held the transparent glass mask, and in the other the marble basin holding the just-manufactured poison. Her eyes naturally large, and painted now for stage requirements looked out straight before her, over the heads of the audience, burning, full of light and a strange, mystic fire; a curious smile curled her lips slightly, a smile of elation, of triumph in her success, and yet half-tender, as if she were moved with pity and regret for what she had done. The people sat motionless in their seats and gazed silent and fascinated at that fac'. To me it showed a perfect conception of the character, and I sat wrapped in an intense satisfaction, feeding my fancy, carried back absolutely to the Middle Ages, seeing her at last, as it seemed to me, in her true form and guise. She stood perfectly immovable; the rich green-blue silk, that had cost me so much trouble, falling in the most statuesque folds and reflecting curious, vivid gleams of light from the heavy, swinging lamps which hung directly above her head. Her hair, powdered till it was crimson as the pictured hair of the Siorza, was pushed back from her temples and forehead, and fell in thick masses just on the nape of her neck and behind her ears. The sleeves of the dress were long to the very wrist, and ruffled according to the fashion of the day; and from their edge a deep fall of lace concealed the hand almost down to its slim, white fingertips. But though her arms were covered, her neck was not. The full, white throat was bare, and the light from above struck the white shoulders where, just at the top of the close sleeve, they seemed to have burst through their silken bands. I sat and steeped my eyes in the sight of her my realized dream standing in front of me.

My care had not been expended in vain on the picture. It, too, was entirely true to the medieval idea. Somber curtains of heavy stuff and color formed all the background; a tripod of bronze, crucible, and furnace stood at her right hand, and on her left a stand covered with glass masks, mortars, pestles, and jars without number, of the most approved medieval shapes and patterns. It made a very striking and curious picture, to which the wonderful expression on the girl's face lent all its life and reality. The audience had the Sforza before them, and their breathless silence and immovability showed they felt the same fascination that was so fatal to her lovers in the past centuries. It was very different from the other tableaux, and met with a different reception. For a second after the curtains closed, instead of the light laughter and applause that had greeted the others, there was a dead silence, then a deafening clamor. The audience realized that the pict- ure had vanished, and that unless desperate efforts were made, they would not be able to recall it. With one accord every one present clapped and cheered. The blase or sleepy elderly officers, and the fatigued and languid women in the front row seemed electrified, while the young, unbridled subalterns I had massed at the back kicked, yelled, and stamped, after the manner of their kind when gratified. In a few seconds they succeeded in making the curtains divide and recalling the seventeenth century.

Catherine gazed over and beyond them, and the light gleamed on her glass mask and her mortar of poison, and her red hair for another seventy-five seconds, and then the curtain closed upon her as before. And the crowd at the back yelled again, and the rows in front risked making themselves hot with clapping.

The poisonous fascination of the Sforza seemed to work as well on the nineteenth century as on the seventeenth. Four times she looked out upon them, calm, triumphant, tender, and vindictive; yet the applause was undiminished. The curtain, however, remained closed and dark. Then, when the clamor and encores from the front and kicks from the back were at their loudest, a sudden silence fell on them, as if a pall had been dropped on the audience from the ceiling. Catherine herself moved in front of the great curtain and faced them. She lost nothing of the character in so doing, and the audience were enraptured; she moved, she looked, she stood, an image of the past.

"I am tired of mixing poisons," she said; and though she did not seem to raise her voice at all, it went all through the crowded room, and it seemed calm and a trifle arrogant such a voice as, indeed, the Sforza may have had. " Please excuse me now," and she bowed very easily and naturally, moved across the stage in front of the curtain, and disappeared before the astonished audience had recovered themselves.

I left my seat and went round to the back of the stage. As I passed the door of the room that answered to a greenroom I heard animated voices inside, and just as I approached I heard Anna's voice saying, with perfect good humor:

"Well, who asked me to come to your stupid old tableaux? You wanted me as much as any one."

I entered and saw the Sforza leaning back in a long chair, with her slim, terrible fingers crossed behind her head and its red hair, and facing her stood an irate little May Queen, in a muslin dress, whose flushed cheeks and puckered-up brows looked the reverse of queenly. Round the two stood the remaining pictures those who had appeared and those who had not. Feeling, apparently, was running a little against Catherine, since she was the only one who had been favored with an encore and she had taken four! They all turned at my entrance and, seeing who it was, looked confused and uncomfortable. The Sforza looked across at me, nodded and smiled.

"Here's Rosa abusing me because I kept her waiting so long that her complexion has all melted off and run down her neck," she said, lightly. " It's all your fault for choosing a picture that took their fancy so. I had very little to do with it."

By this speech, in which she negatived the idea of her own charms having had any weight with the applauders, she evidently mollified the women somewhat. They looked less gloomy, and the May Queen put her crown straight and began to rub more powder over her face. Catherine herself got up and arranged her dress for her, and put a tiny touch of rouge on each cheek, which made the girl of the turquoise eyes look so pretty in the mirror that Catherine was holding up before her, that peace was restored, and the May Queen hurried away to the front. All the remaining women began talking at once, and they soon took the Sforza, so unruffled, so undated by her four encores, back into favor.

I stood listening with impatience, longing for some moment when I should be alone with the Sforza. It did not come in the green-room. There was endless chatter and bustle there, pictures coming in and out, gossiping, arranging their hair and gowns in front of the long glass, talking, laughing, and saying alternately pleasant and spiteful things about one another. In the midst of it all Catherine sat resting coolly, with true medieval calm; and I, not liking to deliberately ask her to come away from the others, stood by her side. At last, when all the pictures had been shown and we were getting hungry, there was a general move made in the room. The curtains were closed for the last time, and the stage was being cleared, when, sudden- ly, to our surprise, we heard cries from the still-seated audience:

"Catherine Sforza! Catherine Sforza!"

A silence fell on the room, and the women all looked toward Catherine with envy mingled with surprise. " Why is all this fuss made about her?" their looks said plainly; " she is not beautiful; she is not half so good-looking as many of the others here!" Which was strictly true, but oh! the charm, the magnetism in her which was wanting in those others! at least so it seemed to me; but then I was prejudiced.

Catherine heard the shouts as plainly as the rest, and, after a moment, she rose indolently from her chair.

"What a bore those people are," she said; "d d bore, I think!" she added, in a mischievous undertone to me, with a laugh that disclosed a flash of her white teeth, and she nodded assent to the servants who came to know if they should set up the alchemistic interior for Catherine again.

I rushed round to the front again and hastened to my seat, not to lose a moment of that to me fascinating picture. And when it had disappeared for the last time and the audience were slowly disengaging themselves from their seats, I found the pictures all trooping out of the green-room, anxious to mingle with the spectators and hear compliments at close range.

It had been decided that each picture should maintain its dress and character throughout the evening, so here they all were the May Queen and Rosiere, Gretchen and the Queen of Sheba, the Dancing Girl, Joan of Arc, and a host of others, and the Paris Gamin. Mrs. Tillotson was delighted; her tableau had been greeted with roars of laughter and genuine applause. In fact, she could have taken an encore had she felt inclined to stand on her head seventy-five seconds longer, but she hadn't. And here she came, sparkling, mischievous and pretty, her short, shock hair tumbling into her eyes, and her ragged shirt, making the excuse for a charming piece of decollete work, which showed very daintily a V of gleaming white bosom; while her little, ivory feet, perfectly bare, tripped fearlessly about beneath her ragged trouser-ends. Next to the Sforza, she was decidedly the most popular picture among the men of the evening. The two crowds met and mingled with much laughter, flattery, and jesting; ancl simultaneously made for the head of the short, broad staircase leading to the dining-room. Half-way down was an alcove leading to the conservatory, draped by portieres, and hidden from view of the staircase. As I saw the Sforza come from the green-room, I took her arm and hastened her down the few stairs to the recess, drew her behind those heavy, friendly curtains and then gathered her up into my arms recklessly, half-choking and bruising her.

"My darling! my Old-World darling!" I murmured, straining her closely to me, and so for a moment soothing the pain and the passion that struggled and tore each other in my poor, aching heart. "You were splendid to-night perfect!"

Was I?" she said, very softly, nestling up close to my heart and putting her arm around me. " I am so glad you were pleased with me."

When with me all her arrogance, coldness, and contemptuous indolence of manner, with which she often treated her enemies or faced the world, disappeared. With me, whatever pride she might possess she put at my feet. To me she was always yielding, submissive, clinging, loving, and simple. This change, this distinction she made for me had in it a subtle and intoxicating flattery.

I crushed her up to me and kissed her again and again, on her red hair and painted eyes and fresh mouth, and she yielded herself passionately to me.

"I don't want to be the Sforza," she whispered in my ear, " nor anybody, except just your own little girl."

"But you are not my own yet," I whispered back, my heart beating so violently that it seemed as if it would leap from my throat.

"I didn't say I was. I said I wanted to be."

"Then what prevents you?" and my voice sounded harsh and strange to myself, it was so strained with nervous passion.

"Hush! There are people coming! Let me go! Be patient with me a little while!"

There were feet passing the alcove, and some one even brushed and almost swept back the curtains behind which we stood. We paused a moment, drawing back and keeping silence; then, as the steps and voices went on down the stairs, I gave her my arm and we went out arid down to the supper-room like a couple in the calmest frame of mind.

The room had been arranged under my own eye, and it certainly presented a pleasing vision as we entered. Hosts of little tables, just large enough for two people, stood everywhere under the swinging lamps that sent out differ- nt-colored rays from their varied glass shades. Wreaths and hanging bands of roses, common in India as daisies in Eigland, were looped from lamp to lamp, so that the guests sat under a veritable canopy of roses, and the air was laden with their fragrance. At one side of the room ran i long table, piled up with large blocks of natural uncut ice. The bowls of punch and all the various dishes and wines for the supper veiled under the shade of innumerable epergnes of flowers. At this table waited a line of native servants, noiseless, white-clad figures, ready to serve. The number of tables corresponding to the number of couples, people found their places easily and without formality; and when they were all seated I joined Anna at the table I had chosen for her one set at the upper end of the room beside a heavy blue velvet portiere, and decorated entirely with white roses, while the Eastern glass casing to the lamp above it shot down violet and crimson rays on the Sforza's hair. Every one was hungry and thirsty apparently; at any rate, the room was soon filled with the clatter of knives and forks, the continued report of flying corks, and the bubbling of laughter and talk across the tables.

Anna was very silent through the supper. She sat gazing at me steadily and earnestly with those wide, innocent, appealing blue eyes of hers, that could be so brilliant or so passionate as she chose; and then quite suddenly, toward the close, when there was much noise and laughter in the room, and much champagne had been drunk, so that nobody was any longer very critical as to what others were doing, she leaned across the little table between us, and looking up quickly and full into her face, I saw her eyes were veiled a little by drooping lids and those long, voluptuous lashes, and a curious fire was burning under them. I recognized instantly something I had never seen in her face before. It was her womanhood looking out behind the mask of her girlhood. Then a whisper came to my ears a little, faint, shy half-whisper, but one that had a new accent in it; and my heart recognized that, as my eye had recognized her expression:

"Gerald, you are loved as very few men are. You are, indeed."

CHAPTEE IV.

THE evening of the tableaux was over and I was alone in my room. I was sitting at the long window looking wth idle, unseeing eyes out into the tangle of foliage and b'os-som in the hot moonlight. Every pulse beat hard svith joy; there seemed one long, triumphal note ricging through my head. Anna's glance and whisper to-night had transformed the air to rose color about me and filled it with music.

There was no question about the truth, the genuineness, the spontaneity of those few words. Everything had been pushed aside for the moment, and Nature had come forward herself and spoken to me from under those veiling lashes and in that quick, half-frightened whisper. I did not sleep at all that night, nor even attempt to. I sat looking out into that fertile wilderness of beauty before me and watching the liquid moonlight spilled among the quivering leaves.

It so happened the following day I could not find one moment for my own in which I could go to see Anna. Duty, business, and the commissioner, who seemed suddenly that day to grow from an ordinary English gentleman into the most exacting tyrant, kept me all day. And when in the evening I went round to the white bungalow in the palms I was told by the servant that the Miss Sahib was lying down and could not be disturbed. I would not go again to make an ordinary call and have to talk, perhaps, commonplaces with her and her father for an hour or so. It was not what I wanted. I decided to wait until she had retired for the night and then steal into her compound and up to her window and gain a few delicious moments with her alone, and say and hear a few sentences that were worth to me, just then, all our other conversations put together.

So, after dinner, I had my long cane chair put outside the bungalow and sat there, waiting impatiently until it should be ten o'clock. As soon as the hour came, the silent sais appeared with my horse; and, slinging my guitar across my shoulders, I flung myself into the saddle and cantered out of the compound with a light heart. My horse's footfalls fell without sound on the soft, red roads; the air was still and heavy; and as I neared the Lombards' bungalow the rich, stealthy odor of the stephanotis hedges crept out toward me and suffused itself all round me, as I approached. When I reached the gates 1 dismounted and fastened the Arab to one of the posts. Then on foot I entered, and, leaving the main path, struck across through the pomegranate bushes and rose-trees by a side-walk that I knew led beneath her room. As I pushed aside the fragrant branches and made my way on silently, the wonderful glory of the night and the scene came home to me, absorbed and fired though I was by other thoughts. Above me rose the white stone pile, snowy as the purest marble in the moonlight and even the moonlight is not cold in India; it seems warm, lustrous, and mellow; unlike the lights of the Northern moon. The open balustrade work round the square, flat roof stood out sharply; and over it in places, drooping to the garden, fell like purple rain the great blossoms of the tropical parasites. Above the roof rose the palms, motionless in the heavy, heated air; and through their branches I could see the wheeling stars and the great, glittering Scorpion, head downward in the violet sky, preparing for his plunge beneath the horizon. As I advanced farther through the tangle of the roses, the heavy breath of stephanotis and tuberose grew more and more oppressive, until at last, when I stood beneath her window, it weighed upon the senses. I glanced round me. There was deep, hot stillness everywhere. The whole of Anna's room was built out from the house being really nothing more than an extended veranda and from the casement ran down to the compound a little, light iron stair-way, which white convolvulus and passion-flowers and magnolia had embraced with their twining arms, till it seemed like a stair-way of flowers. I passed round behind this, and then was standing practically under the floor of her chamber. All was profoundly still. I slipped the guitar round and had it in position against my breast. I bent over it, and was just going to sound one of the strings that I thought might have slipped in coming, when a whisper, a breath it was hardly more struck upon my ear.

I looked up, my heart beating to suffocation. Anna's window was set wide, and from there I knew the sound had floated out upon the tranquil air. For the first moment I thought she had been awake and seen me coming, and my heart leaped up with joy. The word " Anna!" rose in a joyful cry and had almost burst from my lips, when it stayed frozen there. Another whisper came down to me, clearer than the last:

"Ke Wmlsurat ho!" (" How beautiful thou art!")

It was Anna's voice and speaking in Hindustani. Her voice, and yet as I had never heard it. There seemed a deep contralto note in it a vibration of intense passion. Ana I stood beneath, immovable, stunned, and paralyzed. Thick, intense, palpable silence for many seconds, and then again that deep whisper in the air, terribly distinct to my distended ear.

"Tumko asliik karti hun!" (" Hove you!"), and then two long sighs, and then silence again, so long, so absolute that it seemed to mock all sound as a dream.

I stood there rigid, tense. Then I looked up. Why did not the sky fall or the stars rush together or the white wall above me crumble upon me? But no, all was unchanged. The glorious sky looked down upon me and her unmoved. The wilderness of white and pink roses stretched round me. The heavy scent still weighed upon the silent, dreaming air. I can not say what I felt. Looking back upon those moments, I can remember nothing but a horrible blank of pain. I stood there a long time, forgetting I had limbs to move away. Then, at last, mechanically grasping the guitar, I took my way silently back along the little rose-path by which I had come, and found myself eventually at the compound gate. I unfastened the Arab, who stood pawing the soft, red sand and arching his neck, and mounted him. Then I shook the reins loosely and gave him his head, and he plunged forward into a long gallop, like the wind, toward the sea.

At Kalatu, between cantonments and the sea, there lies the desert, a band of it two miles in width. The sand is yellow, and the desert wind passes over it, rippling it with waves like the sea. There are countless green tussocks scattered over it where the coarse, dry grass bends unhurt beneath the burning wind. Across this, with heads toward the sea, we went, and clouds of sand rose silently from the Arab's flying hoofs, and miles and miles of undulating sand stretched away on each side under the starlight. For hours I was mad as mad, I think, as any madman confined in an asylum. Eage, unreasoning anger, jealousy, and disappointed physical passion flung back upon itself s-. vept down upon my brain, and tore at it between them, as wild dogs tear at a carcass. My fingers quivered on the reins, and when the motion beneath me seemed ever so slightly slackened, I urged the animal onward without rest. So in a wild gallop we came to the edge of the cliffs, and here the Arab stopped and planted his feet, nearly flinging me from the saddle, and snorted, as he saw the declivity before us and the silver sands and sea far below.

I paused to let him rest, for I felt him quivering beneath me with fatigue and strain, and stroked his neck with my hand. Eeason was coming back to my brain, reason and self-control and all those qualities that bar the man from the brute. Self-respect rose again from where it had lain trampled, and ordered the dogs of rage and lust back into their kennels, and I grew calm. There was a sandy, winding path down the face of the cliffs, and I put my horse to it and we walked slowly down it to the sand. The tide was receding, and great stretches of wet shore lay exposed and glimmering. The moon was sinking now, and blood-red in the mist near the horizon, it gave the Water a reddish tinge; and the slow, languid, red waves lapped soundlessly upon the slimy sands.

What had I been doing? I asked myself. I had been distrusting her. I ought rather to have distrusted my own senses. And suppose I had heard her murmured whispers. Might she not have been murmuring them to the empty air? Might she not have been reading or reciting some Hindu love-poem or tale? Might she not even have been speaking to some child or some pet in her rooms? It was unjust, unfair, unworthy to let such thoughts enter my mind as had been borne in by those words; and not, perhaps, so much the words as that vibrating accent that still seemed thrilling all the air around me. I was calm now, and the judicial attitude, natural to my mind to investigate, to inquire, to assume nothing was coming back to it. But in my heart there seemed a dead weight, a crushing chill that had stamped out all its ardent life of an hnur ago. The brain may reason and weigh and wait to judge, but the heart is unreasonable and can only feel.

I rode till day-break, slowly now, for that first fierce fire had burned itself out, and with it had gone forever the dew, as it were, of my life; the first freshness of a first lore. When I saw the quivering pallor in the east that precedes the dawn, and noted the lines of the sand-hills defining themselves against it, I turned my horse's head and rode homeward.

To change my clothes and take away all traces of the past night's employment and eat a hurried breakfast was the work of an hour, then I had to bend my mind to statistics of the native States a volume of much importance, which the commissioner was preparing, with my help, for the press for four long hours, and then, feeling almost in a lethargy, such is the effect of overexcited anxiety, I drove to the Lombards' and entered the open house-door.

I went in and found her sitting in the soft, subdued light of the shaded drawing-room, in a low wicker-chair, perfectly dressed in white, as usual, with her feet slightly raised on a low Persian stool, and her hands lying idle in her lap. Beside her on a table stood a spray of white roses in water, and her fair face bloomed through the soft light, fresh and immaculate as the morning. As she sat there she would have formed a good artist's study for a picture to be called " Innocence," " Maidenhood," " Purity," or any other similar and equally suitable title. As I advanced into the room she rose to greet me, and I took her into my arms and kissed her.

She looked up at me with those warm eyes of hers full of soft, caressing light.

"You look terribly pale and ill, Gerald. What is the matter?" she asked, and the voice I had heard last night in those terrible whispers that had scorched life and hope o ut of my heart, seemed to fall strangely on my ears now.

"Yes, I do feel very ill," I answered, sitting down beside her; " but it is more a mental illness than physical. Anna, I have come to say you must fulfill your promise to me now, at once. We must be married within the next few days, or I shall leave for the hills, and when I return we shall meet as acquaintances only."

The light and color died out of her face suddenly; but she took the situation exactly as it was, and answered me as directly as I had spoken.

"I should have said what I am going to say long before now. I can not possibly marry you now or at any time."

"Why?" I asked, simply.

"Because," she answered, facing me, her steady eyes fixed on mine beneath their level brows, " because I should have to tell you certain facts first. This I do not want to do; and if I did, you would not marry me. So it is at an end," and she drew from her finger the band of sapphires I had given her, and laid it on a little console table that stood in front of us.

She was very pale, and her eyes were painfully dilated and looked black; but she, apparently, like myself, was determined to be calm and stifle all emotion which might prevent her saying what she had to say. I had judged her rightly. She did not mean, had never meant, to marry me with lies on her lips.

"And suppose I know already these things?" I said, quietly, leaning toward her across the arm of my chair and looking steadfastly at her face. " What then, Anna?"

I could not be angry with her, wounded, sore, and cut to the quick as I was; and, to my own surprise, my voice was tender instead of stern.

She started, and her eyes sought mine in terrified questioning. For an instant, I think, she believed her lover had betrayed her.

"What is it you know?" she said, in a low voice, and growing paler and paler; but her eyes still looking unflinchingly into mine.

"I came beneath your window last night to serenade you, and heard you speaking in Hindustani to some one who shared your room speaking as I would give heaven and earth, Anna, for you to speak to me. Tell me it is not true. Tell me it was not your voice, that I was mad or dreaming anything and I will believe you."

I stretched out my hands to her. The terrible emotion I was repressing flowed into my voice and broke and choked it.

Anna looked at me for one instant and then burst into a passion of tears and flung herself on her knees on the floor at my feet, laying both hands on my knees and looking up at me through her streaming tears.

"I can't tell you that. It was my voice. It is true. It became so while you were away in Burmah; but all the same, I love you, Gerald, as I do no other human being, as I never can love any one else. That is why I have not broken our engagement sooner. I could not give you up. The other is passion, madness, anything you like, but not love. I love you with all my soul and heart and brain; all those are yours forever and ever."

"They are hardly enough for mo," I said, bitterly. " I am not ethereal enough for those to entirely content me."

"Well, why did you not take me before you went to Burmah?" she exclaimed, passionately. " I was innocent then and willing to become all your own. I loved you the first night I saw you. I told you so by my eyes and smiles as far as I could. If you had spoken then I would have followed you to Burmah, or to Hades if you wished, or I would have waited here for you five years or ten or an eternity. But you did not. You left me without a word to tell me you loved me, and all the presumption I could make was the other way. You were a man. You had the right and freedom to speak if you chose. You did not choose. That was all I could conclude."

"I wrote to you," I murmured.

The sickening self-reproach that swept over me, the sense that all had been in my hands and that I had myself cast it away, to be irrevocably lost to me, seemed to be stifling and strangling me.

"Wrote to me!" returned Anna. " Yes, and your very letters that came, full of everything but love, seemed to me confirmation of what I thought. What was in them? Admiration, understanding, intellectual communion, and sympathy with me. That was all. You never sought my passion or my love. What you sought, I gave you. Could I do any more?"

I was silent. Words seemed useless, inadequate. She was still on her knees before me, and the touch of her hands seemed to burn into my flesh.

"For months after you left, I lived here a tranquil, empty existence. You know how empty this frivolous idle life is; how there seems no depth, no intellectuality, no sympathy anywhere. There seems nothing in if. No emotion, nothing to stir one. Well, then, suddenly, this great passion came across my life. It was like the sirocco entering a rose-garden. Perhaps the roses, tired of eternal silence and dew, like to feel its scorching breath, even though it withers and kills them. So the sirocco swept over me, and I bent to it and accepted it because it had something of life in it, something of the joy of living, and I married this man unknown to any one, of course."

4 Married him?" I echoed, lifting my heavy eyes and staring fixedly at her.

"Yes," returned Anna, looking at me half-angrily now in her turn. " What else? I thought you understood. Didn't you say just now you heard us together last night in my room?"

"Yes," I said, hardly audibly, "I knew that."

I leaned back in my chair and closed my eyes. I was overwhelmed. Thought even seemed dead within me. Anna drew nearer to me and put one arm round my neck, and I felt her stoop and kiss me on the lips with her teais falling on my face.

"Gerald, don't look so ill and so wretched. I love you you know I do better than any one else in the world. You have always been so kind to me, and I love your beautiful face and thnse beautiful eyebrows. Oh, why did you not take me to Burmah with you? I should have been so happy!"

' i)o you mean that you are in love with two men at the same time?" 1 asked, opening my eyes and looking at her. They seemed darkened, and I could hardly see her.

I suppose it must be so, unless you recognize that what I feel for him is only passion, not love not love at all. I would not breathe its name with that of love."

"Passion without love, Anna; even men are ashamed when they feel that."

Her head drooped a little and she colored. Then she looked up again as before.

"I feel it too like that," she murmured, " but it has come so. It is not my fault. When I first loved him I shut my eyes to all his faults. I invested him with heaps of qualities I love, and I could have worshiped him, been devoted to him, if he had let me. But his character in many ways I loathe. He is hard and mean and cruel, and when he shows me these things, I feel I hate him; yet I can not tear myself away from him. His lips lie to me all day, and I know it, and I could strike them; yet, when they come to kiss me, I am only too glad to submit. It is horrible to feel in that way, to feel your soul and body fighting together and your body forcing your soul to submission. Oh, you don't know what it is to lie prisoned in arms that you love and whose touch delights you, to lean your head upon a breast that is heaven to you, and yet to know that the heart beneath is mean and narrow and full of cruelty and treachery! To loathe, to feel an unutterable contempt, to feel your own mind struggling to get away from those arms, and to feel your own limbs and body turn and throw you back irresistibly into their embrace! That is my life now, one horrible imprisonment and degradation, in which I keep longing for you, striving to get out of it and come to you, only, I can't somehow give him up."

She dropped her head upon my shoulder as if utterly exhausted, and I sat speechless still. Her words what a view they showed me! What a terrible vista they opened before me! And was I not partly responsible? Had I not helped, by awakening her dawning emotions and then leaving them unsatisfied, to precipitate her into this?

There was a long, unbroken silence.

"Who is this man?" I asked, at length. " A native?"

"Yes."

"What is his name?"

"Gaidakhan."

Just as she pronounced the name, I heard a faint sound at the side of the room, the familiar click of the glass beads on the swaying chick; and, turning my head, I received the impression of a figure just withdrawn. The chick was still swaying.

Anna looked at me and read my thoughts.

"It doesn't matter if he does see us together. He knows that I am openly engaged to you. What do these blacks not know? It is useless to try to keep anything from them. He recognizes your position and my love for you. I know when you first came back I ought to have told you all this; that I had married in your absence, and I know I could have trusted you with my secret; but, oh, the delight it was to see you again, to hear you say that you loved me, the rapture it is to be with you, to feel you kiss me! I could not forego it. Gerald, you only half- realize what love I have for you. Do you remember what I said the night before last?"

H3r soft face, glowing now with a hot color, was close to mine, her eyes looked appealingly into mine. The clearest truth shone in them. I knew, I felt that, as always, she was speaking the simplest, barest truth to me; however strange, horrible, or criminal it was, still it was the truth. There was no artifice, no talking for effect, no making of a tragical scene with me. Truth, perfect truth, came from her lips, I knew; and to the saddest, most wounded heart, what comfort is there in that knowledge!

I put my arms closely round her yielding shoulders, looked down into those wells of blue fire, as her eyes seemed in their passion to become.

"I do, indeed, remember," I said, in a strained voice. " But how can it be? You love me and him at the same time. I can not understand it; it does not seem possible. I never heard never could have conceived it can not now."

She looked at me in silence for a moment, biting her lips violently as if unable to find words to explain. Then, suddenly, they came to her wildly, impetuously, and she spoke so fast I could hardly follow her.

"They are different kinds of love. I admire you, worship you, love you with a love that makes it ecstasy to be with you, to hear your voice, to feel the touch of your hand. You are the light of existence to me; I can not bear to be separated from you. With Gaida it is different. He is a beautiful toy to me. He is like some pet, some lovely Persian kitten. Can't you imagine that? He is a possession that I value. I like to know he belongs to me; I like to feel I have the right to clasp my hands round his wonderful neck when and if I wish; but I do not care to be with him. I do not crave for his presence, as 1 do for yours. I do not feel ecstasy at his proximity. I care little for his society. As you know, my time has been passed with you. I see little of Gaida. I want to see little of him. What link can there be between his brain and mine? You understand, Gerald, he was first my servant, as far as a man of the hill tribes is ever any one's servant, and I was content to keep him as that; but he he oh! his passion was something terrible resistless. He would go, or he would possess me. He would not stay in the house otherwise. And so, to keep him, I yielded to the idea of marriage with him, thinking you had passed out of my life. Now, if I could turn him into stone and marble and so always possess him, I would be willing to, I swear. Now you can see can you not? how it all is. Suppose " she added, swiftly " I had a tame leopard or panther that I loved, even a dog, say oh, you don't know how passionately I love anything that I love at all yet you would not dream of objecting to that, and Gaida is little more to me."

"Oh, but it is different, Anna, totally," I murmured. " This man is your lover your husband."

"Yes," she said, in a lower voice, and one tense with feeling, "I am married to Gaida, and for that mere reason I love him, I cling to him, I know. My feelings cling round him simply because of that, and in that one way he has a stronger hold on me than you. Oh, Gerald, take me too in that way! Let us marry; then nothing could touch or break the love I have for you."

A throb of unspeakable joy went through me. I strained her to me, and pressed my lips on hers suddenly.

"You will give him up," I said in her ear, in a low voice, suffocated with hope and joy=

Anna gave a sob which seemed to break the slight, lovely figure in my arms.

"Oh, don't ask me! It would be like cutting my heart from me. Let me keep him too, for a little while at first."

A revulsion of feeling, a shock almost of loathing passed through me. I pushed her from me and sprung up.

"Anna, I can not believe it is you who are speaking. You must be mad or I am. Englishmen do not share their wives. It must be at an end, as you said."

And hardly knowing what I was doing, I walked from her to the door. But Anna had risen and followed me, and now stood between me and the cliicks.

"Wait! wait! give me time! Love like ours can not be done with or set aside in a few words. I will try 1 will try to give him up. Let me have time to think. This evening I will tell you. Do not throw me aside. I can not bear it." Her broken, passionate words, still more the agonized look upon her face, turned the terrible impulse of anger to an equally terrible grief.,.

"This evening? You will be at the Delanys' dance? I will see you there. Do not speak to me any more now. I can not stand it."

Then, catching again her grief-stricken and pathetic eyes, I drew her up silently to my heart and pressed her there. Taking up the ring from the table, I slipped if; over the delicate, white, trembling finger.

"All remains as it was outwardly," I said. " What has passed is forever buried between ourselves. I shall never throw you aside, my darling. It is for you to decide if you will belong to me entirely, or only as now."

Then, before she could answer, I passed through the chicks and into the hall.

I found my carriage waiting at the door, but sent it home, and left myself free to find my way back on foot. I felt as if the walking would help my shattered thoughts. It was the close of the afternoon, and, therefore, the loveliest part of the Indian day. I turned aside from the broad, red road, down which my carriage disappeared, and entered a winding lane that, in spite of many twists and vagaries, yet maintained a parallel direction with it and would lead me home in the end. It was narrow and grassy, being little trodden except by the bare feet of the natives; and the rose and syringa hedges came forward from each side at places and entwined their leafy arms and lingered to gossip in the middle of the road undisturbed. Overhead the giant sago-palms towered into the blue sky, majestic and far away from small and earthly things; while, between, the cotton-trees dropped and rustled their little leaves, and threw shade on the mortals passing underneath. Down this silent, fragrant alley I walked slowly, thinking of many things and trying to realize the position I had taken tip. How strange it all was, I thought with a bitter smile; and how the station would stare could they get a glimpse now into the brain of the most envied man in it! What was I, practically, I asked myself. The fiance of a woman living with, loving, and married to another man. It was ludicrous. I laughed aloud, and my laugh startled a cushat on its nest and a green parrot, that flew screaming from the tall hedge above me. I wondered if any man had ever been exactly in my position before or had listened to the propositions and spent the hours I had that morning; and, if they had been, how they had acted; and what the whole set of young officers and civilians in the station, to whom by rank and age I belonged, and yet from whom in thought and feeling I so widely differed, would say of me and my conduct, if they knew all. These thoughts flashed through my brain, and then I dismissed them with a contemptuous smile. What was the world or its opinions or judgment to me? I was, of the world in the sense that I lived in it, worked in it, entertained and drank wine in it, with the rest; but mj mind was not modeled after its patterns.

At the tutor's, where, with six other students, I had read for the service, I was nicknamed " the Philosopher " and " the Athenian' because the problems of life and 1 death interested me more than geometry; and I had been detected more than once reading Plato's " Euthydemus " and " Phredrus " out of studying hours. That, indeed, which had put me into the first place in the examination, as shown by the marks' list, was the extraordinary superiority over all other candidates in Greek; and this was not acquired in laborious construing under a tutor's fostering care, but in long, silent, lonely nights of intense excitement, when I had sat reading the dead tongue for pleasure, and seeming to grasp the very hand of the dead philosopher across the gulf of centuries of modern thought and learning; so that, probably, I looked at the whole matter with different eyes from the average young Englishman. But in the emotions we are all more nearly on a level, and that which I felt most keenly as I walked quietly on was pain hot rushes of pain in which my heart seemed burning to a cinder, succeeded by a cold, sick hopelessness and despair. But I did not regret what I had said or done in the moments of clear reason between those of resentful agony. I realized that nothing could have been gained by thrusting her from me and regaining my freedom.

Freedom! What a mockery the mere word was, when her presence and her smile still meant for me all that was most precious in life. And if, in time, I had learned to put away the thought of her, what then? Was there anr other woman here or elsewhere in the world that could, 1 will not say equal her but, be to me what she was? Where else could I find that exquisite sensibility, that quick response to every thought and feeling, that intellectuality and brilliance that had not made her hard, but had linked itself to the softest and tenderest heart, and the most caressing, yielding ways? Above all, that capacity for passion I do not mean only physical, but mental passion and all forms of intense feeling that showed in her shining eyes and swift, supple movements. She appealed to me, spoke to all the impulses and moods within me in a hundred voices. It was as if the spirit of the Greek Agathon had come back to earth in another form; and, like Plato, I too seemed to feel my soul slipping through my lips and being drunk in by hers when I kissed her. Psychology had always been my favorite study and humanity my favorite book, and here, in Anna, I had come upon a curious yet lovely page. Even if I had not loved her, I should have been fascinated by that page and kept my eyes upon it, until I understood it and could translate, it clearly.

No, it was better as it was. Better to have the nominal right I had. Better this possession by her promise and in public opinion, than none. Besides, had I not much more? I knew, even without that confession of hers this morning, that I was possessed of her soul and heart and brain. All, all, in fact, except and here the fierce pain broke out in me again; pain and anger and fury rising up and obscuring my mental vision like smoke before the eyes. But I crushed them under, and my thoughts fought their way painfully but steadily through the brain. I saw that of whatever length the interim of suffering would be, beyond it there was hope. Physical passion, when it is real and genuine, especially when, from opposing circumstances, it can not reach satiety, is hard to kill and long in dying. Still, it wears thin under the continual battling and striving of the imprisoned soul against it As the unworthy object keeps revealing more and mere traits that shock and repulse its lover, so the force of contempt and loathing grows in the lover's struggling soul; grows until at last it is strong enough to vanquish the clingii g senses. For no new beauties of body or charm of passion have been reinforcing them. They are bound by the same ties as at the beginning, while the soul's loathing, that it brings down upon those ties, has increased a thousandfold. Then is the moment when they break and the lover stands free. Such a moment must come to Anna, Well, I would wait for itj

I saw that without external aid of circumstances, a bondage of soul, such as hers by the senses, could not last.

As she had said, Gaida was tearing huge rents in the mantle of passion she had thrown over him, and soon it would fall in mere remnants from him.

Besides, that was the farthest termination. A hundred accidents might give her to me any day, any hour. With all my help and care and protection for she should have them all the slender foundation on which she had built her happiness might be swept away. How insecure the whole fabric was! How unlikely that secrecy could be long be preserved! And one breath of scandal would blow it down. I would not hasten that hour of grief for her, if I could, by a raising of the eyebrow.

I could work without her knowledge against this man if I chose; have him killed or imprisoned, as far as that went, and Anna need never know. But she trusted me entirely. held her in my hand as one can hold a little hedge-sparrow, and she knew it and did not even flutter in my clasp. She felt safe there, and she was. My conquest would be accomplished in other ways. My plan of action was clear before me as a general's when he takes the field. I would protect them and their secret as long as it was possible, and if the storm broke upon them, I would acknowledge their marriage and receive them into my own house. What I did, the station would do. Was I not the station, in fact? And I smiled in contempt at the thought of the men and women who flocked to my house because I fed and wined them well; and who, for the sake of that food and wine, would condone anything I did.

Yes, Anna should have from me nothing but protection, consolation, comfort, love. She should find that one other besides herself knew how to love, whatever my pain and suffering and ultimate reward. Whatever I might be to others, she at least should never turn to me in vain. I would crush myself into nothing and she should be all. I would, if called upon, give everything and receive nothing.

I came to this conclusion slowly and by careful thought. Then I registered the resolution within myself and steeled myself to the endurance of all it might mean. Yet I had my consolation; it was the knowledge she was worth it by character, by intellect, by grace, by charm, by every- thing that makes a human being of worth in this world, she was worth it. And she could do what so few other men and women can she could understand and appreciate. I knew that not one pang of mine, not the smallest sacrifice, would pass unnoticed and unweighed, or fail to bring me more than five times its value in gratitude and love. What hardship is there is serving such a mistress? To me none. There are instances recorded or at least supposed to exist where men have poured out a life-long devotion at the feet of some senseless idol that cared little for them, nothing for their suffering, and laughed at their love. Such self-abnegation seems to me degradation, and can only exist where the worshiper is as worthless as the idol. But for Anna I would have given up my life as cheerfully as men in all ages have died for their gods, while and because they believed in them. When they ceased to believe, they ceased to die.

When I reached my bungalow, I went into the library, threw myself on the couch, and closed my eyes. I felt sleep would come to me now, and I gave myself over to it. Until my interview with Anna I had felt restless, eager, excited, a prey to a stormy rage of anger; yet full, unconsciously, of an expectation that there would be some explanation of it all; that Anna, in a few clear words, would dispel the whole horrible nightmare, as it almost seemed to be; and that I should return from her presence, calm, soothed, full of joy, as I had so often been before.

But now, now that everything was settled and there was nothing to do but face the blank loss and sorrow I had had, I felt no more unrest, no excitement, only exhaustion and longing for oblivion. The heavy air pressed on my eyelids, and in a few moments I passed into the blank darkness of sleep.

When I awoke it must have been some hours later. It had grown dark outside, and inside the assiduous butler had lighted up all the lamps and left the cliick invitingly parted so that I could see the table laid for my dinner in the dining-room beyond. I stretched myself as I lay on the broad couch and threw my e es round the room, and they rested on the little book-case at my feet, in which I kept different volumes in the various languages and dialects of the East. The most prominent among them, and the one which pressed its title in Gujerati to the glass, wag the " History of Draupadi," and I read it over and over in the curious characters, and it seemed to have a peculiar bearing on my own frame of thought. Draupadi is one of the dearest Hindu ideals. She is the feminine character in their literature round which clings, perhaps, the most sacred reverence. She is the type of pure, trustful womanhood and faithful wifehood answering to the Greek conception and British acceptance of Penelope.

As it is represented in India, the legend of Draupadi is a singularly beautiful one. Yet the principle of it is the subdivision of a woman's love. It portrays the woman in the dawn of life, consecrated, not to one husband, but to fire. To each of the five brothers who wed her simultaneously, and who share her among them, as they share their common tent, Draupadi is a faithful and devoted wife, and eventually bears a son to each. Her counsels guide them, her love and fidelity save them from surrounding dangers, and they unite at all times to protect and defend the chastity of the woman they revere and cherish.

Strange and to Englishmen perverted idea; yet thousands of cultivated and enlightened individuals through many ages have been able to comprehend it and to associate it with an ideal of purity. And was I wholly justified in the revolt and loathing 1 had felt of Anna when she made her final suggestion to me this afternoon?

This query flashed upon me suddenly as I lay there, as if a sudden flash of lightning had revealed a before-unobserved picture on the wall opposite me. But could I marry her and share her with another? I could not, I knew I could not. The blood rushed to my brain. I clinched my hands and pressed them to my head, vainly striving to shut out the thoughts that came and seemed to madden me. Yet there came almost immediately the insidious idea creeping upon me that had been suggested and had underlain her own words to me. As things stood, he was in the superior, I in the inferior position. He was, so to speak, the master of the house, and I but a poor beggar before the door. He was received within the citadel, I was but sitting down before it Naturally, the victory was with him. But let us both be within that house or citadel, and which then would have the power to throw the other out? She loved me as passionately as she did him, and mentally far more; but this last advantage on my side was overwhelmed by his superior position. But let the positions be equal, and all the advantage would be with me.

I sprung from the couch and paced the room, a terrible delirium in my brain in which rational thought was hardly possible. The shock and horror of the first discovery that she loved another, as I supposed, instead of, or better than, myself; had been followed by the hardly lesser one of hearing it was not instead of, or better than, but as well ' as, and in addition to, myself; and then all had culminated in that suggestion of an equal partnership in love that seemed so revolting, so terrible, and yet whispered to the simply passionate part of my love with a secret and poisonous allurement. After all, for how short a time it would be. Could I not, loving her as I did, turn that heart of hers, so full of love for me already, to myself, and fill it so entirely there would be no room for any other there?

What was this love of hers for Gaida? Was it not a mere morbid growth that had sprung up in my absence, a result partly of the awakened and ungratified impulses of that love I had stirred; and would it not be steadily pushed aside as the real love strengthened and developed? But no, no; I could not enter into such a horrible, disgraceful compact with her, whatever its grounds might be and its possible results and reward. I would not and could not desecrate this feeling I had for her, which was something infinitely higher than a mere love through the senses; would not and could not use it as the means to an end, however worthy the end might seem. Where would my own self-respect be? It must be sacrificed, and with it also hers; and with the sense of honor lost between us, our love, instead of being, as it now was, something infinitely tender and holy, might insensibly degenerate into the same mere love of pleasure and self-gratification that bound her and Gaida together. No, I would fight the battle and take my chances of victory from the ground where I stood. The contest should be won by the perpetual contrast ol one love with the other, and there should be no moral compulsion, no coercion, not even that coercion of the sentiments that intimacy produces and that Gaida was swaying her with now. I would wait for that hour when she would, of her own accord, turn to me as her protector and deliverer, her asylum and her hope.

All that I could do by patience and the extreme of fidel- ity and tenderness should be done, bat I would not buy in-fluence over her senses by degrading my love to the level of my rival's. I might have done it with a woman I loved less than Anna; but, rightly or wrongly, reasonably 01 otherwise, Anna had roused and held all the very best and the most selfless emotions that I was capable of. My eye could not light on that delicate, beautifully balanced form, or meet those soft, ardent eyes, without a rush of tenderness and devotion filling me, different far from what most men understand by love. And I had seen her, met her, been loved by her in the first fresh, pure unfolding of her heart, and I had left her. And now I had returned and found her enveloped in a horror and a darkness worse than death.

I saw her, as it were, standing smiling on a gulf of hid- eous, unknown dangers, and I alone knew and saw and could save her.

Could I desert her? Married to a native! One needs to have lived in India to fully understand the horror contained in those words. Aside from the moral degradations of life shared with one who, according to the British standpoint, has no moral sense, of being allied with a race whose vices and lives are beyond description; there is the daily, hourly physical danger from a native's insensate jealousy, unreasoning rage, and childish, yet fiendish, revenge.

A smile bestowed on another, one of those hundred little social amenities or functions fulfilled by his wife, not under stood in its right sense by the unlettered, unthinking barbarian; and a naked corpse, with breasts cut off, and mutilated beyond recognition, flung out upon the meidan, are but likely cause and probable result.

Why had I not taken her with me to Burmah? Oh, fool that I had been, with blinded eyes! How much better that disease and death that I had so dreaded for her from the Lihuli swamps, than this!

My servant entered and stopped, amazed, at the door, to see his sahib pacing wildly backward and forward with clinched hands and the sweat pouring unnoticed from his face. He made a profound salaam as he caught my wandering eye.

"Will not the sahib eat? It is hours past the appointed time."

I wared him away with impatient anger. The sight of w black face was hateful and abhorrent to me, at that moment.

"Go, go!" I said, " and see that neither you nor any one disturbs me till the morning. Clear the table. I shall not eat to-night."

Silent and wondering, the man withdrew, and I heard him and other servants clearing away the set-out but untouched dinner in the adjoining room. Then they returned to their quarters, and I was left alone in the silence. 1 looked at my watch. It was ten. I must dress and go to the dance, or I should fail in my appointment with Anna. I went upstairs and began my toilet with feverish haste.

I was fairly early at the Delanys', and Anna had not yet arrived. For that matter, she generally did come late. I met a girl that I had not seen for some time, and who had aow become a married woman. By her I took my seat where I had the whole length of the room before me, and I could watch for Anna's appearance. At a quarter to twelve she entered, and I could distinguish her in a mo-pient. What was there that made her figure so charming? She was tall, but not of that height which makes a woman formidable instead of caressable. She was only tall when pou actually measured her. At other times, the only impression her figure gave was of extreme grace and suppleness. Her waist was slim and low, her shoulders broad, and hips slight. Perhaps there was something in this proportion that gave the whole its peculiar, insinuating charm.

She wore this evening a gown of heavy, white silk, as usual, with a train of great length and weight; and the whole dress had, or was lent by its wearer, an incomparable distinction. As she came nearer we could see that she was wearing at her bosom a cluster of her favorite white roses, and a small spray was intertwined with the beautiful double plait of fair hair on her neck. I watched her with my usual delight, and then as she came closer I sprung to my feet with an almost uttered exclamation of dismay. Her face was terrible to look at. For a minute I could not believe that this was the rounded, smiling, rose-like face I knew. It was colorless and in some indescribable way seemed blighted. The eyes had a strained look of intense suffering and exhaustion, and the pale lips had a terrible line round them I had never seen,

Wo met and pressed each other's hands in a conventional way, and then Anna said, hurriedly:

"Let us go outside, somewhere, where we can speak for a few moments, and then I am going home. I can not stay here."

We went in silence toward the veranda, which led to the compound beyond and a wild jungle of ilowers and palms, where a hundred couples might walk unseen by one another, and yet where the music of the ball-room would reach them all. As we passed out I heard one woman say to another by whom she was sitting:

"How dreadfully ill Miss Lombard looks this evening."

And the other answered:

"Yes; this season is really extremely trying."

Anna's lips curled in a faint smile; but we neither of us spoke till we had got far away from the house, down by the end of a tiny path that stepped by a rustic seat and pen summer-house, surrounded by a perfect thicket of rhododendrons. Here Anna sat down and I by her side, And the silence between us seemed like some great, palpable curtain which we were both afraid to lift. At last I Baid, very gently for her looks were enough to move the most indifferent to pity:

"You look most unhappy, Anna. Speak to me and let me comfort you."

She turned her eyes upon me and said, in a low tone:

"I have suffered intensely all day, since you left me. I have fought with myself and been defeated. I can not give him up. I feel now that I must lose one of you, and to lose either will kill me."

Her face was such an unconscious confirmation of her words that I could not look upon them as a mere hysterical expression. Only once have I seen such a look on a human face, and that was on the face of a woman suffering from a terrible disease, just after she had learned the truth and three weeks before her death from it. That other horrible feminine face, with the seal of death set on it, rose suddenly before me as Anna looked at me, and my heart seemed literally wrung with fear and pain, as if giant hands had clutched it and twisted it to breaking point.

"If I keep him," she went on, quietly, with an accent of desolation that was pitiful, " you will leave desert me and I shall lose you, 3 '

That was all, and again there was a great silence. In i I thought and ratified my own decision. I am prepared for all men to condemn me; to say I acted wrongly and weakly; to say I should have risen and left her there; to say that I had done all that I could, and that since she had decided upon her course, I had nothing to do but to accept that decision and leave her to follow the fate she had decided upon. Perhaps I was weak. Perhaps, if we look closely, we should see that all unselfishness is a form of weakness. Be that as it may, I saw that she was suffering, I loved her, and I could alleviate her suffering bj speaking, and I spoke.

"No, Anna, I will not desert you. If you can not breat with this man now, I will wait. I foresee that the day will come when you will long to break this tie and will call upon me to help you. Till that day comes I am your pro-tector and your friend."

I put my arms round her and her head fell upon mj breast with a long-suppressed, terrible sob of pain; and W6 sat on, motionless and in silence. From the gay, brilliant windows of the Delanys' bungalow the music streamed oul to us, and we heard occasionally on the other side of tht rhododendrons a laugh or a whisper as steps went by, with the trailing swish of a ball-gown on the grass.

Light feet, light hearts, light love, light flirtations were? passing gayly on the other side of that crimson hedge, and we sat there drenched in an agony too great for words. Deep emotions, great passions are out of place in this little world of ours. They are but for the immortal gods, who possess all eternity in which to suffer and recover from them. Conventionality! How calm, how comfortable, how suitable it is to our little, limited lives! How it might be said of that, rather than of wisdom:

"Her ways are ways of pleasantness, And all her paths are peace."

Time passed. Dance after dance was played and finished, and at last Anna raised her head.

"Take me home, Gerald. To-morrow come and see Gaida. It is justice to me that you should see him. I will be in the drawing-room at two exactly. Come to me there,"

We rose, and to avoid passing through the crowd, I led her to an open lawn that impinged upon the road where all the carriages were drawn up waiting. I went among them and found hers, and then brought her to it and put her in and gave her my promise I would see her at the hour she wished the next day. As I put my hand for a moment on the door, she drew it within the carriage and kissed it. Then the carriage drove onward and I went to seek my own. I could not face a return to the idle, callous, light-hearted crowd within and hear comments on Anna's illness and change of looks. I drove away and reached, thankfully, the lonely darkness of my own house.

The following morning, after a sleepless night, I rose early and went early to my work that I might be free by two, and at a few minutes before the hour I had reached the bungalow and was in her drawing-room.

She met me at the entrance to the room and herself drew aside the chicks to admit me. She was deadly pale to her very lips. She seemed intensely excited, and I did not feel surprised that she should be so. Coming to receive two lovers, both of whom I knew she loved, and to show one to the other! As for me, I felt in a dream. All seemed un' real to me. Were we really two ordinary, flesh-and-blood British mortals? Was this ordinary life, or wore we shades acting in some grotesque farce? She motioned me to a chair, far removed from her and in the darkest shade of the shaded room. I sunk into it mechanically. The chair seemed real and ordinary enough, and there were other chairs and tables and ordinary things round me in this ordinary room, where Anna was wont to laugh and talk society chatter with her ordinary English friends. But what a heart of strange emotions beat under that calm, white breast! What thoughts passed and repassed behind that smooth, white brow, while the lightest nonsense was slipping from her lips! What self-possession and self-control she must have had to meet this curious position and to live this twofold life! What courage and nerves of steel to give herself to a man whose very breath of life is cruelty, whose jealousy means atrocity, whose anger means death! True, she was my Anna Lombard, that I had thought of when I had first heard her name, stepped out of the Middle Ages before me. And I looked at her, sitting not far from me, pale, calm, composed as a statue; and my eyes seemed to see, only through a mist of pain, a shade from those times of blood and lust and passion and crime; times when swift poisons were made by white fingers, and when women loved as men, as strongly, and often as briefly; when they laughed at the idea of one lover, yet were ready to die with, for, or by the hand of any one of the many; times when the very air they breathed seemed charged with treachery, cunning, and danger. From these a shade had returned and confounded itself with the clear white soul of an English girl, in a body beautiful and innocent to look upon as the sunlight of a summer day.

She sounded a gong on a table near her, and almost simultaneously the swaying chick divided, and a figure came into the room a room so large and dark that I, in my far corner, half-concealed by a portiere, would not be seen unless by one searching for me.

I sat motionless, hardly breathing, in my chair in the shadow. All my senses seemed absorbed in that of vision. This, then, was Gaida Khan. He moved into the room like a king coming to audience. He was of great height, and his form evidently, from its motions, as perfect as the perfect face. I sat frozen, rigid, while a great hopelessness settled on my heart and seemed to kill it. A woman whose eyes had been once opened so that she could see that beauty, one whose senses were captured by it, would never be free, entirely free, till death released her. This was the thought that seemed festering round my heart, chilling and crushing it to nothing. At first, when I had heard from her lips that my rival was a native, a feeling of contempt and scorn had given me some comfort and security. His age, too, that of a mere boy; and rank, that of the bazaar.

Everything had seemed in my favor. But now that I saw all arguments, all reasons, all considerations of this and that were swept away when brought suddenly face to face with him. Later, I learned that there were thousands of euch men in northern India, serving in the native regiments: soldiers, weavers, grass-piaiters, men walking with bare feet in the dust of the highway, to be seen and found in all sorts of occupations, to be met every day in the streets of Peshawur; and that Gaida was but a good and handsome specimen of his extraordinarily gifted race. But I, though five years in India, had never before met a Pathan, or, seeing one, had had my eyes and thoughts elsewhere. And now, with my eyes actually sharpened by jealous pain and wonder, I looked at thi man and he seemed almost superhuman. I had again, for an instant, that feeling of unreality as I watched him advance with an easy, stately grace and dignity. Anna made a slight motion of her hand to the jilmil beside her, and Gaida moved toward it and set it wide open, letting a flood of the bright yellow light from the desert in upon his face doubtless, as she intended. It is difficult in the slow, cold words that follow one another on paper to convey any idea of the glory of beauty that the hand of God has set upon this race. The face was of the Greek type in the absolute oval of its contour, and the perfectly straight features, the high nose chiseled in one line with the forehead, the short, curling upper lip, and the full, rounded chin; but curiously unlike the Greek type, which shares, with almost all statuesquely beautiful features, a certain, hard emptiness and fixity, this face was full of fire, animation, and brill iance. The skin was smooth and soft as velvet, of the tint of burnished copper, but glowing and transparent; and eyes full of intellect and pride looked out from dark-marked eyebrows that swept the smooth brow in a wide arch above them. On his black hair, which curled closely round the ears and nape of his neck, he wore a high, scar, let turban, the two ends of which fell as low as his waist at the back, and seemed to add still greater grace to the exquisite poise of the head, that was supported by a neck like a massive column of warmed and tinted marble. What a marvel of humanity, what a chef-d'oeuvre of its Creator! That beauty was like a sort of magic, as she had said. I realized it with my whole soul in those few moments. If that had been a woman, I might have been as faithless to Anna as she was now to me, for his sake.

As it was, I sat paralyzed and gazing at him, feeling crushed and without hope. I knew then what a woman feels who finds herself in the blaze of another woman's beauty which has scorched out light and love from her own life.

"Thank you," Anna said, speaking in Hindustani, " and have you any new fans to show me to-day, Gaida?"

The Pathan smiled, and it was as if a sword cut me. The smile was irresistible, sweet as might be painted on the lips of Botticelli's cherubs. A soft light played all over the youthful face, and the delicately carved lips parted from the faultless lines of even, milky teeth.

"Look at this punkah," he replied, taking from his right hand to his left a fan of plaited grass, worked so finely one could not imagine fingers had woven it together.

"Lovely, indeed," returned Anna, taking it from him. " How long did it take you to do this?"

"Oh, a day and a half, I think," replied the Pathan, lightly. " The Mohurrum festival will be here soon. Do you like my dress for it?"

He turned round before her as he spoke, displaying the festival dress, and with it the magnificence of his shapely form. The dress was exceedingly rich, the attire of the Mohammedan for a fete. The zouave jacket was of turquoise silk embroidered in gold, over a fine white tunic of muslin, thin as a spider's web. The trousers were the full Turkish shape, and of fine white linen, and gold-embroidered sandals were on his feet.

"It is very pretty perfect, I think, Gaida," she answered. " I am glad you showed it to me. You and all the servants, except my own bearer, can have a holiday the entire day. You can tell them."

Gaida nodded and smiled again.

"I want you to be there to see us," he said. " Will you come down to the sahib's office in the city and see us pass by?"

"I will try," said Anna. " And now I have things to Ao; I must see to them, Gaida."

She rose from her chair, and then the two figures were standing close together and made a perfect picture, such s one could seldom see, in the warm radiance of light falling in upon them from the open jilmil. Anna, tall and graceful, in her long, flowing white muslin, with her fair English face and her sunny hair crowning her upraised head, and Gaida, taller still, magnificent in his Oriental dress, with his regal head inclined a little as he looked down on her. It seemed like a page torn from the " Arabian Nights," and put before me.

"Good-by," I heard Anna say gently, and then before my straining, starting eyes, I saw the Pathan take her right hand, very gently and reverently as I myself would have done and draw her a little closer to him. He bent his head down and kissed her on the lips. Every move- rnent of the proud neck and shoulders was grace and dignity incarnate. Then they unclasped hands, and he turned away and walked toward the chick, erect and easily as he had entered, passed through it, and was gone. My hands were clinched on each chair-arm till the bones almost started; my brain seemed bursting, my eyeballs seemed to strain beyond their lids. What had passed before me had been an idyl of purity and dignity and grace. No kiss could have been given or received with more perfect chastity of look, gesture, and action. And every motion of his frame, from the stretching out of his hand to the bending of that kingly head till his lips touched hers, would have been an ideal for a painter drawing a monarch bestowing a kiss upon his betrothed. And he was a barbarian who trod the streets of a bazaar with naked, dusty feet! But, against myself, my instincts, to a certain extent, justified Anna. What wonder that, with her eye so sensitive to beauty, her brain so saturated with poetry and romance of feeling, she should be fascinated beyond power of resistance by this presence that compelled even my admiration I, 'who had lost all through him; I, who hated and loathed him; I, whose life was devastated by him. Yes, even I, looking through her eyes, could see and feel and realize the overpowering influence that rushed through her and dominated her and made her yield to that kiss, even here, now, before my eyes.

What a strange and extraordinarily fascinating mixture he was! That extreme sweetness and most Caressable and appealing youthfulness when he smiled, contrasted how sharply with the cold, serene beauty of his profile in repose, the hauteur of that curling lip, the proud step and carriage, the calm authority of that last embrace.

After he had left, 1 neither moved nor stirred. I felt I could not. There was utter silence in the room between us. Then Anna came over to me, knelt beside my chair, and laid her head down on my knees.

"Gerald."

"Yes."

"What do you think of him?"

"I understand now."

The words were just a hoarse whisper. I could not articulate more. I stretched out my hand and laid it gently on her soft hair.

"Yet I do not love him as I love you," she declared, oassionately, raising her head and looking at me with clear, burning eyes. " But, oh, the influence he has upon me when I see him enter the room, when I look at him, and when I think of losing him"

She did not finish; but the shudder that went over her, and the gray pallor that drove out the rose color in her face, finished it for her. I passed my arm round her and kept it there. I felt as if she had wounded me and I was bleeding to death; yet to caress her was still a pleasure, and she knelt beside me willingly, inclining toward me, absorbed in me. It was strange. She did love me, there was no doubt. What was this horrible mystery of a double love?

There was a long silence, then I murmured, hardly conscious that I was thinking aloud:

"It is impossible, inconceivable, unprecedented! No woman has ever done it."

"What?" asked Anna, with straining eyes wandering over my face.

"Been in love," I answered, mechanically, " really and passionately in love with two men, at the same time."

"If you had stayed and been with me, and I had met Graida," she answered, in her peculiar, trenchant way, when her voice, coming down with each word, seemed like hammer falling true on its nail, "I do not think I should have cared or taken any notice of him, any more than of the thousands of beautiful faces round one, out here. But you were not here, and I had no idea you would ever return to me. I do love Gaida now, and you, too both-of you. It may be inconceivable, impossible, unprecedented, as you say, but it is so. If I could kill my love for him, I would; for I want to be free from him. I love you jo much, I want to be with you, live with you, spend every minute of my life with you; but something some intangible, fearful something binds me to this man, and I can't loose myself."

She spoke the last words, slowly, fearfully, and her face grew pale and her eyes dilated. She gave one fleeting, half-terrified glance round the room, as if seeking to see with physical vision this terrible, compelling force that was. overmastering her.

"How can it possibly be kept a secret your marriage?"

asked, after a moment. " It seems as if such a thing must be known all over the station directly."

"It may be," she answered back, in a half-audible whisper, " at any moment. There is so much chance in these things. They may or may not be found out to-day or tomorrow or any time. There is no certainty. But all the servants are afraid of Gaida. They think he has some supernatural power over them for harm if they betray him, and he has told them that if his secret gets known, no matter how, he will run amuck and kill them all. They are all anxious to cover it up and to prevent any possibility of Us becoming known, rather than to gossip about it. They are terrified at the mere idea of its being discovered. They feel Gaida would not wait to find out who had told. If it jbecame known, he would simply rush upon them, all with his knife and kill all he could. It becomes, then, a matter they all wish to keep from disclosure. They are in terror of him a sort of superstitious terror."

"And how were you married?" I asked after another Jong pause, and which I tried to bend my thoughts on Jthese questions I wanted to ask her.

"Not here," she answered in the same undertone, as if jhe were afraid of the very walls and swaying chicles. " It was when we were on a visit to Peshawur. One night he got me to come away and go through the marriage ceremony among his own people. He took me, veiled, to a queer sort of house, and we went through some ceremonies he said meant marriage. Of course I could not tell nor day if they were so or not; but I think so, because, you riee " and a little sad, bitter smile swept over her face " he is anxious to tie me to him in every way in his power. The next day we were leaving, and after a week or two's travel we came back here papa and I, I mean and all our servants, of course, including Gaida, came back too."

Just at this moment, and before she could rise from her knees, the chick parted and the butler entered with cards an a salver.

"Captain Sahib and Mem Sahib Webb, ay a," he said, nd I rose to go.

When I was leaving the veranda I heard Anna's light, clear, well-bred tones welcoming her guests.

"This is good of you to come and see me. It is terribly hot to-day, isn't it?"

And I went away painfully marveling at her and at it. all.

CHAPTER V.

FROM that day commenced a curious, strained existence which would have been intolerable to most men and was nearly so to me. Yet I had determined on a particular line of conduct. I saw victory at the end, however long and tedious the battle; and at the end of every other course I saw only loss. This thought nerved me again and agair when it seemed I had come to the last remnant of nrjr strength.

At times, the mere anxiety for her seemed to be a strain greater than I could bear. It seemed to me impossible that such a state of things could continue, such a relationship could remain a secret for long and how it would be discovered and what she might be tempted or forced to do; above all, what the man might do when be realized himself to be on the point of losing her were questions that rose in blood-red letters before my eyes at all times and came between me and my work and my sleep. I dreaded to open the papers lest I might see the story there; 1 dreaded to halt my carriage in the bazaar lest I might hear her name bandied about by the native crowd. My heart beat when I saw a group of natives discussing together on the road or in the compound. They might be discussing her. But, so far, my fears and apprehensions were not fulfilled; as, in this life they so seldom are. It is something we do not fear and have never apprehended that leaps out upon us from the future and devastates our lives.

The days slipped by quietly without event, and Anna lived her double life and divided herself between two loveb undisturbed. Circumstances seemed to lend themselves completely to her wishes, and Fate herself seemed interested in keeping her secret. The Lombards' bungalow was very large, and Anna's room in fact, a whole suite of rooms, only used by her was on the opposite side of the house from her father's. The large, open windows that naturally stood wide all night; the outside spiral staircase hidden under its wealth of foliage reaching from her window to the compound; the compound itself, a perfect jungle of flowers and trees no eje from outside could pierce, and that included all the native servants' dwellings all these things made it easy for her to receive Gaida as soon as the general had retired and the bungalow was dark and still. In the day she never saw him or sent for him, except in his capacity as servant; and he was in n way favored in money, dress, or quarters above the other servants. The superstitious terror with which they had come to regard him, shut off that greatest source of scandal native gossip. In the day, Anna was entirely with mo, and if slander could have touched her at all, it would have connected her name with mine and none other. Yet, even so, it seemed to me as if the whole matter must rise to the light in some way; and I waited in dread for the hour oi discovery.

The more I studied Anna the more incomprehensible and terrible this strange dual passion of hers become for me; but, also, I became more and more convinced I had decided rightly in not abandoning her to herself. Neither would she have deserved my desertion. For this miserable love that had overtaken her she was no more to be held responsible than she would have been for any physical malady she might have been stricken with. She loved me with the same faithful, tender devotion she had given me from the first; and it seemed, when we were alone together, impossible to me that she could be living the life she was. But, indeed, her love for Gaida seemed to have no sort of influence upon her love for and her relations with me. II was a thing utterly separate and apart from that self which she gave to me. Within her the two loves, the higher and the lower, seemed to exist together without touching or disturbing the other; just as in a river sometimes one sees two streams, one muddy, the other clear, flowing side by side without mixing.

That such a state of things should have arisen, that such feelings, which would have been designated by the ignorant and unthinking as mere wantonness, should have sprung up in this nature, seemed the more unreasonable and terrible, because it appeared to be one unusually chaste,, pure, and refined. In all her intimate conversations with me, there had never been one coarse word, never the faintest suggestion of a dullness of the moral sense, never even a suspicion of indelicacy in her wit. Moreover, she was an extremely religious girl, not perhaps religious in a very open and ostentatious way, but in that infinitely truer way, religious in the deepest inner life of the soul. I did not recognize this fully at first; but as she admitted me more and more into her confidence, this side of her nature stood out before me so clearly that it seemed to make the situation and her actions incredible. I met her one Sunday afternoon, quite suddenly and unexpectedly, coming down the steps of the church, just after the service was over. It was a quiet, drowsy afternoon, and the neighborhood of the church was almost deserted. Only a few children under the care of their ayah, and one or two old ladies who tottered down the steps and drove off in their waiting carriages, represented the congregation; for the fashionable time was the early morning service, when it was cool enough for the women to enjoy their elaborate toilets, and they knew the church would be full of eyes to admire them. In the hot Indian afternoon one only wanted to lie under a punkah and go to sleep. I was very much surprised, therefore, to see Anna at this time and place; and I stood still, unobserved, to look at her. She was very simply dressed, and clasped in her hands a small, white ivory prayer-book. The sun shone down on her unshaded face, which was a little pale; and her eyes looked very pure and innocent, as if still full of prayer. Thinking in my mind she was not unlike the poetical conception of Marguerite leaving the cathedral, and reflecting bitterly that suffering not unlike Marguerite's lay before her, I went forward and she saw me.

"This is very nice to meet you here," she said, smiling.

"Have you been to church?" I said, abruptly, though the fact was obvious, as I placed myself by her side and we walked on very slowly.

"Yes. I like the afternoon service. It is so quiet and peaceful, with no people to disturb you, no staring faces nor rustling gowns."

"Anna, do you believe all that is in that prayer-book?"

"Oh, no," she said. " The prayer-book is a thing of man, and may, like other human things, be full of errors and mistakes. I don't know that it is; but I, personally, do not feel that I believe in it. But then I believe in the general idea that this Church and prayer-book stand for."

"Do you believe in a God?"

"Yes, Gerald, I do. I believe in some supreme power; something that is above us; something above our own powers and understanding. I may be wrong. There may be nothing, but I feel that there is, and I have always felt very near that God. I am always praying to him, asking him, consulting him about something. If I am miserable, I pray to him; if I am happy, I thank him; if I am in danger, I pray to him; and I feel his hand is round me, inclosing me, and nothing can hurt me."

I stared at the calm, serious face beside me.

"And what about offending this deity?" I asked.

"I try never to do what I feel is wrong," she said, in a low tone.

"And you are satisfied in your relations to this man?" I said.

"A great love came into my heart for him and I married him. I feel sorry because it would grieve my father, if he knew. Otherwise morally, I mean is it any different from marrying any one else?"

"And your deity also approves of your being in love with two men at the same time, I suppose?" I said, with a bitterness I could not suppress.

Anna paused in her walk and turned and faced me. We were quite alone in the sleepy stillness of the Sunday afternoon; the leaves flickered and swayed over our heads and threw light shadows on the little gravel path before us.

"Gerald," she said, looking steadily at me, "I have told you that feelings can not be controlled beyond a certain point. If you came to me and found me suffering with a violent headache and said, ' Anna, this headache is sinful, you must get rid of it," what could I do?"

"You could cure the headache and the love," I answered, sullenly.

"Yes, if the Divine Father willed; and if not, not. I suppose it is some power beyond our own that wills us to love at all. Certainly, love enters our hearts without our own volition; and I, apparently, have been willed to love two men instead of one, and what can I do?"

"Anna, this is all sophistry. We are not reading Plato now; we are looking at life, and you profess to be looking at it from a religious standpoint. If you look upon yourself as being regularly married to this man and as being his wife, how can it be right to entertain love for me?"

"I don't entertain it," answered Anna, wearily; " it forced itself upon me. I loved you for a whole year before I saw Gaida. Do you wish me to banish you from me? I could do that, but I could not destroy my love for you."

"Well, but the other " I said, desperately.

"Gaida has been and is very good to me. Do you think, if I threw him aside, it would be specially pleasing to God supposing God is interested in my actions at all?"

I was silent. She possessed, somehow, the art of confusing one's thoughts as she did one's senses. I found nothing to answer her with immediately, and, after a second, she added, "Two men love me and are very good to me, each in a different way; and I love them both, each in a different way; and why all this is so, I do not know; but I feel I can do very little in it. And for these unknown matters, a God shall find out the way," " she quoted very softly from the familiar Greek.

We both walked on slowly and in silence; and a little farther on there was a stone seat, grown over with moss and shaded by a cotton-tree and climbing convolvulus. Here we sat down by common consent, and I looked at her face with its pale tranquillity and serious calm. It was possible that a God was holding her in his hand and for his own ends made her suffer and feel differently from other women; and it was possible, too, that the same God would, as she said, discover the way of deliverance for her. That was evidently her faith.

"Let us go home," she said, after a silence. " It was a very long service, and, then, talking of these things with you, Gerald, always tires me out."

She rose, and we wended our way slowly back to her bungalow, where I left her and went on to my own, to spend the rest of the afternoon in a gloomy meditation by myself.

Whatever she might say or feel could not alter my own idea of my duty toward her; which was to draw her not violently or by coercion, but gently; and, in the end, with her consent from her relation to Gaida, which she might, but I could not, look upon as marriage. It was not my duty to consider him or care for him. It seemed to me my duty to try and extricate her from this position, so full of dangers and horror that she, in some inexplicable way, failed entirely to realize.

I entertained more than ever. I was constantly devising a luncheon, a dinner, a picnic, a dance. All were given in rapid succession, and then the circle recommenced. Anna was always invited and always came, hardly going anywhere else, in fact, that she might be sure of not being obliged to refuse me. At these dinners or dances, outside of my duties as host, I devoted myself to her; and this, in view of our acknowledged position, was indulgently accepted by all.

In a little while the station began to feel that there must be some complication, which was preventing the course of our love flowing smoothly into matrimony. For weeks they waited eagerly for the date of the marriage to be given out. Then expectation almost ceased, and speculation on the nature of the obstacle took its place. This was all the more excited and curious as, I think, it must have been evident to all that two people were seldom so passionately moved toward each other as we were. Anna's face was only the most delicate screen to her soul, and love, anger, grief, passion were all reflected in it and played over it, if any of these were swaying her spirit; and as she sat beside me or spoke to me, her eyes flashed and melted and grew dark by turns. Her voice had the softness of love. She smiled when our glances met across a table or crowded room. She yielded all or nearly all her dances to me; and showed in every way that she came to my house for its host alone. Moreover, it was not only at entertainments that we met. We passed almost the whole day together, walking or riding or driving, breakfasting on the general's veranda or mine. The station rarely saw one of us, without the other being present.

Then with wealth and youth and health and love and equality on each side, what could this incomprehensible cause for delay consist in? The station racked its brains and had headaches over it, but could not decide the question. Some of the less excitable and curious said it was just a young girl's caprice, to put off a little lunger the serious part of life. Anna had, after all, but just come out from England and, practically, school. She wanted to have a little more gayety and frivolous amusement before taking up a position as a married woman. Others argued that if she was going to be so wholly devoted to one man in society as she was to her fiance, she might as well be married to him; and a great number of mammas and young girls, who had hardly looked at me before I went to Burmah, lamented and wondered over Anna's folly in not immediately seizing upon the prize I presented. Many of them amiably attempted to console me for and lure ma from my unrewarded service. Such efforts caused me amusement, mingled with pain. It seemed a pity they should waste them on me, a pity I could not tell them ho-utterly and entirely my soul was anchored in Anna's, breast, explain to them how all my desires were bound up in this one woman. And she grew dearer to me every day, Her constant society did not weary me nor let me come tc. the end of her learning and brilliance. It only drew m closer and closer to her. Her mind and heart and soul opened more to me each day, and the farther I looked into them the more I loved her, the more restless and desperate I became to have all this empire to myself.

We often began our day together by a ride before breakfast a ride through the great, cool, dewy gardens, where the pomegranate buds were unfolding, and then breakfasted together with the general on his veranda. Then a break through the morning of my official duties; but a return to lunch with her again in the middle of the day, to consult with her on a thousand points of difficulty that had presented themselves that morning or previously and to hear her elucidating them and straightening them out for me or else merely listening to me with great eyes fixed on me, all attention and sympathy. A little more work in the afternoon, and then afternoon tea in the shade of her rose-scented drawing-room or beneath the banana-trees in the compound, from where we could see the miles of desert sand and the dancing, sapphire sea, like a line of jewels on the horizon, and in the foreground a string of camels winding slowly across into the light of the west. Then dinner at my house and a dance afterward, and the intoxication of the music and the movement with Anna held close to my bosom, in my arms, till four, perhaps, in the morning; and then the rending apart, the yielding her up, and the black dejection that would come over me. Sometimes, when she and all my guests had gone, I would fling myself into a chair in the deserted room, and so sit through the night, with teeth set and my nails sunk deep into the palms of my hands; till the dawn crept in, gliding the compound. Those horrible hours passed over my head without count. I was so absorbed in intense thought, intense suffering, that when the morning light filled the room round me it seemed merely like the flash of a few minutes since Anna had left me. Then, knowing I was due to ride with her or share her chota Jtazcri or first breakfast on the veranda, I would go straight to my dressing-room to change my clothes; and for many nights together the mosquito-nets on my bed would remain undisturbed. Food, too, I could hardly touch. The mental anxiety and excitement in which I lived seemed to close my throat against it. Those terrible nights of desperate pain left me for the succeeding day strung up to that degree of nervous tension when one can think clearly, speak well, transact all business, and do all mental work with great speed and ease; but can neither eat nor sleep nor give one's attention to trivial, restful things. I felt strained to the utmost limit. To be with Anna so constantly; to love her so dearly; to long for her so passionately; to see the terrible danger in which she stood; to feel that on me alone depended all hope of drawing her from that quicksand of passion in which she was sinking; to know that a moment's relaxation of my efforts would undo weeks of care; to feel that, strive as I would, my position was infinitely less powerful, less advantageous, than the man's who could take her in his arms, hold her to his breast, and call her his; to know that after a day of painful effort, when she had been drawn toward me and much had been gained, he, in one embrace that night, would probably regain her wavering will and chain her to himself again all this strove hard (and how nearly successfully I shall never know) to turn my brain from its balance. But I tried to keep my firmness and coolness, tried to dismiss the thoughts of Gaida and his influence, and merely exert my own to the fullest; tried to see the proofs that I was succeeding and draw fresh encouragement from them. But at infinite cost. I hardly recognized my own eyes now, when they looked back from the glass at me. They looked so large and burning in the pale face, and I often wondered, dully, as I was shaving, almost as an outsider would, how the whole thing would end. If I could have felt certain that I was on the right path, it would have been different; but great doubts would seize me, and the knowledge that a few moments with

Qaida was perhaps enough to undo hours by my side, stared me in the face. In fact, a certain night came which jhowed me how little way I had actually progressed, and vhat a terrible uphill, stony path rose yet before me.

Toward the end of the month a great fete was to be given in the commissioner's gardens, for both Europeans and natives. Now, these mixed fetes are naively supposed by the complacent Indian Government to bring the two classes together. They are a concession to that section of the community that thinks the native should be brought up to the level of and treated as a white; and to the uninitiated, to those who have never been to one, this form of diversion seems as if it might bring about a delightfully social and friendly intercourse at least for that particular afternoon or evening. The reality, however, hardly impresses one that way. What happens is this. The gates of a magnificent public or private garden a trifle of two hundred acres or so are thrown open to black and white alike, but not the house of the host; that is for the whites alone. The natives come in and pour over the grounds, looking exceedingly picturesque and beautiful in their Oriental dress, and crowned with flowers, as the Greeks of old time. A little later the whites begin to arrive. The natives loll and Lunge about and stare at them, but they are not allowed, on pain of arrest, to speak to them or as the Government calls it to " annoy them." Nor could the whites, except a few of the men in official positions, understand a word of their many languages, if they did. Refreshments are served from the house, but not to the natives. They have to buy theirs, at little native stalls at the gates. There is a band playing; but all seats, stands, and inclosures are reserved for the whites. The natives can stand outside or hang over the rails if they can get near enough. For the rest, wherever seen, however occupied or idle, standing, walking, or sitting, the native is hustled out of the way by a policeman, should a white or whites be coming down the same path or approaching the same bench. And the whites move about as if absolutely unconscious that such a thing as natives existed. He looks through them and over them, walks by the aid of a preceding policeman through them and over them; and, in fact, the natives have about the same place in the fete that the tropical flowers in the grass beneath the white men's feet have; which flowers they greatly resemble, lending beauty and local color to the gee tie.

On Lieutenant Blundell and myself, the commissioner's practical aides-de-camp, fell the burden of all the arrangements, decorations, and commissariat. Anna seemed delighted at the idea, and showed so much animation that all the ennui I usually felt over such work left me, and I threw myself into it with enthusiasm. She never met me now without asking what I was doing for the fete and saying how much she was looking forward to it. On one of these occasions, her motive flashed upon me suddenly and my heart died within me.

"Is Gaida Khan going to be there?" I asked, abruptly.

A flood of crimson swept over her face as she looked down and murmured, half-inaudibly:

"Yes."

"So that is why you are so interested in the fete!" I said, bitterly.

"Not entirely," Anna said, hurriedly, and with the deprecating air she always had when this name was mentioned, as if imploring me not to be angry wiui her. " But there will be a sword dance by the Pathans and he will be in it. It will bq very beautiful. I want you to see it."

"I m aware that Gaida is very handsome," I said, coldly. " I have seen him once."

This man and the horrible, triangular position we were in, though always in my thoughts, were seldom touched on Between us; and the pain of hearing her speak of him and in this eager way was, to a certain extent, unfamiliar and almost overpowering.

Anna grew pale and silent as she always did when the least displeasure crept into my voice, and the thought shot through me that she ff-ared me, and fear is the road to hate, not love. With an effort that seemed almost beyond my strength I crushed back the anger and sense of injury and said, gently:

"Well, Anna, when will you be there? I shall be at your service all the evening to see dances and everything olse. Blundell will do all the honors overlooked by the commissioner."

A smile of confident pleasure broke over her face again.

"I think about nine," she said, softly, and with a grate- ful inflection that said plainly to me, "Thank you, for not being angry."

The evening of the fete, that was to begin about five and continue till midnight, was exceptionally lovely. The breeze from the sea died away, and, though the heat was consequently intense, the calm of earth and sky in their porfection was singularly beautiful. When all was ready and the commissioner had thanked me for the special service I had rendered to the cause, and a few of his guests had already arrived, I strolled away to the lower parts of the gardens, leaving him and Blundell on the steps of the veranda as a reception committee. The sky overhead gleamed like mother-of-pearl with rose color. The languid branches of the palms, steeped in gold, drooped motionless in the still air. In the west shone already a planet with silver radiance, and the moon rose slowly, pale, ethereal, a transparent disk in the roseate sky. I walked down a narrow alley between masses of pomegranate-trees and roses and hibiscus and rhododendron, growing all over one another, and stifling one another and fainting in one another's embrace, walked away from the direction of the bands and lost myself at last in the heavy quiet of the garden. I wanted to find a little rest and pull myself together. A dreadful tiredness, like coma, seemed creeping over me. Nights of sleepless pain and thoughts, days of anxiety and torment were beginning to tell. I felt as if the store of vitality I had been drawing and living on was exhausted. I walked on slower and slower, soothed, unconsciously, by the perfect tranquillity around me, when suddenly the scent of sandal-wood and attar of roses struck me, and I raised my eyes from the path, expecting to see natives near me. There was a single figure only a short distance from me, and advancing in my direction. One glance seemed to drive all the blood in my body to my heart, and there it seemed held and freezing. It was Gaida Khan. He was not in such rich holiday dress as the last time I had wen him; in fact, there was nothing notably festi about it, except that the full, white linen trousers were brilliantly white, the loose, blue tunic he wore over them seemed new, and the scarlet turban on his head Vas of silk instead of cotton. I controlled myself sufficiently to walk calmly on, though my feet almost stopped and seemed rooted to the ground at the first sight of him; ijut I went slowly that I might see him well as I passed. He advanced without changing his pace, with his head held high on its superb column of neck, and the evening light falling softly on the delicate and perfect face. He camo up to me and passed, glancing at me full as he did so; and it seemed to me he raised his head still higher, and a suspicion of an arrogant smile replaced the exquisitely sweet expression that was natural to the face. For a moment our eyes met across the rose and golden light, in the perfect peace and stillness of the garden. We looked at each other. Two men who represented nearly completely the two extremes of humanity; between whom lay a gulf as wide, perhaps, as could exist between two creatures of the same species and the one on the lower side was the one that was victorious and triumphant. I, rich in all the world values; with my brain crammed with all sorts of learning, useful and useless; accustomed to the best this world can offer. He, without one anna or a hut; unable to read or write or understand any tongue but his own and a few words of another. We, the rivals, looked at each other.

He had something for which I would have exchanged all had. He was the envied, the fortunate, the rich. He had passed me, and the way was so narrow that his clothes brushed me and the scent of sandal-wood flooded me. He was taller than I, though I stood six feet; and his disdainful eyes swept over me contemptuously from beneath the crimson turban as he went by. In that moment all the ibaxon blood rose in my veins and seemed to be living fire. The impulse came to spring at his throat and bear him under me to the ground. It passed before me in a flash: the opportunity, the place, the quiet, the solitude; the certainty, the impunity of my vengeance. I was older and, ioubtless, stronger than he; an accomplished athlete and, besides, had the strength at that moment of mad fury. He was, probably, of the usual weak, native constitution and untrained. A short struggle and I could leave him strangled in the narrow way. When his body was found, Who could know or prove it was I that was responsible?

And even if that were known, the slightest excuse of mine an insult offered to me; momentary anger on my part, leading to an unfortunate accident how easily it would be accepted. What was the life of one miserable native, a cletai-wattah, a man who walked with bare feet in the dust of the highway? But I restrained myself and he walked by unharmed. Then I turned and looked after him as he continued his way with the incomparable majesty and grace of movement that is the special gift of the Pathan. "With eyes dim with anger I followed his figure and Kipling's lines went dully through my head:

"He trod the ling like a buck in spring, And looked like a lance at rest."

I paused there till the thicket of rose and magnolia had closed between him and me. Then I walked forward, feeling almost blind and, suddenly, dizzy, sick, and hopeless.

I did not regret in the least that I had let Gaida go bj unharmed. If I wished for his death, there were othel ways of accomplishing it then by a personal struggle. The impulse I had felt had been merely the natural physical impulse of jealousy and hatred. I did not wish his deathj that is to say, I did not intend to bring it about. I had decided that long ago; and nothing in the world is more fatal than reversing in a moment of anger, or any similar madness, the decisions we have arrived at in cold hours of logical thought. If, when the madness comes, you can not remember your reasons or your logic; if, in fact, these then seem to you like folly, at least you can remember you have made such a decision and adhere to it simply because you have made it. This feeling it was and this mechanical remembrance that had allowed Gaida Khan to pass by me in peace.

I found a gardener's water-tank beside my path, and some moss-covered stones. On these I sat down and buried my head in my hands and rested. Yet I can not clain that I thought much. I allowed myself, as it were, t. drift on a blind stupor of fatigue and pain. An hour, per. haps, went by, and I knew I must be returning to my post of duty. I rose and turned back along the path I had come.

When I had retraced my steps to the bungalow the air had darkened, the rose in the sky had changed to purple, and the stars burst forth in it. Beneath, among the blossom-laden trees, hung countless thousands of colored lamps and lanterns, and figures began to pass me in the narrow paths. The commissioner's, house was in a blaze of light. Light poured from all the windows and from the decorated and illuminated veranda, so that the lawn was bright as day.

Throngs of people, Europeans and natives, covered it, and were crowding up the shallow, white steps toward the long windows. One of the bands was playing, and laughter and voices mingled with the strains of music. Servantf, flitted here and there with trays of wine and ices among 1 those who did not care to leave the freshness of the garden for the house. Groups of natives, looking like animated Greek statues in their white clothing and with garlands ol white clematis on their heads and round their throats, lingered and leaned and talked and gazed toward the house while carriages dashing up to the lower end of the lawi deposited every moment fresh consignments of young English girls in white silk and muslin, and young men in nineteenth-century attire; and behind the white corner of tho bungalow roof and the palms the great, mellow., voluptuous moon climbed steadily and looked down upon it all. Exactly at nine, Anna arrived. I was waiting o, the veranda to receive her. Coming into the strong light; she stepped upon the terrace looking fair and fresh as one of the immortals.

I went forward to greet her, and I felt my face was pale and grave and there was a pained smile on my lips. 1 suffered so much mental pain now and so continually that I seemed growing old under the strain of it. Life and its. joyousness, even youth and youthful impulses, seemed dying within me. But, as her affianced lover, I went forward, as a hundred eyes were turned upon us in the brilliant veranda, and welcomed her and drew her arm through mine. She looked up at me with a smile full of love and pleasure that all those eyes could see, as floods of light were falling on her fair face and white-clothed figure, and, doubtless, many men present hated me as one supremely blessed and favored.

"What time does the wonderful dance begin?" I asked, gently.

"About a quarter-past nine, I think," she answered, " and it will be at the farther side of the gardens. Those people passing down the lawn are going now, I think. Come with me round the house. I know a lovely path down the gardens, that will take us there."

There was a general stir among all the guests, natives and Europeans, and Anna and I separated from the general mass and went round to the back of the bungalow, where, as she said, a narrow and lovely alley, arched completely over by the bending cocoanut-palms, opened in front of us. Here and there the moonlight fell through their fan-like branches and seemed to splash like molten silver on the path before us. In one of these irregular pools of light Anna slackened her footsteps and I saw her raise her face and look at me steadily.

"You looked so handsome, Gerald, this evening," she breathed, softly, " when you came forward on the terrace to meet me. So dark, so pale, so beautiful! Kiss me," she added, and stopped short in the path.

I stopped too, and took her wholly in my arms and kissed her.

"Give him up for me," I said in her ear. " Am I not worth it?"

I felt her bosom strained against mine heave spasmodically, and her arms tremble against my neck. At last a choked whisper reached me:

"Oh, I do want to, you know; but, somehow, since I have given myself to him you don't understand, perhaps, but it is such a tie for a woman."

I put her from me suddenly.

"Anna, we must not talk of these things," I said, with a suppressed vehemence that made her shrink from me, " if you want me to remain a reasoning being. I am strained to the utmost limit as it is."

We walked on in perfect silence through one cool, fragrant alley after another, where the moonlight, filtered through the palms, softened and silvered the heavy-scented air, till we arrived in the open again and the crowds of figures told me we were near the appointed ground.

When we reached the spot I saw at once that our clever, little commissioner had selected and arranged it with his usual incomparable taste in such things. The luxurious undergrowth, the long, rank grass and rampant parasites and blossoms, had all been cut away for a large, circular space; which had then been swept clean and surrounded by a light iron railing, about three feet high. Outside this railing a grassy, lawn-like space stretched away till a ring of cocoauut-palms, and all their accompanying under- growth of rose and pomegranate, pressed forward again, making the natural, verdant, fragrant wall. Raised on the grassy lawn, facing the clean-swept ring, a grand-stand came into view; and line upon line of chairs in it were being taken up as we approached. On the opposite side, the Grenadier band had taken its position; while natives and English pressed up all round the circle to the railings. It was as light here as at noonday, thousands of colored lamps being swung in long strings of light from pole to pole above our heads, and the roof of the grand-stand itself beingone blaze of rose and gold.

"Where will you go?" I asked Anna, as we came up.

"Oh, to our seats in the stand," she replied, indifferently, as if she had no other possible interest in or connection with the spectacle than the merest onlooker. No one, certainly, could have dreamed, as she quietly descended the crowded stand to its two best seats, reserved for her in the very front, and calmly crushed the white silk of her costume into their narrow limits and took her place with a certain cold grace that was all her own, that this fair-skinned, light-haired Saxon girl so thoroughly English in every look and gesture, and with, apparently, all the cold pride of the English had come to see her husband dance nis barbaric dance there in the dust before us. I felt a bitter pain as I watched her and took my place beside her, and yet I was glad in a sort of bitter way. I carried a wound a raw, terrible wound in my breast; but, if she could prevent, none should ever know it, none of those eyes round us should peer delightedly into its bleeding re-eessss.

The stand was quite full, packed from end to end now, and might itself have been some beautiful tropical flower, it so glowed with silk and bright colors and brilliant, laughing faces. The band opposite began to play, and trays of sweetmeats, ices, and champagne were brought and passed along in front of the tiers of seats. Anna would not take anything, and, looking at her closely, I saw that though the center of her lips was of the usual bright rose, the corners were white and burned-looking. The commissioner and Bundell had their seats in the tier directly above and behind ours, and toward the half-hour past nine he bent down to Anna and murmured:

"Here they are."

We looked toward the ring. The band had ceased its English airs, and in perfect silence forty Pathans, each with a flashing, naked swoid three and a half feet long and carved slightly at the point like a cimeter, walked slowly into the circle. They were all of great and uniform height, dressed entirely in white, full Mohammedan trousers, straight tunic over to the middle of the thigh, with loose, wide-open, falling sleeves;

on their heads, surmounting their magnificent faces, was wound to the height of a foot, perhaps, a snow-white turban.

A little shiver and flutter passed in a ripple over the stand. Whatever the men may have thought of the " dogs " and " pigs " of natives before them, the women were not and could not be quite unmoved by the sudden display, for their benefit, of this male beauty, this physical perfection. Fair, fluffy heads leaned suddenly together, and whispers were exchanged behind fans. " Aren't they handsome!" "Beautiful!" "Just like statues," ran in feminine murmurs from seat to seat. The Pathans advanced slowly till they all faced the stand, and the full glare of the rosy, yellow light fell on them; showing to us all distinctly the splendid foreheads of pale, burnished bronze; the narrow, delicate, sweeping eyebrows over the lustrous, flashing, midnight eyes; the perfectly modeled noses with the carved, proud nostrils; the firm, cruel, yet exquisite mouths and beautiful chins.

They looked up at the eager, surprised, admiring white faces above them, salaamed and smiled. As before I had noticed with Gaida, the smile is the last touch of the Creator's hand upon their marvelous faces of beauty. The cruel, beautiful lines of the lips dissolve, the lips part from even teeth of flashing pearl, and a sweetness that can only be faintly represented by saying " as of heaven " is lent to the irresistible countenances. A little shiver of delight swept over the women as that smile, like sunlight on a brook, passed over the faces of the Pathans. And I, sitting in mv place, thought wonderingly, "How strange and deceitful Nature is at times! Who could believe that these men are the most bloodthirsty, perhaps the most fiendishly cruel, and certainly the most depraved and vicious race of the earth?" and I passed my hand over my eyes for a moment to shut out those god-like forms and faces, while I thought of all I had heard and read of them stories that would almost sear the paper they were written on, and scorch out Saxon eyes with shame to read. And to think that she this girl beside me, whose slender, delicate, white fingers held my soul and brain and heart in their hold, who controlled the very rush of blood through my veins; she, with all her delicacy and refinement of thought and feeling, was in the hands of one of these! I turned to her now with all this savage pain confusing my thoughts, and, altering some of them enough to give her sharp senses the clew to them all, I said something about the men before us being mere devils; and she turned her face fully to me, meeting my gaze with her eyes full of cool, insolent courage. It was the same look that shone in her father's face when he led his men up the defiles of death in the Border campaigns; the same look that shines in the eyes of the Saxon the world over, and makes him what he is the world's master.

"I am not afraid," she said, simply, answering all she knew was in my thoughts; and she turned to look down to the arena again.

I followed her eyes and at that instant the dance commenced. The Pathans had all fallen into line, one behind the other, forming a circle the entire circumference of the inclosure. At the first crash of the opening chord of music, forty flashing swords leaped into the air and were whirled, each one gleaming, round the head of each white-robed Pathan as he plunged forward, breaking into a wild, musical chant in unison with the music. Now, I do not know what step was used in that dance, nor can I possibly conceive any European foot making one like it. I can only say that the Pathans moved round in that perfect circle, of which the proportions never varied, with marvelous rapidity, the broad blades of their swords playing like lightning above their heads the whole time, and their gait in the dance was the gait of the Pathan when he walks, somewhat rolling and sensuous, but when fitted to such forms of extreme grace and symmetry, one that reaches the climax of beauty in motion.

Their curious, swaying movement from side to side seemed to bring into play every one of the muscles of those shapely forms. The powerful shoulders and flanks, the line of the spine, the somewhat too-developed muscles of the hip and waist, all were moving; and their play could be seen distinctly under the one surface of fine white linen over them.

As the dancers swung around the ring, it was a sensuously beautiful sight; and, as such sights are generally rendered by women for the benefit or otherwise of men, I glanced round with a faint feeling of amusement, questioning in my mind what the women thought of this reversing of the order of things, in their favor. The stand was mainly filled by women, and that they were affected by the unexpectedness and beauty of the scene before them and moved by the sudden call it made on the senses, was evident. Their faces, as they leaned forward, were pale; and a dilated eye, the slight, nervous movement of a fan, the parted lips or sudden flush of color on the cheeks told the emotions that the otherwise coldly well-bred crowd failed to betray. I brought my eyes back and they rested on Anna. She was pale, too; and I saw her nostril quiver, dilate, and beat nervously. But for that, she was motionless, calm as a statue.

There was nothing, one might say, voluntarily sensuous or sensual in the spectacle. The dance was not a licentious, but a martial one; and the management of the swords that they kept whirling and flashing in horizontal and vertical circles round them, was magnificent.

There was perfect order and concert in each movement in spite of their intense rapidity; for each man was so closely following the other that the slightest misstep, stumble, or lagging of the pace on any one's part must have resulted in a fatal accident. Each whirling sword was timed to a second to rise and descend, and each only cleared by an inch or so the white-turbaned head directly in front of it, and its backward whirl over each man's head as they swept triumphantly round their circle cleared by hardly so much the brow of the man behind him. It was a splendid, inspiring sight; breathing of courage and bravery, dexterity and skill, and the madness and triumph of victory. And what of sensual element there was in it came involuntarily and unavoidably from the wonderful physical beauty displayed, and the sumptuousness of Oriental form and outline, not from studied trick and gestures as in the Nautches.

I looked on fascinated, and drew my breath still with a Curious feeling each tune that Gajda passed, with his flung upward on its column of bronze throat, beneath its white turban, and between a sword and a sword.

And as the music grew louder and faster and the danoe nore abandoned and the encircling swords more dangerous in those flying, glistening circles, the faces of even the quiet British officers flushed up with animation. On Anna's left sat the colonel of the regiment to which most of the dancers belonged; for, with the exception of Gaida and a few others, chosen for their personal beauty and skill, the men before us were all soldiers enrolled in one of the Pathan regiments and officered by Englishmen who are able to turn the splendid fighting qualities of these men, their love of danger and death in battle, their reckless courage, their very appetite for blood, to the best account. This old colonel, who had mixed with Pathans, studied and commanded them for twenty years, gazed down now at his men with flushing face and queerly glittering eyes. They were his children, practically, and he had seen their irresistible rush in battle, their fierce onsets, their mute, smiling courage, their unmurmuring deaths; until, by the side of these things, their horrible lives, when not in war, and unspeakable vices seemed to grow small to his almost parental eye.

Anna leaned toward him and murmured:

"What splendid fellows, colonel. Are you not proud of them?"

"I am! I am!" he returned, with beaming eyes, and raised his hands to clap them loudly.

This was the signal, and a perfect storm of applause broke from the crowded stand. At the same moment the music ceased, as it had begun, with one sudden crash; and on the instant the almost flying forms became motionless and the lifted swords made an arrested wave of gleaming light round the ring. Then the swords were lowered. The Pathans smiled and salaamed as before, and filed silently a procession of kings one would have said out of the inclosure.

The stand full of whites began to flutter and whisper and laugh, as they rustled out of the seats; and Anna and I very slowly followed in silence. Almost without a word we walked through the grounds and entered her carriage. When we arrived at the house, the general alighted first and went up into the veranda, and we were left alone at the foot of the steps, while the carriage drove away.

"You will receive him to-night?" I said in a low voice.

"I suppose so," she said, raising her hand to her lips, which parted in a little, nervous yawn; " he is my husband."

My brain seemed scorching as if with fire.

"And what am I?" I asked, in desperation, standing so as to bar her farther path.

She stood still and looked up at me. Then she opened her arms to me tenderly.

"You are my fiance; so we must kiss and say goodnight."

I turned from her in a silence too bitter for words; felt, rather than saw, that her arms dropped to her sides, and that she, too, turned and went into the house.

I walked away toward my own bungalow, feeling that I had drunk up the draught of life; that my mouth was full of bitter lees and dregs; and that the cup was empty.

When I reached the house I went straight to my room, undressed, and threw myself on the bed. I felt the round patch of burning fire, that foretells Indian fever, kindled in both palms, and I knew that in an hour or two I should be mercifully oblivious for a time of all surrounding things. My days and sleepless nights of suffering, capped by this terrible evening, the mental fever in which I had been living so long, had culminated at last in physical fever. My finger-tips were still of normal temperature, and doubling them into my hands I felt the little fire growing in the palms and extending its circle every minute. I felt chilly aad languid, with intense pain in the back; and I drew a thick, soft blanket all over me, though the thermometer marked ninety-six degrees. And then I lay still, dreamily giving myself over to that strange sensation of growing heat and languor, that intense fiery stupor creeping insidiously all over me, and melting away one's mental feelings, perceptions, and pains, as in a natural crucible. I lay still, sinking deeper and deeper into a sort of heat coma, in which I seemed wrapped round and round with flames flames that did not burn, but only heated heated to a point where bones and limbs and brains were all fused together, and one was nothing any longer bub an inert mass pf dreamy heatt

Then came a blank of unconsciousness, and my next memory is that I was struggling like a madman, at the open window, with my trembling Afghan bearers; and some one, that they afterward told me was myself, was screaming with a queer sort of laughter that rang out over the quiet, moonlit compound. After a little while I was back in bed again with some one holding me down by both arms; and the doctor was there beside the bed, with a wine-glass in his hand. I knew it was the doctor, for 1 remembered his long Roman nose, and now so funny! his nose had grown so long it reached out as far as the bed, and I tried to wrench my hand loose from the bearer's hold, because I knew I was expected to shake hands with it. Then he put the wine-glass down to my lips, and I seized the rim with my teeth and bit a piece out of it. Glass is a queer food to give a sick man. And then a stream of icy liquid splashed all over my face and throat, and I fought desperately because the icy drops seemed killing me. Then they bound me down to the charpoy with cloths, arid enormous hands came down on my face and held my mouth open, and something went cold and freezing down my throat, and I twisted and strained and wrenched, and there was a loud creaking, and I heard a voice saying, far off in the distance I think it was at the end of the world:

"He will break up the bed."

And there was pain at my wrists and ankles. They came arid sawed at them with red-hot saws, and I screamed and twisted and they sawed the faster; and then there was black, black night, and nothing more.

In the morning I opened my eyes. There were two servants by the bed and the doctor sitting beside me. I felt very quiet and very weak. I stretched out my hand and touched the chair beside me. It felt warm. Then I knew the fever had left me. I looked at the doctor and smiled.

"You had a pretty sharp attack last night," he observed, " and, by Jove! what strength you have! I never recognized fully your splendid physique until now."

"Thank you, doctor," I returned, weakly; " I am afraid it was rather troublesome than otherwise last night," Then, as a thought of fear suddenly struck me, I added, "Was I delirious?"

"Delirious!" exclaimed the doctor, " well, I should rather think so. First you tried to jump out of the win- dow, then you bit up a wine-glass, then you tried to break down the bed, screaming all the time. Ve had a lively time with you, I can assure you."

"What did I say in my delirium?" I asked, paling. Good God! Suppose I had betrayed Anna's secret!

"Oh, nothing coherent at all. You were past that. Don't be alarmed, my boy, you have not given yourself away. You just shrieked like a maniac and strained so when we bound you, I thought you'd break your wrists."

I glanced at my wrists. They were livid and swollen double. Then I closed my eyes. How inestimably thankful I was that I had uttered nothing about her.

Then I was given some beef-tea and left to myself, covered up with blankets: and I sunk into a long, restful coma.

I was roused toward noon. My bearer stood by my bedside with a great bunch of white roses on a salver and a card.

"The Miss Sahib Lombard was here and would so much like to see the sahib," said the servant.

I was too weak to lift the flowers; but I motioned the servant to set the tray, card, and flowers on the bed, and said I would see her.

I glanced round the room. Like most Indian rooms, it was large, with an infinity of windows, all standing open to the fresh Kalatu breeze, and more like a sitting-room than a bedroom. In fact, my one narrow, wooden-frame charpoy was the only thing in it that suggested a sleeping-room. My bearer closed the doors into my bath-room and dressing-room, drew an easy-chair to the side of the bed and retired.

I watched the door by which she would enter, and in a few seconds she came in. In white, and with a white sailor hat on her bright hair and a faint, pale rose glow on her cool, white skin, she looked, as usual, a type of the morning.

She stopped short at the door with a look of dismay. I suppose I may have had a ghastly appearance, after the efforts of the previous night. Then she advanced, almost running, and, stooping over the bed, would have kissed me; but I put both my hands on her chest and held her from me.

"Did you receive him last night?" I asked, looking up at her. And I felt the fever beginning to awake in my veins again.

"Yes."

"Then don't kiss me. Your kisses are loathsome to me," and I turned my head away from her on the pillow.

She drew back as if my hands had been daggers that stabbed her breast, and sat down in silence in the chair close by me. There was silence, and I felt the excitement, resentment, anger, grief, and sorrow that her presence caused in me, rushing through me and relighting the devouring fever in every tissue. I turned my head to look at her, after a minute. She was sitting silently gazing at me with wide-open, pathetic eyes, and great tears were forming in them and overflowing and pouring down the long, black lashes.

I stretched out my hand a little nearer to her on the coverlet.

"Forgive my violence," I said, gently. " I was like a madman last night, and my brain has not recovered its usual balance yet."

She ungloved one white hand and laid it over mine.

"I heard you were very ill," she said in a trembling voice.

"No, not very ill," I murmured, turning my head restlessly on the pillow for a furious pain was beginning there. " Only a little Indian fever and other kinds."

Anna did not answer; she only sat and cried more.

"Don't cry," I said, " that does not alter things."

Then I closed my eyes. The fever had taken hold of my head and it was being held in a vise of steel, while red-hotpincers tore slowly at the brain-tissues.

When I opened my eyes again I saw the sunlight had shifted its position in the room, and I knew an hour or more must have passed. Anna still sat by me, holding my hand and still crying; only now the fair skin was colored red with tears, the blue eyes were lost in a red mist and had dark, purple patches round their lids.

"Find the doctor and tell him to give me more anti-febrine," I muttered, " and then go. Don't sit here and cry, spoiling your face."

Whether she went or stayed, I don't know. The rest of that day and night is a blur to me. The next clear point to me was the following morning, when I was calm out of pain and I saw the doctor's face again above my bed. It was much graver than on the previous morning in fact, I laughed a little as I saw it. It reminded me of a London undertaker.

"You have been so much worse than I anticipated," I heard him saying after a minute, "I think change of air is imperative. You seemed to grow suddenly worse yesterday after Miss Lombard's visit, and you raved terribly in the night."

Again that fear! What was he saying? Change of air? Go away! Certainly! Yes, that was it. Go away, before I had betrayed Anna. Go away among strangers, where what I said would not matter.

"Yes, doctor, yes, I think so. Get me away. What did I say last night?"

"I really don't know," returned the doctor, rather crossly, I thought. " I don't pay any heed to fever patients' rambling; but you mentioned Miss Lombard's name a great many times.""

It was time to go! I started put of bed and stood upright for a second. Then I fell in a heap, and the doctor gathered me up and put me into a chair.

"You are very, very weak," he said. " I don't think you can go at present."

"I tell you I am going to-day. The bearer can carry me to the carriage, if I can't walk. Help me get dressed, doctor, and tell the men to put up some things for me. The commissioner will give me a fortnight's leave, I know. Then you put me on a train for the hills. Get me away, doctor, or I'll die on your hands; I will, indeed, and be a lasting discredit to you!"

The doctor looked very grave, and felt my hand.

"You have no fever now," he said, doubtfully, " but you are so deplorably weak. Where do you intend to go?"

Oh to Peshawur."

"Why take such a long trip as that? I would suggest ""

"No," I interrupted, angrily, "I am going to Peshawur. Call in my servants. Let me see that black trunk yes, that will do. Now, doctor, just hand me my socks. I can't get up for them."

I was intensely weak and most anxious to use all my mental faculties while they were clear. I knew that even- ing would bring back the fever and incapacity; bat then, if I were on the train, without a soul to near my ravings, it would not matter. And Peshawur! Yes, that idea fascinated me. I would go up to the capital of the Pathans, to Gaida's birth-place, and learn something of the wonderful race learn something of him, too, perhaps. I began feverishly to pull on my socks. My fingers trembled and my bones cracked loudly as the fever had licked up the oil in their sockets. Everything was intense fatigue, but my mind urged me on and kept me up to my work. I could rest on the train. Once on the train I could lie and lie, and rest and rest, until they picked me up and carried me out at the other end. But now I must work. The doctor had left me for a few minutes, and I had to dress myself as well as I could, and get about the room bv clinging on to the furniture. Then he came back, bringing my butler and bearer, and they packed my trunk, and I sat on the edge of the cliarpoy with a brain rocking queerly as it does after fever, as if a seesaw were in your head and my vision all distorted. But I managed to write a check for the butler, who would take all the tickets and would want money for the journey, and one for the doctor, and a note to Anna, and one to the commissioner. The end of it all was, at five o'clock that evening, in a giddy mist of pain, I was put on the train, in a private compart, ment with my two servants, and shipped up to Peshawur.

CHAPTER VI.

FOE weeks I lay ill at Peshawur. Simple Indian fever would have given way quickly and easily to the keen, light air of the hills; but no cool winds nor mountain air could sweep away in a day or two the ravages of those long, terrible nights of mental anguish, that long strain of anxiety and restless passion that had been put upon my brain. Days without food and nights without sleep, Nature deeply resents; and at last, if you continue that treatment of her, she strikes you down in a passion as she did me.

My servants had secured a good position for my bungalow; and from the sick-room, in which I lay through the long, fever-stricken days and nights, I could see, without raising my head from the pillow, the light, turquoise sky and the deep blue Hues of the hills. It was rather pleas- ant, rather a relief to me, this intense physical weakness, in which the brain ceases to bother one with its ideas and pictures, its thoughts and desires. This bodily preoccupation with bodily pain and sufferings swept one's brain clear and left it blank, like a little child's. After hours of delirium and fever, there came long hours of blank, quiet weakness; in which I lay content to be without sensation of any sort gazing out through the open jilmils into the clear, light, placid air beyond. Then I slowly began to get better; and I almost dreaded recovery. Recovery meant taking up again the burden of responsibility and anxiety that the utter helplessness of disease slips from one's shoulders. I gained strength slowly each day; and I knew that with my strength would come back desires and longings and hopes and cares without end.

In all this time I heard constantly from Anna, and her letters had always the same burden: her love for myself, her gratitude, her devotion, and her piteous longing to be free from " her bondage," as she called it. But it was a bondage that none could free her from; and no one could understand that better than I. Let there be no misunderstanding here. It was Anna's own love that held her captive. She wished to crush out that love, to annihilate it, perhaps; but she could not; and no human aid could help her. As the drunkard longs to kill the desire for drink, yet goes on drinking; so she might wish to kill her love, yet she continued loving. Had the bondage been any other than this; had she been tied to this man by the tie of marriage without love, I would and could, possibly, have freed her. But in this case, since her love was the disease and her captivity but, as it were, the symptom, it was useless to attack the latter and set her free until the disease itself, torn from its roots, was eradicated. Forcible separation from Gaida would not free her; it would simply martyrize and idealize him in her thoughts, and she would be bound to him by the chains of a thousand memories; and for the one who caused that separation she would feel nothing but resentment. Even if she gave herself to me, it would be with that memory of him standing like a shield between us. And that should not be. No, the terrible passion must be killed or die; and until that time came about she could not be released. And I, forced to remain passive, yet was comforted, knowing that one man had the power to kill it; and, he, probably, was working surely to that end and that man was Gaida himself.

I could not answer her letters fully; but I sent her little pencil notes as often as the fever, the dysentery that followed it, the recurrence of the fever, and all the weakness in between, permitted.

And then at last there came a day when I left my bed and was dressed again with a white collar round my neck, and I sat up by the window of my room and looked downward, instead of being on my back and looking upward, as I had for so long.

There was a pile of newspapers on the chair beside me, and I looked at one printed at Kalatu and let my eye stray over it from column to column. Ever since I had shared Anna's secret with her, I had never been able to take up a paper, European or native, without a vague dread that I might find her name in it, coupled with suspicion, some veiled story or even open scandal; and so, from habit, my eye flitted nervously over both sheets until all the headlines had been noted, and I was about to lay the paper down with relief when I saw in an obscure, out-of-the-way corner of the last page, two or three lines headed " The Epidemic," and read as follows:

"The cholera epidemic remains at present unabated, despite the stringent measures adopted for its suppression by our able commissioner. Three hundred and twenty deaths were reported yesterday, against two hundred and ninety of the day before; and there are seventy-five fresh cases today."

That was all absolutely all. Just that little foot-note at the end of the sheet. I turned over the four pages of the paper vainly to find some other allusion to it. There was none. Political articles were there as usual; complaints against the corrupt municipality; and, in the local news columns, account after account of this dinner, that garden party, this little dance, Mrs. So-and-Sp's picnic, gay jokes, Ion mots, descriptions of gowns, with list of successes or failures in the weekly gymkhana. These things filled up the sheet; just as if Kalatu was the healthiest station imaginable and in the gayest and most light-hearted of humors, with no deadly stream of disease flow-log round it and stealthily lapping up its victims at an average of three hundred a day. Well, not for nothing have we British our reputation for phlegm. And Anna was there, and, like the true Briton she was, thought the plague too insignificant a matter to be mentioned in her letters. Then I recollected she had not written to me for a week. Could the general have sent her away for safety? t was not likely. I had experience of these things. I know how the British in India treat the plague. I had been through an epidemic before in another station and had noticed their demeanor when I was fresh from England, too, and, therefore, I had noticed it; from England, where, if a navvy dies with stomach-ache in the hot August weather, somewhere down by the docks, the morning papers have big head-lines, set in capital letters: " Case of cholera in London. Great alarm felt. Message from the queen." But things are different in India, and this is how they do them there. First, in a native paper, appears a statement of five deaths from cholera. A week goes by, and then, in a European paper, one reads that by order such-and-such wells have been closed and the public tanks and wash-houses shut up " as a precautionary measure." The following week the public is informed, without comment, that " deaths from cholera are now averaging one hundred and fifty a day, and bounds have been established, the line being set at the native city " which is, perhaps, five miles from cantonments. This means that no white person shall drive in his carriage, ride or pass by on foot, or in any way whatever cross the set line and return. All beyond the line is infected. Day by day passes, and the number of deaths per day creeps up steadily, and that line is drawn tighter and tighter, closer and closer round the whites as that deadly black sea of cholera encroaches and encroaches on all sides. The line or boundary being set down by the native city at first, one can ride or drive from there to the coast, one can still canter through the public gardens, shop in upper town, attend the band-stand, or visit distant bungalows out on the desert. Presently, the line is drawn up into a narrower loop, and one by one cuts out the upper town; for the advancing tide of cholera has crept into that. Next, the gardens go, the line is put between them and you; next, the drive to the sea or the desert is forbidden, and the line contracts into a puny cir-cle, which embraces the principal bungalows, half a mile, perhaps, of level ground for driving, and the band-stand. Within this you trot and canter and your coachman turns twenty times in half an hour, and cholera stares you in the face from every side from over the line.

Meanwhile, in spite of the strenuous measures adopted by the sanitary inspection committee, the board of health, the health commissioner, and many other untiring and conscientious officials; in spite of quarantines and isolations and closed wells and disinfectants, the deaths reach, perhaps, four hundred per diem; and the English go on with their dancing and dining, picnic in compounds because everywhere else is beyond the line and charade parties. It is not considered etiquette to allude to the plague in any way or at any time; and any one committing such a solecism is immediately frowned down by the rest of the company present. If an expected guest is absent from his place at a dinner-party, and his sudden death is handed to his hostess as his excuse, no inquiry is made as to his illness. It is taken for granted it is the prevailing epidemic; and, of course, no one would be so ill-bred as to mention that. Very few of the women or children are sent away; at any rate, not until the mortality among the whites is very great. Beyond the line, the native population sickens and dies; and the list of its losses are sent in, day by day, as an item to the newspaper; and within the bounds, the whites laugh and dance and flirt and listen to their bands playing dance music and read obituary notices of their best friends, and the funereal tom-toms never cease throbbing over the line.

Well, so it is in India at least in the stations where I have been and so here it evidently was in Kalatu. And General Lombard and his daughter were among that gay, insouciant crowd, listening to dance music and reading obituary notices like the rest. But, though the British may scorn danger and deride death, the Briton has to die like the rest of men; and though he die with a smile on his lips, that does not comfort any particular friend who wanted him alive.

All these reflections and recollections passed quickly through my brain, as I sat with the open paper on my knees and my eyes staring vacantly out toward the Kaiber hills. Then I turned and called up my servants and bid them pack up my trunks and make all ready to go down to Kalatu the following day.

There were one or two little hand-cases that I always packed myself, and, as I bent over these, the thought would keep driving through my brain: " I have not heard for a week. Suppose she should be ill!" And a companion thought followed quickly: " Suppose she should be dead!" And yet a third: "Suppose she should be dead and buried!" One never knows in India. An eighteen-hours' absence, for the matter of that, is unsafe. Twelve hours is enough for cholera to do its work in, and six hours after that the corpse is buried. So that, on Monday evening one may hold a form close in one's arms, alive and brilliant with health, and on Tuesday, at noon, on going to call, one may learn that it is shut away with eight feet of cemetery earth barring one from it forever. Leaning over my trunk, I d d my weak foolishness for having such thoughts. Were there not three hundred white women and girls in Kalatu, and why should Anna be stricken more than they? And would not General Lombard have wired me if my fiancee were ill? Yet that horrible, haunting possibility, that idea that I might never again feel that soft heart beat against my own; never see those eyes deepen and darken as they looked into mine; never have those gentle, slender arms clasped about my neck again, stood beside me or behind me all that day, goading me.

"The sahib packs badly," observed my bearer, judicially, from over my shoulder, as he stood watching me throwing in my things recklessly. " Even I can pack superior."

It is a tedious journey down from Peshawur; and the train, when it does arrive, brings you in at five in the morning not the most convenient hour. Kalalu seemed unchanged as I drove from the station. Its broad red roads, with their border of emerald-green moss at the edges, looked cool and pleasant enough to the eye, in the early dawn. The bungalows had their customary quota of servants moving about them; and the sun, climbing over the edge of the level plain to the east, threw long, cool shadows from the broad-leaved banana-trees.

I learned from the coachman that Lombard Sahib and the Miss Sahib were both well, and perhaps that made the drive seem very supportable. At nine o'clock, tubbed and shaved, I was turning over the papers in the club reading-room and having the absence of several familiar faces explained to me; by half-past I had reported myself to the commissioner; and at ten I was ready to make my way over to Anna's.

CHAPTER VII.

WHEN I reached the bungalow, breakfast was over and the general had already left. Anna met me on the veranda, and I looked over her critically, expecting to see some change in her, after a month of the kind of life she had been leading. But no; there was all that same slim grace and freshness unimpaired, and the pallor and grief of her face was evidently only the result of sudden and recent shock. She was pale, and her eyes looked very large and dark; but that only seemed to make her face even more expressive than usual.

"Oh, Gerald, why did you come?" were her first words. " I do so wish you hadn't. It would be safer to keep away, for a little while."

"Since I came down from Peshawur entirely to see if I could be of any use to you, I think my presence here is quite natural," I answered, smiling.

It was very sweet to me to even see her again. After all, the mere sight of the loved one is a great and precious thing.

"Did you really really? How good of you!" she said, looking up at me with melting eyes. " Isn't it horrible? The whole station is down with it. No one knows who will be the next one. We have it here in the house among the servants."

I guessed the truth from her voice and accent, and my heart almost stood still as I put the question:

"Has Gaida it?"

"Yes; he is the only one who has at present."

My heart seemed to give a great bound as I heard; but the throb of exultation and triumph, if it were really that that went through me, was checked instantly by the look of blighting anguish on her face.

"I believe he is going to die," she said.

The words are simple enough; but she spoke as the pris- oner may speak who is stretched on the rack, with writhing lips and every nerve wrenched with agony.

I looked at her face and understood how the approach of death had raised all her waning, dying passion again to its highest pitch. All his faults and offenses were forgotten, doubtless, when he was stricken before her; and her whole being was clinging wildly to its love for the beautiful human frame, the source of so much passionate pleasure to her and now claimed by disease and death. 1 saw it all, and ground my teeth that it should be so; but still, being so, my own line of action was clear.

"Let me see him. I have some knowledge of the disease and its treatment."

Anna started. 'You? Why? What would you do?"

"I will bring him through, if I can," I answered, sim- piy-

"I think the danger is too great. You might get it from him." There was a minute's silence, while we both looked at each other. Then her eyes swam suddenly in tears, and she caught my hand and pressed it up to her breast. "Oh! you know, you know, if I had to choose between you, it would be you. Your life is infinitely more to me than his. You are always first. However much I love him, I love you more. I can't bring you into the contagion."

Her voice was so passionate, her whole face and form so expressive of her strange, double emotion that, for a second, I felt unbalanced and longed to gather her into my arms and kiss her. Then I recalled myself and said, merely:

"I don't believe in contagion through the breath or touch. I shall not eat or drink in Gaida's room, so I shall be all right. Take me to him."

She hesitated for a moment, then, apparently, the pressure of my will in the matter overcame her own as was usual in our intercourse and she turned, and we went down the steps of the veranda and round the house, across the rose-garden, by the very same little track I had taken on that memorable night of whispers. And the memory of all those terrible, savage emotions swept over me; but not the emotions themselves. I understood now so much better. The girl's respective passions of the mind and body were one of those terrible, complex problems that life is continually holding out to our gaze. It was something beyond her own power, will, or comprehension. She was but the innocent, will-less plaything of some of those extraordinary forces that govern and sport with humanity; that push it and pull it hither and thither, and can suddenly wrench asunder the strongest ties, though their victim bleed to death at the severance.

I was not now the deceived and cheated lover of a faithless mistress. I was simply her co-sufferer from the hidden, relentless laws of life.

My feelings did not differ very widely now, I think, from what they would have been if I had known her stricken with some fearful disease. There was the same sorrow; the same crushing resentment against destiny; the same sense of selfish, personal loss; the same anxiety, pity, and sympathy for her.

The ancients, indeed, considered passion and all love a disease, and openly called it such. But as such though in this case the effects upon my feelings were much the same I do not regard it. Passion is, rather, the effect upon us of some mysterious, hidden power in Nature that sways irresistibly the senses, but has no control over the soul. And so our body is driven often, as it seems, with intangible blows and irresistible coercion, as Anna's was, toward some object that the soul rejects and abhors. Subsequently that same power, invisible as a storm wind and as powerful, often with the same blows that one can not meet, but yet can feel, binds down the body there, and with it the struggling soul.

If I had seen Anna carried from me by some beast of prey, crying to me for help, holding out her arms to me, and longing for me in her death-agony; I could not have understood more clearly or felt more free from anger with her than I did now, now that I had once gazed into this problem and read it.

So I followed calmly her light, quick footsteps for she was almost running now, like a deer to its mate in the thicket and in a few minutes we had reached the quarters of the natives at the far end of the compound. No one was stirring. It was high noon, and any of the natives not engaged in the house were sleeping behind the grass mats hanging before their hut doors,

At one of these, in no way marked out from the rest, Anaa stopped, and, lifting the hanging mat with her hand, stooped and passed in underneath, and I followed. Never, as long as I retain memory of anything, can I forget that scene of desolation, squalor, and misery, as it seems to Europeans, that seemed to burn in upon my eyes. The hut was perfectly square, with unpapered, uncovered brown mud walls. There was one unglazed aperture a foot square, in the wall opposite, which let in the only light; the mats over the door having fallen again after our entrance and blocking out the sunlight there. The roof was of mud and laths, and, perhaps, half a foot higher than my head. The floor was of soft mud, trodden by many feet into a sodden paste. The whole of the center was taken up by a large, square charpoy, that possessed no drapery, no bedclothes of any kind save one thin, gray blanket. There was only just space for one person to pass all round the room, between the bed and the mud walls. Other furniture there was none. One cracked china tea-cup and a bent tin spoon were stuck upright in the mud of the floor by the bed. And there, stretched on the bed, in the dim twilight of this human stable, with a few, white cotton rags on him, lay Gaida, dying in the grip of the black cholera. He had turned his head toward the entrance as Anna raised the mat. I made a step forward and stood by the bed. As his eyes lighted on me their narrow oval filled with a fury of anger and scorn.

"Son of a sow!" he muttered, raising himself, and then fell back with a groan of agony. His lips were blue. Then he turned to Anna. " Why dost thou bring him here?"

he said, in a hoarse voice. " Is it not enough that I am leaving thee to him? Canst thou not wait till I am dead?"

Anna knelt beside him on the mud floor, stretching aar arms out on the bed in a passion of tears.

"He has come to aid thee cure thee," she answered. " Allah has sent him."

"Men do not aid and cure their rivals," the Pathan muttered in reply, turning his head wearily from side to side.

"The English do," returned Anna, between her heartrending sobs. " I tell thee he is a medicine-man. He is skilled in many things. He will restore tliee to life for my sake. Accept him. Allah sends him."

"True. What Allah wills is. If he has sent him to kill, I die. If to cure, I live. He may come."

Anna rose joyfully from her knees, and I advanced to the bed and looked keenly at him. He was still in the first stage of cholera, and could bo saved, I thought.

"Gaida Khan," I said, gently, "I am going to cure you for your wife's sake. You know Englishmen do not lie. Trust me."

A semblance of that former smile, which had been the crowning beauty of that marvelous face, passed over it.

"My trust is with thee," he murmured, and clused his eyes.

I opened a pocket medicine-case and took out a preparation of opium and gave him a few drops. He took them calmly and lay motionless. I turned to Anna,

"Give your servants orders to carry him over to my house," 1 said. " I can treat him better there, and air and space are essential."

Anna clasped her hands against her breast in dismay, and looked at mo with streaming eyes.

"Do you want to take him away from me now?"

"You cai come there stay there, if you wish," I said, hurriedly; " but he must be moved. Give your orders at once. Seconds now mean life or death."

Anna grew paler, if that were possible; but she did not hesitate longer. She raised the swinging mat and slipped out into the burnished light of the compound. I stood by the bed ready to give more opium, if there should be the slightest sign of an approaching cramp. But he lay still, and there was no sound within or without save the gay call of a maina, now and then, swinging on a bough outside.

In a few seconds Anna reappeared wilh four servants, two of whom went to the head of the charpoy and two to the feet, and they lifted it with ease. Anna and I tora down the mats from the front of the hut, and left a free and open way for the charpoy and its bearers to pass out. The compound was silent and deserted in the blazing solitude of noon, and we threaded our way across it between the pomegranate-trees and out to the side-gate that opened on to the road leading to my house. This, too, was quiet and empty, lying arid and parched under the pitiless glare.

Anna drew one of the thin, cotton cloths entirely over Gaida's head and face, as the natives themselves do before going to sleep, and so we passed swiftly up to my compound with our burden, that lay motionless under the coverings as if already a corpse. When we reached my house, I had him taken to one of the rooms on the west side a large, cool, lofty room with a wide veranda beyond, into which its windows opened. This veranda being filled with palms and ferns, hourly watered by a watchful gardener, formed a natural thermantidote. The fierce desert wind blew through it, and its scorching breath came into the room, a cool zephyr, bearing the moist scent of ferns. From his own cliarpoy Gaida was lifted to a bed of stretched canvas, cool and yielding as down. He opened his eyes, as he sunk back upon it, and gazed round. The tranquil, shaded quiet, the refreshing atmosphere seemed to surprise him, after the close heat of the mud hut with the sun rays pouring down upon its cow-dung roof. Anna had to retuni, to be present at the house when the general came back and preside over his luncheon; so that I and Gaida were left alone.

I worked against the disease all through that day, and toward evening seemed to have made some headway. I had had great experience with cholera, having nursed many of my servants and others, usually natives, to recovery. I was absolutely without fear of the disease myself; why, I can not say, except that fear is such a curious, relative emotion. No two people seem to feel the same degree of fear for the same thing. I have known personally a young lieutenant who fled from his post in abject terror before the cholera, and shortly afterward picked up an unexploded shell, with the lighted fuse attached, and carried it some distance in his hands with unshaken coolness and bravery.

As that long Indian day a day of splendor and gorgeous color wore away beyond the luminous green of the veranda, I worked and watched, never leaving his bedside for a moment. I did not dare to let my thoughts dwell on the relative positions that would be mine if he died and if he recovered. I shut out everything from my thought, except the strenuous desire to save him. It was the easier to me to do this, since it was but the consistent following out of the policy I had decided upon from the very first, and had been pursuing through so many weary months.

To servo Anna, to protect in every way this man since that was her wish and leave the ultimate issue entirely to powers beyond my own, had been the line of action from which I had never wavered. How often the old Greek cry co the Deity rose in my heart. I did not wish to stretch out my own hand to the rudder of my fate. Loving Anna as I did, made it impossible for me; since my reaching the port of my desires, might mean her shipwreck. I sat, therefore, as it were, a simple oarsman, rowing humbly in the boat, obeying orders, and trusting blindly to the hand upon the helm. So now my immediate duty was to save this life that was ruining my own. That was my last order, and I was obeying it even cheerfully and with my utmost strength; for I had beaten down my own desires and my own self to a point which made it possible.

Toward evening, as I sat watching him, I saw that some stimulant was needed. There was improvement, certainly, since the morning; the great coolness, the perfect rest, and silence and pure air had all helped him; but now he seemed failing and sinking; and I saw I must bring about a reaction or he was lost. Eaw brandy was what was needed, and I crossed the room to my chest and uncorked a bottle. Then I looked at it doubtfully. Being a Mohammedan, he would not touch it, I knew, unless I could successfully disguise it. I selected an empty medicine-bottle with a large, attractive label, and filled it with the brandy, pouring some essence of peppermint into it. Then I walked to the bed with the bottle and glass, and aroused him. He seemed heavy and sleepy.

"It is time to take some more medicine," I said; and he rose a little, obediently, and I filled the glass and held it to his lips. He swallowed two mouthfuls, then, as the brandy burned his throat and chest, he recognized in a flash and intuitively, what it was. He sprung to a sitting position, with his eyes blazing, and dashed the glass out of my hand to the floor, where it broke to atoms.

' Base born and cursed! Dog! Thou wantest to steal my soul from Allah! Thou wouldst have me live, but in sin; drinking what he has forbidden, like an unbeliever."

"Gaida," I answered, bitterly, in the same tongue, " you talk foolishly. It would be better for me if I let your soul depart immediately to Allah. I have no wish to keep you here in sin or otherwise. But to drink wine for medicine is different from drinking it for pleasure. Drink it now to get well, but abjure it afterward. Allah will forgive you."

"Thou wouldst seduce me," he muttered, sullenly, eying me suspiciously.

He was still sitting up, and I noticed he pressed his hands low down on his chest, and I knew the frightful internal cramps were beginning.

"If you will not take it, you must die," 1 urged.

"Then I die," he returned, and flung himself back on the bed.

He had hardly spoken, before a horrible convulsion seized him. His head bent backward till the veins in the purple throat seemed cracking, his spine arched upward till nothing touched the cliarpoy but his feet and head. His hands were knotted into balls beneath him, and his arms turned livid to the elbow. The next moment he had rolled over on his face, with a muffled scream of agony; his knees drawn upward to the chin. I turned to get my hypodermic injector, and as I did so he was seized with vomiting and that vomiting of cholera! Surely there is no other sickness like it. It seems to rack the whole body and stretch every nerve to splitting point. I put my hand on his forehead to support his head, from which the wild eyeballs seemed literally staring. At first, in the basin over which he hung strained and quivering, there was only a dark, almost ink like fluid; but in a few moments it became brightly stained with blood, and I saw that some vessel in the throat or stomach had been ruptured. A red stream, mingled with the darker one, continued to pour from his lips, as spasm after spasm of vomiting passed through his tortured frame. Then he sunk back suddenly, almost slipping through my arms, to the pillow, and lay as if dead, drenched with sweat and a red froth of slime and blood covering the blue lips.

At this moment Anna entered and paused at the door. I looked at her, my heart wrung with pity and alai'm; but she neither screamed nor fainted nor gave any sign. On her face was the look of one who has gone through the acme of human agony, and who expects nothing, hopes nothing more from life. Sne crossed the room calmly and looked at the bent, crooked, blackened remnant of life and beauty on the bed; that lay there as a young tree lies in the forest, that has been struck and shivered by the lightning, burned, blistered, and useless; and then at the basin I held.

She bent over him, and with her handkerchief wiped his lips dry; and I brought her a small piece of ice to put between them. After a minute she straightened herself by the bed and looked at me, as if inquiring an account of my charge.

"He was improving steadily," I answered, " and would have done so up till now; but I could not persuade him to take any stimulant. It will be difficult to save him without."

"No," she answered, looking at the broken glass and spilled brandy, " he would prefer to die, I know."

"So he said."

"Is there no substitute?"

I thought for a few moments.

"Nothing, I think, so good; but I will try this," and I took a bottle from my cabinet and poured out a dose from it.

This he took submissively enough; and as Anna took a seat by the bed he looked up with a smile and clasped her hand feebly in one of his. He turned toward her on his side and closed his eyes; and for one hour he seemed to rest in peace, while we sat in silence. Then the light grew a richer shade of gold, and a clock chimed somewhere in the house.

"I must go back to be present at dinner," Anna said, looking at her watch, " and stay with papa through the evening; but, as soon as every one is in bed, I will come back here."

I felt it was quite useless to try to dissuade her, to warn her of her own danger or the risk she ran in every way in leaving her own house at such an hour as she proposed and walking over to spend the night in mine. But even to me, things looked so differently under the wing of death that was spread over us all, from how they would at other times. Everything that was not life or death seemed small.

So I assented, and Anna left me toward six and drove back to her bungalow; there to be tender, quiet, and calm; to listen to the account of the general's doings during the day; to sit at the head of his table and take soup and drink wine with smiling lips, and ask and answer ordinary ques- tions with a natural voice, while her heart was beating itself to death beneath that smooth, white breast.

It was past eleven before she returned. I had ordered all the doors of the house to be left open, nominally that we might have more air; and so she stepped straight from the compound into the veranda of the sick-room and then into the room itself. She sunk into the nearest chair, closing her eyes; and I saw her face was white, while the sweat stood out in large drops on her forehead. The way between the two houses was short; but it was over a heavy road of soft dust; and in the oppressive heat of that air, which it was labor even to breathe, the exertion of walking that distance was very great. I went to her and lifted her drooping head against my breast.

"How is he? How has he been?" she asked, lifting her heavy eyes to mine. " Will he recover?"

I looked down at her.

"I can not say," I murmured. His powers of resistance are wonderful; but I am afraid"

"So am I," whispered Anna, with trembling lips.

She remained with us through the night, sitting with her eyes fixed on the bed; and I, in the intervals of waiting upon him, sat and watched her. Outside, the moon rose slowly and poured its cold, clear, silver light down on our pestilence-stricken station. The stars rose, wheeled, flashed on their courses, and sunk again behind the horizon. Hour after hour of the hot, silent night rolled heavily by; and we waited and worked in silence. It was a curious situation: Anna here in my house with me through those midnight hours, the woman I loved and whom all the station thought mine; and the man, whose life stood between me and the sunlight, lying on my bed and my hands trying to wrench him backward, as he slipped toward the grave; and me, myself, if I really were myself Lucky Ethridge watching them both, dazed and tortured and battling against this death, that would be the only thing to deliver me. Yet so it was, till the white light of the dawn broke in through the jilmils. Anna staggered to her feet with a face as terrible almost as the one on the pillow; and, drawing a veil over her head, prepared to go back to her bungalow. Gaida was sleeping. She came up to me and put her arms round me and kissed me, a burning kiss on the neck; then she stepped out through the veranda down into the blighted, withering compound, and took her way through the dust to the road.

The kiss seemed to speak to me in a language I can not translate. I only know that I prayed then, fervently and honestly, for the power to save this man to be put into my hands. And I worked and watched strenuously by his bedside every golden second of that long, golden day. But the fiat had gone forth against him. There was no longer any rally or response. All that I could do kept back, weighted, and made slower those steps; yet, in spite of me, they crept onward, onward persistently to the shadow.

It was five o'clock on this, the second afternoon.

Gaida was sinking rapidly; his feet were already cold. The last glory of the afternoon sun was rushing into the room through the western window and filling it with warm radiance. It fell all over the bed and over Anna sitting beside it, crushed and hopeless. Her face, always wonderful for its power of reflecting what was passing in her soul, had now upon it the stamp of absolute horror and despair. Cheeks and lips were bloodless, and the eyes so unnaturally dilated that the black pupil almost eclipsed the blue iris. She sat drooping, smitten, helpless beside him; and I watched them both. In a few minutes his eyes opened on the splendor of the sunlight that filled the room, and he looked at her. It was the rally before death.

"I am leaving thee," he said, in the hoarse, choleraic whisper; and stretched toward her his pinched, blue arm only three days before so powerful and shapely.

Tears came gushing to Anna's strained eyes and fell in drenching rain down her white face as she flung herself forward on the bed and put her arms about him.

"Tell me that I shall not lose thee; that thou wilt not forget me for the houris of Paradise. Tell me thy soul will wait there for mine." Gaida opened wide his dying eyes, and there was a look of love and tenderness in them. He raised his hand and put it softly on her head. " Thou art a female; thou hast no soul," he said; and I heard a low, anguished sob break from her breast, as if he had driven his knife there. " Farewell, thou light of my eyes," he said; and Anna, in a frenzy of grief and agony, bent her face to his and kissed him on his blackened, cholera-tainted lips. " Go from me," he murmured, feeling the supreme moment approaching; " let me die."

1 drew Anna from him. His breast was arching in a horrible paroxysm of death; his teeth were clinched, and the black, blistered lips rolled back from them. There was a moment's tense struggle between that noble frame and its despoiler, then his nostrils dilated suddenly. " Allah! Allah!" he called, raising his right arm. It fell, and he lay motionless.

"Gerald, he is dead! dead!"' and Anna flung herself full length upon the floor and struck her forehead again and again on it, like one mad.

I caught her up in my arms. She was insensible. It was a whole hour before I brought her back to consciousness. I had taken her into another room, and when she opened her eyes she was in my arms and met my gaze looking down upon her. She turned to me, clung to me, and wept on my shoulder in a flood of frightful, scalding tears, that I thought would never cease. At last, however, she raised her head and looked about her. It was growing dark.

"Gerald, I must go back. Take me back. Nothing of this must be known, for your sake. My life belongs to you now. Let us go home."

I ordered my carriage, locking the doors and windows of the room where Gaida lay, and we went back together.

She sat beside me in the carriage, rigid and pale, quiet and wonderfully controlled. I held her ice-cold hand in mine and pressed it hard; but we did not speak. She gave her directions to the coachman perfectly clearly when she alighted.

"I will rejoin you in a few moments," I said, as she ascended the steps of the veranda.

She inclined her head, and I drove back rapidly to my bungalow. Here I made all the arrangements for the burial of Gaida, exactly as if it had been one of my own favored servants who had died. My servants were devoted to me, and orders were obeyed as soon as given. Within a couple of hours I was free to return to Anna, and I went to her; being afraid of things I could not name to myself.

When I reached her sitting-room and parted the chicks, I saw her lying on a low couch at the opposite end. In her hand she held a little bottle that she was holding against the light and gazing at. I went forward and saw it was a vial of chloroform. I put my hand on her wrist.

"Anna, what were you thinking of?"

She raised her ghastly face and looked up in my eyes.

"Of how nice it would be, if you would let me die," she said.

"But you have promised me."

"Yes, I know. My life is not my own; it belongs to you. Could you give me a little; so that I might be insensible, just a little while?"

"I will give you this," I answered, taking away the chloroform and putting another little bottle into her iand. " Go upstairs and to bed and drink this, and you will know nothing for some hours."

Her hand clasped on the bottle; and she rose and went out of the room, as if in a dream.

I took down word that she was not feeling well and could not be with us at dinner; and I and the general sat down alone. When it was over, I told him, as gently and cautiously as I could, that there was great likelihood of Anna being attacked with cholera; and I begged that I might remain in the house that night, to be with her the first moment.

General Lombard heard me with perfect silence and composure. He seemed, like his daughter, able to draw over his face a mask of stone, when he wished. He called up a eervant and gave orders that a room was to be prepared immediately for the sahib next the Miss Sahib's room; and when the man had withdrawn, he turned to me and said, quietly:

"Where do you think she has taken the disease?"

"Possibly by attending to the servants here," I answered; " and, then, the whole air is full of it."

"I should have sent her away," he said, as if to himself; and then I noticed how all the ruddy color had died away from his face, leaving it gray; and sudden lines stood out, making it haggard and drawn.

"You acted like all we British act," I answered; " scorn danger and brave it, and sometimes the danger has its revenge."

He sighed heavily in reply, and, after a minute, rose from his seat.

"I will go up and see her," he said; and I was left alone, staring through the open door into the luminous, hot darkness of the night.

I felt a strange, curious triumph and cnlin. All around me was death. It lurked in every shadow. It was behind each rose-petal; the breath of the syringa was poison. There was death in the heavy, languid air, the whole atmosphere was feeding one with death; but I did not think I should die, nor she. I believed she would pass through the shadow; but I did not think the time had come for her to die. I can not explain this confidence; but it flooded my whole soul, and I watched the great, glittering Scorpion plunging through the sky before me, and felt tranquil and secure in the great stillness around me, which I knew was the stillness of desolation and death. Where lights had gleamed out through the foliage of the compounds, now there was blackness. The indefinite sounds of distant music and laughter, that had formerly floated up the flower-laden alleys, were replaced by a brooding silence in the poison-laden air. There was not a house from which the occupants had not fled or were preparing to flee or was not full of mourning or terror. Kalatu, in all its glory of tropic beauty, was but a pest- and charnel-house.

Yet I felt calm. Gaida was dead. Nothing now but grief stood between her soul and mine; and grief for the loss of physical passion is as short as grief for the loss of a passion of the soul is lasting.

When I reached my room that night, my head seemed reeling. I craved nothing but sleep. I saw the doors leading into Anna's room, that communicated with mine, and I knew she was sleeping behind them. Sleeping or weeping? But all was dull except that great longing for sleep that obliterated all else. My eyes were dim and my eyelids seemed fallen on them already. Without any power to raise them I descried in one corner the outline of the bed and staggered toward it as if blind or drunk. Then, fully dressed, I threw myself, face downward, on it and fell asleep. I awakened suddenly with a violent shock. It was still dark. A terrible cry of agony came from Anna's room:

"Gerald!"

I sprung from the bed and to the intermediate door and threw it wide open. A night-lamp burned on the table and shed its light through the room. I saw Anna standing in the centre in her white night-gown, with her fair hair falling to her waist, her hands pressed to her sides, her figure bent nearly double to the floor in a paroxysm of agony. I rushed to her and raised her in my arms. The spasm passed over, and her body lost its tenseness and leaned heavily against me; the head fell to my shoulder; the face was piteous, pinched, and blue.

"Oh, those terrible cramps!" she murmured. " And this is what he suffered!"

A rain of tears burst from her eyes and fell warm on my hands that held her. The next instant she had struggled from my arms and thrown herself on the bed.

"Oh, Gerald, let me die!"

I bent over her and raised her hidden face, blue with the shadow of the disease and drenched in her unavailing tears.

"Anna, do you not owe me something? Promise to try and live for me."

She could not answer. Suddenly her lips were drawn back and curled up from the perfect white teeth, and her body arched from the bed in a writhing, horrible convulsion. I took out two morphine pills and passed them between the blackening lips; and after a second or two her body fell inert, and, as if lifeless, back to the bed. Her eyes were closed. The sweat rolled heavily from her face and fell to the pillow, and the linen grew dark with it all round her head.

The room was full now of figures. The servants had all heard that terrible cry and were standing mute, submissive, waiting to be used, by the doors and at the bedhead. One had summoned General Lombard, and her father came now across the room with a steady tread and that same set look with which he faced the bullets and the Afghans' knives.

"Brandy," I said to him as soon as he reached me, " and champagne. Let me have bottles of it and a tin cup, lest she should break the glass; and tell the servants to bring boiling water large tubs of it and the heaviest blankets."

He turned away to give the orders, and I leaned over her and whispered in her ear: "I can not save you, if you wish to die. Will yourself to jive, Anna forme."

She opened her eyes and looked into mine. Perhaps something of all my burning agony was in them, and she read it there and pitied me. Her voice came with difficulty and was low and hoarse. It was the voice of cholera that spoke through her lips.

"I will it, then, if you do."

That was all; but it poured new life and energy through my veins. My soul was prostrate in an agony of prayer to God.

When the servant brought the wine and brandy to the bedside, I poured out half a pint in equal parts into the cup and held it to her lips. She lay collapsed and cold. I put my hand upon her bosom. It was cold and drenched in clammy sweat. I saw the disease in her case would run a short and violent course. She had already passed the first or convulsive stage and entered the second or cold stage, within two hours. In twelve hours, or perhaps less, all would be decided. I slipped my arm beneath her head and raised it. She drank the contents of the cup and the same quantity twice again, and the liquid which would have produced intoxication in health was all lapped up, as it were, by the disease. Her ejes were clear as they met mine. She lay passive, inert, cold.

"Those blankets," I said, turning to the silent servants, who had brought in a bath of boiling water from which the steam rose in clouds, " plunge them in for two or three seconds, then wring them out and give them to me."

They did as I ordered, though it must have left their hands almost raw.

"Here, sahib," they said a minute later, holding out tho blanket, and then I lifted Anna from the bed.

Her night-gown was heavy and black with sweat, and the touch of her body through it was as ice. With one hand I tore it from her, from the neck downward, and it fell with a heavy plash to the floor; and so, for one brief instant, the lovely form met my eyes which had ached so long for the sight of it in vain the exquisite casket of that soul I loved far better than my own.

Strange that this should be my first sight of it; my first, and perhaps my last. It was but a flash; the next instant the blanket enveloped her in its folds. I held her in my arms, and through the clouds of burning steam that rose between our faces I saw her open her eyes and seek mine. She put her lips close to my ear and I heard her murmur; o

"I am glad your eyes have rested on me once, before the grave closes over me forever."

I bent my head and put my burning lips on hers, now nothing but a shriveled, blue line; and for one second human love, the love I had for her, conquered the sense of danger, the presence of disease, the nearness of death.

"Not even the grave shall shut you from me," I answered. " We will lie in it together."

She sighed it seemed to me a natural, relieved sigh and, after a minute, murmured: "I am warmer now; it is nice to feel warm again."

I called for another blanket and wrapped that tightly over the other one, and then placed two dry ones that they brought burning and scorched to smoking straight from the fire.

"Dry and heat the bed," I said to the servants; and when this was done, I laid her back on it.

Her head sunk to the pillow, with a weary sigh. I looked at her keenly. Still there was not that reaction that I wanted, though her face now seemed whiter and less blue. I filled the cup again to the brim with brandy and she drank it, as a child drinks water. Then she turned a little on her side.

"I am sleepy," she said. " Give me your hand and let me go to sleep."

She was swathed in the coverings and her arms bound by them straight to her side; but I laid my hand upon her shoulder and she seemed content. The next second she was asleep. 1 motioned silently to the general to approach.

"She will live, I believe," I whispered. " This is the sleep that ends, not in death, but recovery."

The old man, who had stood silent, with set face, beside us all the time, clasped his hands involuntarily, suddenly, and turned away.

Anna slept on for ten hours, and I sat without stirring in my place. The dawn, had long since broken before she fell asleep, and I saw it break into the glorious Indian day. Noon came, with its deadly heat and stillness. The servants came and went in the room, with their noiseless steps, their bare feet unheard on the matting. Sometimes they slept on the floor beside me; but more often sat on their haunches watching, with great patient eyes, the figure on the bed.

It was two hours past noon, when the glare of the day was beginning to soften ever so slightly, and a faint, hot wind off the desert came sighing through thejilmils, that she awoke and turned to me with a sigh and a smile.

"Gerald," she said in a whisper, " you followed me into the Valley of the Shadow and brought me back. I am all your own now, forever and ever."

And, feeling as if some perceptible bond were put round us, drawing us together, that nothing cauld break, from which we ourselves could not escape if we would I stooped and kissed her.

CHAPTEE VIII.

regained her health very slowly. This surprised her father, who expected the rapid rebound natural to her youth and strength; but it did not surprise me. I knew it was the weight of the previous shock and grief, which was crushing her vitality under it. It was that that she needed to recover from, far more than the cholera.

In those days immediately following her illness we were inseparable. The fact that I alone knew everything, and that there was no necessity for disguise or constraint with me, drew Anna to me; and she clung to me and found comfort in my presence. The general noted this and pressed me to stay on in his house; so that Anna and I were almost constantly together. She was extremely weak, and would sit for hours in a cane chair in the veranda, doing nothing; with her eyes circled by a bluish shade and often brimming over with tears, gazing out into the sunlit compound. At such times it was a consolation, she told me, to have me near her; and her little, cold hand would steal into mine and often her head would drop on my shoulder.

"The mere contact with you, seems to take all the pain out of me," she said once; and constantly she would fa!7 into a quiet sleep thus, with my arm for a pillow.

Those days were very sweet to me and inclosed a happiness all their own. Every hour of them welded our two souls more into one, and Anna opened her heart more and more to me. My attitude toward Gaida and my last efforts to save him, however unwise and, perhaps, reprehensible they had been, had, at least, secured me one thing, and that was Anna's complete and absolute confidence. I had become almost part of herself, and she withheld none of her thoughts from me. They became mine. She talked freely to me, when we were alone, of Gaida and her relations to him; and I let her do so, even encouraged her, knowing that is the only way to treat and finally heal a deep sorrow.

The constant talk, the long stream of confidences, poured out from a heart full of pain and grief, is as the blood flowing from a poisoned wound, which carries the poison with it, and allows the wound in time to heal. And in that time I realized very clearly that she had yielded to his passion for her, and not to hers for him. Her feelings had been rather an indefinite, abstract love of his beauty; a romantic, poetic sentiment which he as man invariably does had dragged down to the level of physical desire.

She was very sweet to me, indeed, during all these days; and so grateful for all I had done, that I began to feel ashamed of myself and wonder I had not done more for her, been more patient and more kind.

She said to me, laughingly, but with serious eyes, that I had made her my little slave-girl and chained her to me with chains of gratitude for all time. And day by day I watched her freeing herself more and more from the old ties, memories, and feelings; and becoming more absorbed in the present and in the enjoyment of my love. She waited and watched for my coming, and would run down the house-steps into the compound to meet me with face and eyes alight with pleasure; and when others were present with me she hardly noticed them. As she grew better and stronger each day, I realized what an infinite relief it was to know that she was free and safe, with her secret, in all probability, forever buried with the dead Pathan. I could not help sometimes the shock of asking myself whether, when I tried to save him, had 1 not been really working against her? Was it not foolishly inconsistent of me, knowing and fearing and feeling all I had, to exert myself to fight against his death; which was unquestionably the best thing that could have happened for her? Yet to my nature it would have been impossible to have acted Otherwise, The eternal question is ever presenting itself;

Are we to act as we think best for one we love, or to act as the loved one wishes and commands? I do not pretend to answer this question for others; but for myself, and loving Anna as I did, the last was the only way possible to me. Love in the highest sense makes the lover only a subordinate part of the loved one. The lover asks nothing, expects nothing, wills nothing, and he has no rights, no claims; the loved one's will is all; and often how often! does this highest love conquer irresistibly and end by enslaving the loved one, as Anna declared now she was enslaved to me.

I could not shut my eyes to the fact that if I had succeeded in saving Gaida's life, as I had tried to do, the practical result would have been to prolong her dangerous position. But, even then, the theory of doing all that the loved one wishes, might have been vindicated in the end. Who could say how much my action would have strengthened my hold on her and loosened Gaida's? Who could say that feelings might not have sprung up in her; feelings as powerful to free her from him, as death itself had been?

"These things are all so very curious," she said to me one afternoon, when we were sitting under the shade of a heavy stone, magnolia-covered porch, looking out into the burning desert. Our chairs were set close together, her hand was in mine, and her head was leaning against my arm. " We are surrounded hedged in, as it were all our life long by invisible forces. We have no idea how helpless we are, until we get into opposition with them. Passion, for instance, is so strange. It seems to me like a great monster possessed of one long tentacle, with an immensely powerful claw at the end. When we come into contact with it, out shoots the tentacle, and the claw comes down upon us with tremendous force and holds Us motionless; it has fastened us firmly. As long as we remain perfectly still and do not struggle, we hardly feel it; we do not recognize what strength it has nor how it is holding us. But try to get away, try to throw it off; then you feel the claw upon you. You feel that it has sunk into your being and paralyzed you; that there is no getting away from it; that, if you struggle, the claw will reduce you to a bleeding, crushed mass beneath it. Sometimes, of course, by strong will one can cut the tentacle and be free; and then one has to carry about the horrible claw inside one, festering in one's heart. It is terrible, when one really thinks of it all and realizes how helpless one is. That claw may come down on one at any time, and one does not notice it at all, until one tries to get away, any more than you notice my hand on yours now; but if you were to get up, then you would know I was holding you."

I was silent; feeling how much truth there was in what she had said. Had not this very claw she spoke of come down upon me and fastened itself into my breast and bound me to Anna; so that, though my life might hate been sp iled through her, I could not tear myself loose. Even had I cut the tentacle, the festering claw would still have poisoned me.

"And then, again," and she went on, dreamily, " love is a different organism, floating about in life's ocean, that seems like one of those shining, iridescent sea-anemones, armed with a thousand little soft, clinging tentacles. And it stretches out first one soft, little feeler and then another, and at last you find them all clinging round you and yourself bound fast by them. And if they are very numerous and all have fastened round you, you can never get away. Love has thousands of those little tentacles. For instance, one is attraction, another is gratitude, and another is memory of joys together, and another is memory of griefs together, and so on."

And I knew there was truth in this metaphor, also.

"I don't think we could very easily get free," she added, looking up at me with a smile beneath her arched eyelids, "The claw has come down upon us, and all the little, soft feelers in addition."

"I like my captivity," I whispered.

"Yes, the claw and the feelers both hypnotize one into an exquisite trance, when one has not to struggle against them. But when the claw of passion came out upon me from Gaida's beauty and pinioned me and I wanted to get away from it, that was horrible."

She had grown quite white, and shivered in the hot, dry air. I bent over her.

"Don't dwell on it. What does it matter? It is over."

Yes, I think it is over," she answered. The next minute she closed her eyes. " I feel so tired; I should like to go to sleep."

I resettled my arm behind her head, and she turned her cheek on it and fell into that sudden sleep of physical weakness.

A few days later I moved back into my own bungalow. I had many things to arrange there. Anna seemed sufficiently recovered now to return to her normal life. She had persuaded the general to give a ball to the station, to celebrate her recovery; and I hoped that our marriage would follow it in a few days.

She improved now at a faster rate each day; and even the week that intervened before the ball, made a great difference to her. On the morning of that day, I saw her for a few minutes, and she seemed to have regained almost all her former glow of color and life.

"Come into the drawing-room," she said, " and I will play you a little thing and sing you something that seems to express the feelings in my heart."

We went in together, and she sat down at the piano and played. There was something electrical in her way of playing, that morning. The music sounded like the opening of a triumphal march. Her fingers rose from the notes sharply, and there was an eclat and fire in the piece, whatever it was, that arrested and held the ear. Suddenly the music changed to a joyous accompaniment for a song; and her voice, unusually clear and resonant to-day, swelled through the room.

"Vitoria, Vitoria, Vitoria, Non lagrimare piu E scholta d'amore, La Servitu."

That was all. There was a truly victorious roll of chords, and then she sprung up and closed the piano. She smiled at me and I smiled back. It had been a very beautiful burst of music and song, exactly such as one might catch through an open window when a victorious army was marching by; and I knew all that the words meant to convey.

She looked animated, fresh, and vigorous in her simple morning cotton dress, and I wanted to take her in my arms; but she receded, smiling.

"Not now; not now. I know you are busy and must go back to the office; but this evening come early and wait for me in the second drawing-room."

So, early, indeed, that evening I went to her and paced impatiently the little, second drawing-room, as she had indicated, that led into the larger one beyond.

When she had finished her toilet she came to the door between the two rooms and opened it, standing in the frame of the door-way. Her dress was white and long, very long, as usual; cut at the breast lower than I had ever seen it, and entirely sleeveless; the whole responsibility of the bodice being thrown on two narrow, slender shoulder-straps. I looked at her, and the magic that the sight possessed for ine emptied itself slowly into my veins. It was not that the figure was exceedingly opulent, or that there was any remarkable development; quite the contrary: but there was something in the wonderful purity of the skin, whiter than the satin below it and absolutely unstained by the faintest course of a vein or the smallest mole, and something in the modeling of the shoulders and the turn of the neck that seemed to speak to one. The beauty of her body, like that of her face, was not in the form, not in the flesh. It was the beauty of intense expression. The cool courage of her spirit seemed expressed in that firm, smooth expanse down to the curve of her low breasts; and all the passionate abandonment of which she was capable, in the pose of her shoulders and the long, soft, white line from shoulder to elbow.

She came toward me, faintly smiling, and gave herself into my arms; and her face and body spoke to me so clearly there was no need of words between us. She meant to convey to me and I understood her that she had for my sake conquered her grief and broken her memories; that she was no longer sacred to another or to the contemplation of the past; that she had come back to life and the enjoyment of it; and that my period of self-restraint and self-denial was over. And I, seeing that she wished and expected it, permitted myself the touch and the kiss of pas sion.

A little later, when Anna, with an old general, led off the dancers, she was radiant; and the eyes of the crowd followed her instinctively, attracted and held by the curious exuberance of vitality that seemed speaking in face and form. As we danced together and she gave herself up to me, fitting all the smooth undulations of her movements to mine; as my arm pressed the warm, bare flesh of her shoulder and our eyes looked into each other's and our breath intermingled, my thoughts were borne back to the first evening we had met, and I contrasted that slight, loose bond of attraction, based on the pleasure of the senses, with the steel-like chain that held us now.

How infinitely dearer to me now she wa?; after the pain and the sorrow gone through together, after the suffering and the waiting, after the exquisite trust and confidence, the intimacies of the soul, and the birth of that gratitude and love in her heart which is deathless. At the end of the long waltzes together, we went out and sat on the darkest, quietest side of the lawn in silence, unwilling to speak or to be spoken to.

At four in the morning when the daylight had already broken over the plains and filled the lawn and gardens with its cool, white light, though it was shut jealously from the ball-room we stepped through the windows for the last dance. Anna was claimed by the colonel of the regiment, and I went to seek my partner. At the close of the dance a galop I had just passed Anna and the colonel, and she had smiled at me over his shoulder, when she fell suddenly and her whole weight, thrown unexpectedly on her partner, brought him to his knees. Every one thought she had simply slipped on the polished floor; and though she was immediately surrounded, the general expectation was to see her rise directly herself without, or with very little, aid. I was at her side the first, and as I bent over her I saw it was no question of slippery floor or lost balance. She had fainted; and she lay now before us all, white and unconscious, helpless, oblivious of everything, on the shining floor.

I felt a curious shock pass over me, a prescience that in some way the incident was more serious than it seemed. As I lifted her, and, with the help of another man, carried her to a divan at the side of the room, she lay unconscious, with her head supported on my arm.

One of the women with unnecessary haste, I thought cut open her satin bodice, that could not have impeded her breathing in the least, and unbuttoned her slays; but, as Anna's figure was one that needed no compression or artificial restraint, and received none, this measure hardly helped matters.

She did not recover until a couple of glasses of water had been thrown on her face, and then she slowly opened her eyes. I looked into them and was stai'tled by the expression of terror and mental distress that met me. It seemed incomprehensible. Then, the next moment, she sat up, and realizing where she was, forced a smile, and gathering her cut and disordered clothing together over her breast, thanked those nearest her for their help. Her father was beside her and also a doctor, one of the guests; and they supported her between them from the room, while the crowd, with expressions of sympathy and allusions to the great heat and the fatigue of so long a ball just after her illness, began to break up and depart.

I followed the general, after a few moments, to her room, and was surprised to hear that Anna had gone to bed and would not see me again, just then. The general told me this outside her room, so, after a good-night to him, I turned disconsolately to go over to my own bungalow.

I was leaving the Lombards' hall when the doctor overtook me and offered to go across with me, his house being in the same direction as mine. He seemed to think Anna's fainting fit was not at all to be wondered at, considering the heat and exertion of dancing so long.

"But all that might make her tired, but it shouldn't cause her to faint, if she is all right?" I objected.

"Are you a doctor, my dear sir, or am I?" returned the little man, snappishly. " I examined that girl, a little while ago, myself. There is nothing the matter with her. She has a marvelous constitution, wonderful vitality, every organ perfect. You will be very foolish if you allow a little fainting fit like that to alarm you."

"I don't know that it does alarm me," I answered. " I merely don't understand it, and I don't think the explanation you give of it adequate, that's all."

The doctor edged up nearer to me and stuck his elbow into my side. The general's champagne had made him loquacious and facetious.

"Well, if you want another reason for her faint, I'll give it to you. Nervous excitement that's more to do with that young woman's health than anything else. Dances with you. Kisses on the lawn. Eh? And so on. Thought so. Go ahead and marry her just as soon as you can. That's the best thing you can do,"

It is so extremely pleasant to be told that one ought to do what one wants to do, and so extremely rare also, that I forgave the doctor his familiarity on the spot and felt quite friendly to him and inclined to believe all he said. When we came to my house, I shook hands cordially and wished him a good morning's sleep.

CHAPTER IX.

I WAS just finishing breakfast the following day and in the happiest frame of mind. Everything seemed now to promise sunshine in the future, bright as that streaming golden light outside. I sat back in my chair and gazed with satisfaction round the room. For weeks past it had been my employment and delight, for all spare hours, to work upon the beauty and the comfort of the house she was so soon to enter. All that money and care and orders from the largest Bombay furnisbing-house could command had been obtained; and now, as my eyes rested on the floor, it gave back the glow of Persian and Turkish rugs, velvet cloths worked in gold of Burmese art draped the tables, and curtains of the finest lace floated beside the bay-windows. The drawing-room and Anna's boudoir had been the objects of much care and thought; but the point where every energy had been concentrated to bring about perfection, had been the room which would be our sleeping-room. I occupied still the veranda-room on the opposite side of the house; but every day I came and looked into this one, to see if anything struck me as wanting or if any improvement could be made.

The bed I had designed and arranged after the manner of my own in Burmah, where I had passed so many lonely, wakeful nights; only the draperies, instead of being red, were blue, to match my Anna's eyes and contrast with her fair hair. And when it was finished it was a thing of beauty, with its silken curtains and its fine veils of azure-tinted mosquito-net. The goddess Parvati, the Indian Venus, molded in silver and supported by silver chains from the roof, swung above it, holding in her hands a lamp of scented oil, where the flame burned in a perforated silver globe.

Everything throughout the house was ready for the presence that was to light and beautify it all; and as I re- viewed things in my mind this morning and could recall nothing that was wanting, I pushed back my chair with a satisfied smile.

"The Mem Sahib is here," said the servant, suddenly, behind me; and. turning, I saw Anna step over the threshold. With a cry of delight, I stretched out both hands as I went to meet her. She put hers into them and said, in a strained voice:

"Send all the servants away, Gerald. I have something to tell you."

Her face looked deadly white in the morning sunshine; and with a sick sinking of the heart I ordered all the servants to leave us. Then I sat down in an arm-chair and drew the trembling girl into my arms.

"Now, what new trouble is it?" I said, gently, stroking her soft hair with one hand.

"Oh! so dreadful, so utterly dreadful that I can't tell you," she muttered, with both hands clasped over her face; and her voice had all the accents of shame and terror.

"Gerald, I am nothing but a worry and a misery to you. Why didn't you let me die when I had the cholera?"

"Because I wanted you for myself," I answered, gently; " because I shall always want you, whether you are-a worry or not."

There was silence for a minute; then I pressed her a little closer, and said, softly: "Well, what is it?"

"I can't say it. I can't breathe it," she replied, in the same desperate voice. " Can't you guess what I have discovered?"

Then it all flashed upon me, and the reason of her swoon last night; and for an instant the whole bright, throbbing sunshine seemed blotted out; the worth and use and beauty of life all seemed obliterated. For a second I could have thrown her from me in anger and loathing; so bitter was my disappointment, crushing in just now on my bright hopes and expectations. But only for a minute, for my love for her was something more than love and hope for my own pleasure.

"You are angry," she said. " Kill me; strangle me; I am ready to die. I should be glad to."

Her voice and its stricken despair roused me.

No, I'm not angry. This is but the consequence of the past. I forgave your marriage long ago. It would be absurd to quarrel with the consequences."

I spoke mechanically, and what I said was logical enough; but yet, in this world, is it not always the consequences and not the sins that we do quarrel with? Sins we can forgive; it is virtually the results that are unpardonable.

"I can't understand it," she said, in the same smothered voice; " and after the cholera, too, Gerald. 1 accepted that. I was glad of it. I thought it made this impossible. Oh, it is horrible; I can't bear it."

She was sitting on my knees, where I had drawn her; but now she tried to rise. I caught sight of her averted face, and the unutterably agonized look upon it was terrible. It went to my heart. I knew she had been made for better things.

"Just when I was trying to free myself from all that abasement in the past, when I thought 1 was free, and giving myself entirely to thoughts of you and loving you as I do and wanting to wholly belong to you; then to be forced back, as it were, into all that has gone by; to live it all over again for months to come; now, when all the passion that held me to Gaida is dead, at last. It is something beyond words. I could tear myself in pieces. You understand, don't you?" she went on after a moment. " If Gaida had been worth it worthy of my love I should never have taken it from him. I should not have cared what I had done for him, what I had suffered. I gave him all that I had in the world; I threw all that I had at his feet; but he was not worthy, and in a little while my love died. Then still, for a long time, the passion lingered on; but it could not survive; it is dead, and I loathe the very memory of him his very name; and now Good God! His child! What can I do? I feel I can not live and keep sane."

She really looked so intensely ill, so peculiarly different from her usual self, that all other feelings were swallowed up in alarm for her life and reason. Strangely enough, I had seen her once before look like this, and that was when there had been the threatened severance from Gaida.

"There is nothing to be done but to accept it all and as bravely and as calmly as you can. After all, what are a few months out of a life-time? They will pass over and you will forget them, as you have been forgetting your days of cholera. And it is not as if you had to bear it alone. I am here, knowing everything and sympathizing with everything. Do you think there is anything we can not meet together?"

I had pressed her head to my shoulder, and she let it stay there, hiding her face against the shelter.

"I think our marriage had better take place at once. The whole station is expecting it"

I broke off, for she had started in my arms as if an electric current had passed through her.

"Marriage!" she exclaimed; but her voice was only a dry whisper. " Oh, I can't, I can't marry you now. How can I? Accept every advantage from you, take everything and bring you nothing, nothing but this What can you think of me?"

"Why," I said, with a sad smile, " after all this time, we do not seem to understand each other a bit. If you are in distress, is not that just the time to come to me? When others are likely to reproach or misunderstand you, you come to me because you know I never shall. If you were in a storm, should 1 not hold out my arms to you and try to cover you with my cloak? That is my idea of love, Anna. That both should give everything and expect nothing in return. You gave all to Gaida; you would have given all to me, but for my folly. What has happened since, I look upon as my punishment for that. This is part, it seems to me, of our mutual punishment. Let us accept it and bear it together."

Anna had clasped both her arms round my neck, and was lying passive and quiet.

"You are so very good to me that it seems I can not let you"

"No, it is not goodness," I answered, sadly. "I am only doing what 1 must. You have become a part of myself, and I want to shield you from everything that would hurt you and end in your loss to me; just as I would try to save my arms from amputation."

"It is such happiness to be so loved," she answered, under her breath, " and it is so terrible to give you nothing but unhappiness in exchange."

"I am glad I am here to protect you," I answered, drawing the cold, trembling form still tighter against my breast. "That is not unhappiness." I did, indeed, feel such keen pity for her, that all sense of the part I would have to bear in the punishment was lost. " Are you quite sure it is so?" I asked, stroking one of the little, ice-cold hands.

"I can't be absolutely sure," she answered, half-inaudi-bly; " but I think so from several things, and especially from last night. Oh, don't ask me about it, it's so dreadful!"

I was silent. My great fear was for her reason. I knew she was differently organized from the majority of women. 1 knew that to her exceptionally excitable and sensitive brain circumstances unfortunate enough in themselves assumed an additional horror. She undoubtedly felt more keenly both the pleasures and the pains of this life than the average human being is intended to do, and both were exaggerated and magnified by her view of them.

"Listen to me, Anna. You have read and studied philosophy by the bookf ul. Now is the time to practice some of it."

"I could, if this only affected myself," she murmured in a stifled voice.

"That can not be helped. We can not, either of us, consider ourselves separately any longer. When we love another, we double our pains and sorrows just as we double our pleasures; but that is quite fair. We must face this, just as we would any other trial, together, and as calmly as we can. I shall give out the announcement of our marriage this afternoon. How soon will you be ready? What day shall I say?"

"I don't know."

"It must be done at once," I urged. " After your marriage you are, to some extent, secure; and life itself is such an uncertain thing, Anna, we can only count on the moment in our hands. I may, for instance, meet with some accident. I might die, and then you would be left as you are now, and unmarried."

"It would not matter," said Anna, who was sobbing now. " I should come with you."

"But, my sweet, it would make me very unhappy in my last moments to feel that I had not done all that lay in my power for you, while I was alive. I know this is not a thing to be put off. It is all important now that the mar- riage should take place at once, before anything intervenes which might make it impossible. Once married, you are safe from the outside world, at any rate; whatever private griefs and sorrows we may have. The world can know nothing and say nothing."

"I was looking forward to it so much, I wanted it so much till now," she sobbed, brokenly.

"So did I," I answered, " and now I want it more than ever. So it is settled," I added, kissing her. " The wedding takes place at once, and I will make all the arrangements for it."

"Let me get up; I feel stifled; I believe that dreadful fainting is coming on again."

She struggled out of my embrace, and I rose. Her face was white and her eyes uncertain and unbalanced.

I put my arm round her waist and drew her toward the table. The spirit-lamp under my coffee-urn was still burning, and the coffee abore boiling unnoticed. I poured her out a cup of it and pressed her gently into a chair. She drank the coffee obediently and began to look more natural again.

" We shall soon be having our breakfast together, as an ordinary matter," I said, smiling.

My great idea was to turn her thoughts into a lighter vein. I saw that she felt the position acutely, felt it to a degree that might affect even her reason; and I felt I must, if possible, lift the strain from her brain; if only from moment to moment. She played with the little, green coffee-cup, turning it round in the saucer, and her eyes wandered about the room.

"It is so nice to come to you," she said, softly. " I feel so rested, almost happy, when I have been with you a little while; and I dreaded this telling you, I mean. Last night I suffered so; I felt I could never, never tell you nor see you again, and yet, through all the suffering, I longed for you so much."

"I wondered why you would not see me last night," I answered. " Dear child, you would have slept better if you had told me at once, and let me comfort you."

"You have been so very good to me and done so much for me one thing after another; but it seems as if you, even you, must get tired of it all, must feel angry with me, must fail me some time. I keep on disappointing you so."

"Well, this is the last," I returned, smiling. " You will be my own after this, and I will take care of you better."

She was sitting in one of my large arm-chairs, leaning one elbow on the table and shading her face with her hand. She looked up at me now.

"I don't think we can marry immediately," she said, with a painful blush. " I mean not hurriedly at all. That would only attract attention. I have been so much, so very much with you, and all the station has talked so of our attachment, that that they would never guess the truth if they thought anything they would think it was you it was your fault."

I bit my lips suddenly. I saw in a moment the truth of what she said.

"What is said of me matters very little," I answered, after a second. " But, of course, I don't wish to make it seem hurried, so as to throw suspicion into people's mind. I want to save you from anything of the sort, whether connected with me or in any other; but a fortnight hence I think would be a reasonable date. Don't you? I feel a little anxious now about delaying it as long as that; but, perhaps, as you say, it must be so."

"Yes, I should think a fortnight from the ball yesterday, when I was supposed to have recovered, would be about what they would expect," she answered in a low tone.

"That shall be so," I said. " And now you are here, Anna, come and see the house, and tell me what you think of all I have been doing. I forbid you absolutely to think of the future any more just now, or what it may have for you. The anticipation of everything in life is the keenest part, both in pleasures and trials. Things are smaller when we actually come to face them. Each day brings its own strength with it."

Anna got up from the chair, and, in obedience to my wishes, gave a little, faint smile; and we went out of the dining-room together through the different rooms of the house on the ground floor; then up the staircase to the upper rooms and verandas; and, last, I brought her to the bedroom at the end, which covered the whole width of that part of the bungalow. She sunk in one of the chairs, and I went over the windows to open them and let in the light and air.

There was a long pier-glass at the end of the room, and as I walked toward it I caught her reflection. She was sitting contemplating the bed with such a look of hopeless misery on her face that I left off what I was saying about the flowers on the veranda and went back to her.

"What is the matter? Don't you like it?" I said, gently.

Her eyes filled with great tears which rolled slowly down her cheeks.

"Oh, yes, it is beautiful, too beautiful," she said at once, taking my hand, as I stood beside her. " And I see you have put there Parvati. She is suitable for me."

"Why, dear?" I asked, disturbed at the bitterness in her tone. " What are you thinking of?"

"Don't you know the legend of Parvati?" Anna answered, gazing at the little, silver figure, absently. " She was sitting waiting in the forest one day for her lover Shiva, I think it was and a little, gray squirrel ran by her. Parvati stretched out her hand idly and caught it, and the squirrel ran through her grasp and escaped; but her fingers were so burning with the fire of love that they scorched the fur on its back; and forever after, to this day, the squirrel bears three black stripes along its back where the fingers of the goddess burned them. My hands used to burn like that when you were away at Burmah."

And she put them over her face.

"I didn't know the legend," I said, simply. " But I will take down the image and throw it in the garden if you wish."

"No, no! not for worlds; let it stay there."

"You should not regret that fire," I said, putting my hand on her downcast head. " It is a gift of Nature to you, just like your red lips or curling hair; and it gives you much of your power over men, Anna, and makes them your slaves as I am," I added.

Anna looked up.

' No, not a slave, an idol," she murmured, passionately, taking my hands and kissing them. Then she rose. " I must go. I have been here too long already."

I made no effort to dissuade her; and we went to the door and left the room together.

"Did you have no hat?" I asked in an ordinary tone; and we passed into the dining-room again, where the butler was arranging the sideboard.

"No; I came in a gharry, and had it all closed," she said. " How long the coachman must have thought me!"

I went with her to the door, and there her servant was waiting with a large, white parasol, to shade her with it to the carriage, waiting at the foot of the steps. I waited till she had disappeared and the carriage had driven off. Then I retraced my steps into the dining-room and sat down.

There was almost a smile on my lips as I thought bitterly how life seems to get hold of some men and play with them, mock them, cheat them, toss them about for sport. It had done so with me; but I would conquer life in the end; I would come out the victor. This woman, whom I had desired when I first saw her, and who had been removed and removed from me by various devices of circumstances, each time I had thought to possess her, should be entirely my own at last; with not the shadow even of a thought I did not know, between us.

I went, as usual, in the evening to the Lombards', feeling full of anxiety; but my apprehensions died away, as soon as Anna entered the room. She looked pale and subdued, but quite calm and mistress of herself, and I saw she had summoned all the strength of her nature to meet the situation. There were only a few people present familiar friends. Mrs. Tillotson, the Paris Gamin of the tableaux, among them. I smiled to myself as I saw her peering sharply at Anna. Keen-witted, as I knew she was, and keen-sighted, I felt that Anna could defeat easily any one who tried to pry into her life; and that once she had gathered up the reins and fixed her eyes on the goal, she would drive her chariot and steer her course straight through the gaping crowds that line the ways of life, watching for the accidents of those who do more and dare more than they can.

That evening she was orthodoxly charming. She laughed the requisite amount, neither too much nor too little, and talked the prescribed idiotic babble of ordinary society which I knew was always an effort to her with the greatest fluency and ease. She played and sung for us the most delightfully twaddly society songs, and did not even touch her favorite Wagner till the clo e of the evening, when she gave us the " Festspiel und Bruutiied " from " Lohen- grin." It was Liszt's arrangement, and she played the opening in fact all the " Festspiel " with the magnificent energy and fervor of her temperament; and I, listening, thought, "Anna is speaking to me now. This is the first glimpse of her real self that I have had this evening."

Then, from out of that intricate maze of brilliant chords and arpeggios floated suddenly, softly, and delicately as an evening breeze, the Bridal Chorus. The melody filled the room and fell like a charm over us all. The faces of the married women took a dreamily reflective expression, and the unmarried girls one of eager hope and expectancy. When she had finished there was much smiling applause.

Anna rose.

"That's what I feel like," she said, simply, and with a glance at me.

The announcement that our wedding was to take place two weeks from the night before, had been given out that afternoon, and every one laughed indulgently; and there was a great deal of whispered confidence and hushed laughter between her and all the women, as they broke up for the night.

Anna, standing, saying " good-by " to them, was the happy, innocent, unthinking bride-elect to perfection. When they had all gone and the general had retired, we stood for a moment alone together.

"You don't misunderstand me?" she said in a low tone. " You don't think me callous, nor that I don't feel the horror of the whole thing; but this is what you wish me to be, is it not? This is how you wish me to act?"

"Do you think we could misunderstand each other?" I said, looking into her eyes, so sad now that the affected mirth had died from them. " I think you are most good and brave. I want you to be inwardly as philosophic and resigned as you can, and outwardly as bright and nappy as you can. Nothing we can do can alter things now, and we must try and minimize them, not exaggerate them to ourselves."

"You poured courage and life into me this morning. You were so good to me, and I am so grateful."

Nothing else was said; but her tones were weighted with feeling and, as I folded her gently in my arms for a goodnight kiss, I felt that each new trial, which might have sundered others from each other, had only brought us into a more exquisite relationship.

During the next fortnight the final preparations for the wedding occupied both of us. For me, a great deal of the life and spirit had been taken out of them. I had had a blow and received a wound that I could not recover from; since the wound must, necessarily, remain an open and bleeding sore for months to come. At the same time I did not suffer so much as a man whose love was differently constituted. For me, Anna's presence near me in itself, even if sick, sorrowing, and burdened with the chains of her dead passion, would still be a delight beyond words. Moreover, having once fully determined to accept the situation as it was, I rarely allowed myself to dwell on it, and tried as far as possible to put away the thought and remembrance of the secret she had given to my keeping; and which seemed mocked and made unreal, each time I was with her, by her fair, innocent, girlish look. I think she herself had determined in the same way to crush it under silence now; for she never alluded to it when we were together, and when others were present she showed a soul of gayety and happiness, not, I think, forced; and seemed interested in the selection of all the countless treasures submitted by the Kalatu merchants for the Mem Sahib's wardrobe.

One morning, rather early, I entered the drawing-room a little unceremoniously, and found her trying on a just-finished gown; because, as she naively explained later, "There was a long glass there and none in her bedroom, and she had not expected visitors."

The gown was one of rose-colored silk, and suited admirably the rose of her skin. She was just surveying herself, as I came in; and the eager, happy, interested look in her eyes, bent on her own reflection, delighted me. When she caught sight of me, however, the dress seemed forgotten, and she responded eagerly to my caress, crushing up the delicate lace and ruffles on her breast against my coat, dusty with the ride over.

"Gerald, when I woke this morning, a bird was singing exquisitely at my window, and a maina was calling from the banana-tree. I felt so happy to think only three mornings would go by and then I should wake up under the smile of those serious eyes of yours, that never do anything but smile upon me."

Another morning I found her leaning back in a long chair surveying the goods of a native dealer in Oriental trimmings, who had his wares opened out in a circle on the floor all round her. And another time I came in to see her the center of a crowd of young girls of her own age, who were all eating sweetmeats and drinking iced coffee and discussing the approaching event; but each time she was gay, contented, smiling. So the time passed till the eve of the marriage came; and then, by prearrange-ment, I went to her to take her for a drive with me before sunset. I found her sitting in her chair waiting for me on the bungalow steps; a delicate, charming figure with a large, white hat that turned up at the side, where a few tiny, soft, light curls lay against it.

"Let me sit on the left side, where your hat turns up," I said, laughing. " I don't wish even a hat-brim to be between us."

And she laughed and obeyed.

"We will drive to the Burra Bagh or the Great Gardens," I said, and so directed the coachman. The evening was still with a heavy, dreaming stillness, that the drone of a thousand insects seemed only to intensify. The carriage-wheels made no sound on the soft roads, bordered by emerald turf; the hedges gave out their heavy odor of syringa and tuberose. All around the sunshine fell in a burnished golden haze, deepened and enriched by the approach of the sunset. Overhead, through the fan-like, spreading branches of the cocoanut-palms, that the sun burned into glinting gold, the sky was beginning to blush softly; and small, gold-tipped, rosy clouds floated across it. Occasionally, a huge, heavy, black, carrion bird flapped lazily across from side to side, too indolent to croak and too lazy to even fly properly and in a straight line. He just flapped heavily and obliquely through the warm, still air from one syringa-laden hedge to another. I leaned back in the carriage, giving myself up to the restfulness of my surroundings and letting my eyes rest on the soft, cool cheek of the girl beside me, rising, as it did, above the white ruffles of lace round her neck.

We were quite silent for a long while, as we often were When together. Conversation is pleasant, but there is no actual need of it between minds so closely linked as ours were.

After a time she slipped her hand out of her glove and laid it on mine.

"I shall never forget how good you were to me the morning I told you," she whispered. " You must never think that because I don't speak of it, that I forget"

"I think you were very brave and good to come and tell me," I answered, quietly " Many women would have left me no choice. They would have married and said nothing about it."

"Would they?" returned Anna, turning upon me a startled gaze. " Oh, I could never have done that, any more than I could marry you as you wished, and as I longed to, while Gaida was alive, and not told you of his existence."

I looked into the wide-open, fearless eyes, truly great wells of living light, with truth at the bottom of them.

"I know you could not," I said, simply. " The lying and deceit that come naturally, it seems, to most women are not among your faults, my Anna."

"I have enough without them," she answered, sadly.

"You're not to be sad now," 1 said, authoritatively, " on the eve of your marriage to me. I can't have it."

"I am not," she said, smiling. " I can not help feeling so pleased to think I am going to belong to you after to-morrow. Fancy not being one's own mistress any more, having no will indisputably of one's own. Fancy not being able to get up when one wakes and feels ready to, but when some one else wakes and is ready to; and no longer being able to ring and order luncheon when one feels hungry, but having to wait until some one else is hungry; and having to sit up at night until some-one else gets tired. How funny it all seems, and, to me, very delightful."

"Is that your idea of married life?" I asked, smiling.

"Is not that what it must come to, practically?" she returned, smiling, too. " You know, when two people live together there can be only one will between them, and I think it is the woman's place to give way. Nature has given her the part of submission in the whole drama of love. She can't take the initiative; she can only respond. She is fitted to do that, and that is where she gets her best happiness. When I marry you, I put my will in your hands. I make you a present of it. I have no further use for it. The only thing of importance henceforward is yours. And, it seems to me, that is only a small part of the whole surrender a woman makes in marriage. JEven now, for instance, you decide the moment when you shall kiss me, and I am very glad to submit. Well, on the same principle, I can submit when you decide other things for me, and find pleasure in it."

"You are terribly unfashionable in your views," I said, laughing. " Just now, when woman is fighting to take the lead in everything. You don't seem to belong to the nineteenth century."

"I don't think that I do," she answered. " The nineteenth century is nearly over, any way. Perhaps I am a product of the twentieth, and come too soon."

It was growing dark all round us, the beautiful, luminous dark of the East, full of mysterious rose and violet.

"No, not too soon," I answered, and as our eyes met each other's, through the soft-colored dusk, there was a moment's keen realization that all the centuries to come could not give to each other two that were as nearly one as we were.

The following day, late in the afternoon, we were married; not quietly as we would have wished, and in Anna's drawing-room, but in the presence of all the station. So far did we sacrifice ourselves for the sake of the people who knew us. There followed a long reception at my house; and then, at last, we were alone.

It was a little after nine. In a few hours more the night would be over and the light would be dawning on the plains. Anna turned to me, and we stood for a moment together, when our guests had gone, under one of the lamps which threw a veil of light over her and turned her hair to flame color.

"Surely I am the least deserving and the most fortunate of any one in the world," she said in a low voice. " Gerald, in spite of everything, I am so happy."

We passed out of the room and went upstairs to the one in which I had worked so hard for her sake, and which she was entering at last. It was full of a soft radiance of light, such as she delighted in, from swinging lamps in slightly veiled shades; and the great pier-glass at the op- posite end of the room, facing the door, reflected her figure as she stepped over the threshold. I closed the door behind us. The windows, with their jilmils, stood wide open to the four quarters of the violet sky, studded with different patterns traced in blazing stars, so that they looked like four slides from a kaleidoscope. The servants had all retreated to their quarters; the sea wind, that sweeps restlessly over the desert sand all day, had sunk. Not a breath disturbed the heavy, sultry air.

We crossed the room involuntarily to the mirror there, and stood looking into it at her reflection; and she put up her hands to her neck to unfasten the necklet I had given her. Then she dropped them again.

"You do it for me," she murmured; and I unclasped the diamonds and replaced them with kisses.

Then I took the great, doubled-up plait of her hair and, untying the white ribbon that held it double, began to un-plait it, letting each soft strand slip through my fingers, as 1 released it.

"And so you love me?" I said, softly, when it was all loosened and fell like sunlight over her neck and shoulders.

Anna leaned back against me and put her arms round my neck, turning her face upward so that her mouth, like an opening flower, was close beneath my own.

"I do not love you," she said, with her voice quivering and the pulses beating hard in her throat. " 1 worship and adore you."

And it is not a little thing for a man to hear from the woman he loves.

Hours later, wide awake, I raised myself on one elbow, where I lay beside her and gazed down upon her. The dawn was just beginning to softly fill the room. Anna had fallen asleep; fallen with her face turned and her arms a little extended toward me, into the happy, trustful, innocent sleep of a child beside its mother. And I, to whom she was as sacred now from the approach of passion as before she became my own and held my name, looked down upon her and realized that in self-renunciation, self-abnegation, self-denial 'for another, lies the keenest, purest pleasure of humanity. This was my marriage night, and what had it brought me? No abandonment to personal pleasure, no sensual delight of any sort, no gratification of the desires or the senses; nothing that the promise of its name implies; only self-repression and self-restraint, a total denial of the physical will. Yet out of all this rose a supreme happiness; and, I suppose, no man ever felt at the final abandonment to him of a mistress or the possession of a wife the same passion of delight and triumph that I did when Anna lay down beside me and sunk to sleep with a happy, contented sigh. Out of the stress and the violence and the selfishness of passion, she had come to the shelter of an absolute love. She was happy, protected, safe; and I was the one who gave her that happiness, protection, safety. In the whole world there is no privilege that Fate can give equal to this: the power to bestow these three where one loves. I gazed down upon her now in the quiet room, where the soft light was diffusing itself, seeming like the presence of the Divine Spirit sanctioning our union; and my heart swelled within me with a peace and calm and joy that nothing in my life has equaled. She slept beside me tranquilly as a child, with her loosened hair thrown back and straying over the pillow and her breath coming and going softly, almost imperceptibly, in her glad, confident slumber.

What did it matter to me the unappeased longings of the senses, the gratification of which has but one final end, satiety, and the absence of the falsely designated " real," that is, physical, pleasures?

In that mental exaltation that filled me, as I gazed at that calm face and form wrapped in the mystery of sleep, I was unconscious of my physical being; and it is in these moments when the soul and brain take up the supreme command of man that he discovers the essence of joy.

CHAPTER X.

THE note that had been struck on my marriage night was the key-note of my married life self-renunciation; but, as on that night it had brought me nothing but the height of happiness, so it continued to be from day to day the source of delight to me. It was Anna who was dissatisfied with herself.

"I am no good to you, dear Gerald," she would say. " What can I do?

And I could only answer the simple truth, "You are every tiling to me, Anna. I am more than satisfied."

It was so. Her presence alone seemed to fill up my life with contentment. There was an extraordinary tie, as it seemed, between us; invisible, but, at times, almost tangible. It was as if she held one end of an elastic thread and I the other, and that this thread would not stretch beyond a certain distance, nor for longer than a certain time. If either strained at it, it pulled us irresistibly together again. There seemed a curious balance of electricity between us; one must have possessed just the amount which the other lacked.

When we were together, both felt calm and satisfied; but for those hours in each day if there were any in which we were separated, there was always a sub-consciousness of restlessness and discontent till we were together again. Thus it often happened that when I went down into the city to attend a trial or other business, if I were detained there, a knock would generally come on my office-door; and, on opening it, I would see Anna with a deprecating look on her face.

"Why have you come down, dear?" I would ask generally, pro formdj though I knew by my own instinctive feelings why she had come.

And she would look at me, helplessly, for a moment or so, and then laugh and say, "I don't know."

She would install herself quietly in one corner of the room and read, or often do nothing until my work was over; and then we would both descend the stairs, get into the carriage, and drive home together; and that simple little detail of every-day life would seem something delightful to me, because it was done with her. I could not shake myself free from the feeling of pleasure it gave me; though it seemed unreasonable, even to me, to feel it so keenly. I can not explain why it was so except by the theory that we exerted some force each over the other, that some electrical condition in me had been disturbed by her absence and was put right by her presence, in the same manner as some people suffer from headache during a thunder-storm and feel relieved and soothed when it is over.

And existence has no more perfect charm than this duality, than this feeling of the strong, elastic thread binding together the two lives; yielding, giving, and stretching as the individuality of each requires, but always drawing them toward the other.

People in the station began to look upon us as the most extraordinary couple possible, because, even after we were married, we were hardly ever seen, except together; and the average Briton seems to expect a man, when married de facto, to seldom appear with his wife.

"I don't know how it is," said Anna to me one day, with a puzzled smile, " but other people don't seem to love at all in the same way we do, or live the same life. They aren't together, as we are. There's Ella Barrington, you know; she never sees Barrington all day. In the morning she goes down to the town and shops, then she drives back for luncheon; and he doesn't come back for that, because he is so far off. Then, in the afternoon, she pays calls all alone. He does come back to dinner; but then in the evening she very often goes to a dance and he goes to bed because he is tired, or he goes to his work again and she goes to bed because she is tired. I could not lead that life."

"Perhaps they don't hit it off very well," I suggested.

I was writing in my office, and Anna was at a little table by my side copying the official correspondence for me, as I finished it. I had three clerks, but they had not her accuracy and speed, and then also

We had just paused for a moment in the work to drink a large glass of soda, in which the ice clinked musically, and to give ourselves up to the fanning of the punkah. Outside the closed jilmils the thermometer registered one hundred and fifteen degrees Fahrenheit, and inside here the short curls on Anna's forehead were wet.

"But that is the life of all the married women in the station," she objected. " It's most funny. You've no idea how different we are. And other people think it is so odd, too, that we should want to be together, now we are married. It's becoming quite a scandal," she added, with her eyes full of laughter. " It is fortunate we had such a big wedding and every one saw it with their own eyes, otherwise they'd get up some story that we weren't married. They would, really."

I laughed. " Quite likely," I answered.

"It's so intensely nice being with you," she continued, pushing her chair a little closer to mine. " If I go down to choose a pair of gloves, you come with me, and that makes choosing the gloves as much pleasure as going to an opera. Then, when I make my calls, you come too, and that makes it all interesting; just as when I used to meet you at the places when we were engaged. And in the evenings, think! I should never go to a dance, while you went to bed or to your work. I would much rather be where you were. But every one thinks it awfully funny, and so, perhaps, it is. I noticed Mrs. Pearson looked quite surprised, and, don't you know, almost well, shocked, when I refused to drive home with her and Captain Green, because I was waiting to drive you back from the office. Surely, my dear," she said, ' your husband doesn't expect you to drive him back every evening?" and I said, ' I don't know, Mrs. Pearson, but I like to do it." And then she raised her eyebrows and Captain Green stared at me through his eye-glasses, and they both drove on with the air that they considered me a harmless maniac."

I nodded and laughed.

"The men think it odd, too, that they never see me at the club now, and that I won't stay the whole afternoon gossiping with them or reading the papers; but prefer to come back to walk or ride with you. They are nearly all married men. I suppose we are different from other people," I concluded.

"There is not one married woman here who lives the life I do," she said, meditatively. " She is interested in her children, her house, her servants, her calls, her golf; and her husband is interested in his work, his horses, his duties, his club. Their lives are quite apart and full of different ideas and aims. We are just like one person, are we not? And," she went on after a pause, " the people who are only just married are only a little better. Even they are rarely together. One does not seem necessary to the other at all."

"I give it up," I said, laughing. " And now we must get back to work. The Government, I'm afraid, will object to paying me for using its time to discuss metaphysical problems."

And we emptied our iced soda-water glass and went back to the correspondence.

About three months after our marriage we were transferred to another station a hot, dry place out on the plains. It was large; and I think I have never seen so many handsome faces among the English girls in India as were crowded into that one station. On the second day after our arrival, when we had to be at home to receive calls, I saw Anna looking from one to another as they came in; and to me, who knew her face so well, her thoughts were perfectly clear. Nothing, however, could make her ungracious in manner; and whatever irrepressible envy she might feel, it was not in her nature to stoop to the spiteful meanness, the petty warfare of sneering words that most women adopt to their rivals. She was graciousness and gentleness itself to them all, and moved about the room and dispensed tea to her guests with her usual quiet ease. That same evening, after dinner, we were sitting on the couch together, looking over some papers that I had brought up from the commissioner's, for her consideration as well as my own, when she said, suddenly, to me:

"Gerald, I wish you were not so handsome."

I laughed; knowing quite well what was in her thoughts.

"Why?"' I said.

"Because all these girls and women will be falling in love with you, I know."

"I don't think that is at all likely; but suppose they did, would that matter very seriously?"

"No no " replied Anna, hesitatingly. " Not if you-"

And then she stopped, looking at me. The blood seemed beating up to my head in great waves.

"Do you think that I don't know the exact value of a pretty face or smooth shoulders?" I said, quietly; trying to overcome the strange excitement that was rising in my veins. " The passing trifles good to help one through a tedious hour. Do you think, for the pleasure they would bring, that I would throw aside a love like ours?"

Her face, at the end of the sofa, seemed to swim before me, with its arched brows and eyes welling over with light. They looked a little startled, a little surprised. Iloavens! Did she not know, did she not realize what my life beside her was? Was it possible that I had overacted my part of self-repression, which I had taken up for her sake? A horrible moment of weakness came over me. It was so long, this trial. Perhaps my attitude was misunderstood by her. Perhaps it was unnecessary, absurd. An insidious temptation was at my side, fiercer even than that of my marriage night. I was strung up then to a pitch of exaltation, in which everything was possible. The first onslaught of desire is far easier to withstand than its slow, continued pressure eating into the brain through weeks and months. Why, I do not know; but it seemed as if in that moment, when she spoke so lightly of the other women, all the long struggles of past nights, all the anticipations, the longings, the visions of feverish moments in the day, reached their culminating point. Other women! Other faces! The passing physical pleasure of a mouth that pleases, of a touch that stings. What were they to me?

The flesh has but one voice with which it calls to kindred flesh; but the soul, the intellect, the brain, have a thousand voices, and all of these called to me from the wi-man before me.

It would be worth something to feel those lips quiver beneath one's own, to light up a torch in those eyes, to feel that breast heave beneath one's own. It would be the final, the only adequate and satisfying expression of our love; and it was possible, if I delayed, it might never be ours. Had she not in a few months months! to descend into the shadow of death, from which she might never return to me? And she was my own, my absolute possession; and there was no bar between us. No one could reproach me. I was her husband.

At that second I was sitting upright at the end of the couch, looking at her, and bending to breaking point a paper-knife between my burning fingers. The next I had thrown myself forward on her. Mv arms were round her. Her face looked up at me from the couch. I seemed to see it through a mist. The lips were faintly smiling, the eyes were luminous with a new light. She gave herself to me willingly. As she had said, my will was hers. Her conscience, also, she was content for me to guard. What I did was right. And it was this that saved me. Had she resisted me in the least, that resistance would have challenged the brute force within me, that longs to dominate by force. Her passivity, her trust in me spoke to the mind that seeks its victories in other ways.

After all, what would this pleasure be in which the soul could not share? Nothing would give me the real joy of possession, but the future. I let her fall from me suddenly, and drew back.

She put her hands over her face and burst into tears.

"Forgive me," I said. " It is so hard to keep one's self-control unbroken. And never speak to me again about other women. If you had any idea of all I suffer on your account, you would know it was quite unnecessary to be jealous of any others."

"I am so sorry," Anna sobbed from the couch; " but, do you wish"

"I don't wish," I said, coldly. In fact the reaction was so strong that ice seemed to have replaced the fire in my veins of a moment ago. I sat down beside her, calmly now, and took her hand. " You know, as well as I do, what I really wish. In our final union I want you to come to me free of all previous ties. I want to be able to take you for my own, without a shadow between us. Nothing else will satisfy me. To take you now is but to discount our pleasure in the future. A pleasure which will bring no reproch with it, as it would now. The nominal right the law has given me is as nothing, to my view, beside the law of Nature. While you are bearing Gaida's child you are still his. I can not understand why I am so weak today. I do not think it will happen again."

That night I did not go to her room, but walked about until past midnight, and then went to my own former veranda room where the hot, sand-laden wind was driving through the slits of the jilmih, and threw myself on the cliarpoy of stretched canvas, beneath the windows; and, after an hour or two, fell into a restless, nervous sleep.

The following morning, when I woke in the narrow camp bed and looked round the bare, unfamiliar room, a curious sense of loss seemed to come over me. I got up and went to Anna's room, turning the handle of the door and going in; for the key was never turned against me. I went up to the bed where she was sleeping. It seemed that she had sobbed herself to sleep, for there were blue nnd scarlet patches round her eyes; marks which I knew the tears always left on her light skin. She opened her oyes after a minute, and there was a cry of delight as she saw me standing looking down at her. She stretched up her arms to me.

"Oh! I had such a wretched night without you. I couldn't sleep at all. And I did not like to go and try to find you. Please, come back to me. You will come tonight, won't you?"

And I promised I would.

Owing to our official rank in the station, we had incessant invitations and a great deal more society than we desired. I kept watch upon myself in all this time that I should not seem to be drawn away from Anna by all these social functions, most of which were forced upon me. I knew she was acutely sensitive; and, as she had given mg the index to her thoughts, I was put on my guard. I do not mean that she was tiresomely or childishly jealous. She never sought to bar me from other women, quite thfo contrary; and if I expressed the most casual admiration for any particular one of the station's favorites, that one was always invited by Anna to the house. She herself would often urge me to accept invitations I should have declined.

"You must get tired of being so much with me," she would say. " Do go, if you like, and see any of these people."

But, as a matter of fact, I seldom wanted to leave her. Most people nearly everybody seemed to bore me and tire me; and it was always with a sense of relief and pleasure that I came back from them to her.

The passion that we had for each other was a passion of the brain, as much or more than one of the senses; and no amount of custom, no time, no familiarity, had any effect-on that, except to strengthen it. All physical pleasures de cline with gratification; but those of the brain increase. When the body is hungry, food satisfies and then stops ite hunger. How different is the brain when hungry foi knowledge! The learning and study given to it as food ut terly fail to satisfy. They do no more than stimulate an increased craving.

Before our marriage I had been content to sit with Anna through a whole evening; because, for one reason, she made a very beautiful picture sitting opposite me, and my sense of vision had been delighted and satisfied. That was one reason, but not the only one. The far stronger one was that my brain was moved and fired by all she said; it was satisfied and delighted by her presence, just as my eyes by her face. And now that the lines of beauty in her form were blurred and distorted, when only a pale face met my eyes, it was still a keen pleasure to return and sit opposite her; keener far than any afforded me by the pink cheeks, the idiotic babble and senseless giggle of the belle of the station. And I was inexpressibly thankful, sometimes, that no evil fate had thrown one of these to my lot as a life's companion. One may gaze on a pink cheek fo-half an hour; one may listen to babble for an hour; one may stand insensate giggling even for two; but in days and weeks and months and years, how shall these satisfy all the longing, straining, striving, restless, nameless desires of the human brain?

The curious, or what to most men may seem the curi ous, part of our existence now was, that as weeks passed on and Anna's condition became evident, it drew me ti her, rather than repelled me. I became infinitely attached to her, and more and more in proportion as I sa. v the situation grew more depressing and terrible to her. She entirely lost her health; and, as she said to me one-morning, she only awoke now to suffer. But with that loss of health, with long hours of pain, periods of sickness and weary, restless nights, came none of that peevishness and irritable fretfulness that most women combine with their suffering. Anna's nature seemed to become sweetei and gentler, the greater the strain that was put on it; and the yielding, unquestioning docility and tenderness she had always displayed toward me, linked themselves now to an almost painful humility,

I saw, as plainly as if the thoughts that came and went in her brain were visible objects, that she dreaded, in her ill health and in this strange position, to become repellent to me. That she felt in some way my debtor, and to show her gratitude, in some way to make even the score she fancied was so much against her, she made use of all the seductive charm that was her gift from Nature. She never complained; it was only from my own observation that I knew how much she suffered, both mentally and physically, but far more the former than the latter. And this suffering united her to me in a far greater degree than the loss of all her physical charm could sunder her. I loved her infinitely more now, and could be far more tender and patient than in the time before our marriage, when, so to speak, she was arrayed with Gaida against me. Now she was suffering with me, and she and I were arrayed together against a common sorrow. The sight of her bearing a long punishment, day by day, wiped out utterly from my mind all remembrance of any fault she might ever have committed against me, roused all my sympathy and pity, and drew the deepest love out of the reserves of my nature. And, in spite of the religious scruples and moral ideas that opposed themselves to possession in the commonest acceptance of the word, yet, in the highest sense, I knew she was altogether my own. The passionate hate, that, she confessed to me, would rise in her, in spite of all her efforts, of the child she was to bear, seemed like a seal on her love for me. Moreover, it was ingrained in my nature to care for and lean toward anything that depended upon mo and clung to me; and Anna, nervous and excitable as she was, viewed her coming trial with a mental terror and turned to me continually for comfort, like a frightened child in the dark.

As day followed day, we were each more and more bound up in the other. Nature can make a habit of loving as she can of anything else. And with some temperaments as with mine love nourishes itself. It is the memory of what we have done for another, far more often than the memory of what that one has done for us, that softens us in reflection. And when love is poured out as mine for Anna, for one who longs for it, demands it, lives by it, and gives back tenfold, there is an intoxication and delight in the exchange, enough to fill two of the blankest lives.

Anna made such a wonderful companion. I had felt that she would do so, during all the time I had known her; but I had never realized what a mere, poor foreshadowing that broken-up companionship had been of the perfect, smooth, intimate union in the life lived day by day, night by night with her.

When she accompanied me to my office, I found she was of more use to me than my three clerks together. She had such a gift of grasping the sense and import of things. It was never any trouble to explain to her. Whatever mental nut, as it were, was offered to her, her intellect seemed to grip it at once and split it open; and the kernel, neat and round, was lying before you. I have found this to be a very rare gift. The brain that can do and create, can form ideas and hold opinions is less uncommon than the one which can really understand. As a rule, explaining to one's subordinate what has to be done and how it is to be done, is so much effort and attended with so little, success, that to do the work one's self is the lighter task. One day I had spent the whole morning in endeavoring to put my assistants in the way of making for me a precis of some native evidence, which was required for the following day; and the result was an intolerably confused document, utterly useless to me or the court. I told them to leave the matter alone; that I would see to it myself in the afternoon; and, having already an impossible amount of work on hand, that prospect did not improve my temper. Tired and savage, I drove home to luncheon, not without a delightful consciousness that for an hour at least I should have perfect rest and peace, arid found Anna, as usual, waiting in the cool, shaded dining-room. She came herself to my side and poured out some wine for me and asked me why I looked so tired; and, during luncheon, I told her. My nerves were shaken by overwork and the peculiarly irritating kind of work I had had that morning; and I upbraided the Government for giving me fools to work with, and lamented the idiocy of mankind in general and the hard fate that made me an Indian civil servant. Anna listened very quietly, making hardly any remark; which was wise, for any remark would have irritated me then. But when I had quite finished and was exhausted, she agreed with everything I had said, which is something; and sympathized with me in every look and tone, rather than in words, which is tranquillizing. When I rose, I said, remorsefully:

"I am sorry to have been so annoyed. I expect I spoiled your luncheon. You look very white. What have you been doing all the morning?"

And, indeed, her face had a settled look of pain on it, that was distressing.

"It is nothing much," she answered, smiling. " I have had a dreadful pain in my side, but it has gone off now. " Then she came close to me and said, timidly, "Please let me come down this afternoon and do the precis for you."

"Dear child," I said, gently, in surprise, "I don't think you can."

"Well, let me try."

"Come, by all means, if it will amuse you; but I am afraid you can't help me in any way."

Anna made no reply, but put on her hat with a delighted air; and we went out to the carriage and drove down to the city together. It was a pleasure to have her beside me. Even when she did not speak she looked intelligent; and I knew, if I spoke to her, I should meet with some other response than the bewildered and vaguely questioning " sahib?" of my clerks. When we reached the office I gave her a chair and a table to herself, in one corner, and piled on the latter the material from which the precis was to be made. Such a pile it was! Fragments of old, torn letters; a dying deposition taken in an opium den of the bazaar, and of which the paper was yellow with smoke and dirt; columns of notes taken from testimony in court, and loose odds-and-ends of papers of all sorts that might or might not probably not throw light on the case. All these in the native tongue Hindustani and written in the Hindustani character by hurried, careless, or inexperienced penmen. Anna looked over them coolly.

"Now, Gerald, tell me exactly what you want," she said, fixing her eyes on me, in which I noticed the pupils beginning to widen and dilate, as they always did with special activity of the brain. I explained to her what I wanted and the previous history of the case, and it seemed to take five minutes, whereas, in the morning, I had expended as many hours; and it was no trouble to explain to her, either. Her large, bright eyes seemed to lead one on. Her keenly interested voice: "Yes, I understand." "I see." " Go on," was encouraging. Her acute attention, absolutely given to the matter in hand, was inspiring. One seemed face to face with an intelligence; whereas, with most people, the fleshy screen between their brain and yours seems terribly thick.

"I understand it now," she said, finally. " I will work it out for you."

And I went over to my own desk. Four hours of the long, golden afternoon wore away in silence, and I managed to get through most of my own work. Then I looked over toward her and saw she was still absorbed. I leaned back in my chair and watched her. The table before her was a model of neatness and order. The papers had, apparently, been classified, and were now all ranged in separate piles. She was working on a large sheet before her. I got up and went over to her.

"Don't work too long upon that, You'll make yourself so tired," I said.

"Just finished," she answered as indeed she had and she blotted the last line and then gave me the five large sheets of the precis and leaned back in her chair with a laugh, to see my surprise and pleasure.

It was admirable. Every paper had been translated and the pith of each extracted and set down with perfect clearness. The letters and testimony were translated and copied with the greatest accuracy; and correct references had been put against each item, by which one could find at once the original.

"Thank you," I said, very earnestly. " You have done that wonderfully. Far quicker than I could. How have you attained such a faculty fur grasping things?"

"I don't know. I suppose I always had it. I remember my mathematical tutor said to me, when I was first learning Euclid, that I could always see the propositions quicker than any of his other pupils; and in reading Tacitus I often saw what the passage meant before the tutor did. Anyhow, I am awfully glad I helped you with the precis; and now let's go home. I want my tea."

The next day the deputy-judge complimented me on the " very masterly way in which the evidence had been condensed and reduced from a mass of confusion to a remarkably clear and lucid statement."

But it was not Anna's knowledge of Greek and Latin, nor even her capability of precis writing that made her so infinitely valuable to me each day of my life such an incident might only occur once in many months. It was her intense sympathy. A sympathy that emanated naturally from her, as perfume from a flower. And the fount of that sympathy was in those clever brains of hers. Now, the sympathy that comes from the brain as well as from the heart is infinitely more comprehensive and satisfying than that which comes from the heart only. That good-natnred sympathy that is offered sometimes by a warm heart beating in an uneducated person's breast! How often is it galling and irritating in the extreme! It is uncertain, also. It reaches out to a toothache and extends over bad colds and accidents. It stretches into the region of linseed poultices and physical comforts. But to those deeper wounds and keener pains of the soul it can not reach. To a brain like Anna's, there was nothing in the human emotions too difficult to understand. Knock in any way you would at the door of her soul, and it would always fly open to you immediately. She would never meet you with the blankj dull stare of hopeless non-comprehension. You knew she. would never disappoint you. The little troubles of life and the large, the physical pains and the mental, she could understand them all. All r. f I hem fr: m;, finger jammed in a door or an insult from the head of a department, to the loss of an appointment or the destruction of an art treasure came wiiliia her province cf sympathy. And, under her influence, I felt that my own character was changing too. Unconsciously to myself, at the time, I grew less selfish. It never seemed any trouble to do anything for her, she was so grateful; and, insensibly, her habit of throwing herself always into my mood, whatever it might be, and interesting herself in anything I was interested in, gradually taught me also that secret of sympathy with another that alone is capable of smoothing out the rugged lines of life. And in this way the weeks and month? passed by of not the happiest period, but still a happy one, of my existence. The cloud of the dread that I might so soon lose her, hung over it and obscured the sunshine. The last day of November came, and in this station of the plaina it was terribly hot and sultry. The air seemed to thicken and thicken, as night approached, until one felt suffocation in breathing it. Toward dark, as I was standing for a moment by an open window, watching the great tridenu of lightning playing on the horizon, Anna came up to me and touched my arm.

"Gerald, I am in such horrible pain," she whispered.

I turned instantly and looked at her. Her face wai white to the lips, and an ungoverned terror looked out of her eyes. I put my arm round her, and I felt she was trembling as one trembles in ague. As I drew her closei I could feel her heart was leaping in great, irregular beats her hands were cold and as wet as if they had been dipped in water.

"Hold me," she whispered. " I am so frightened. I don't know what it will be like. And the pain, Gerald, you have no idea; when it comes on, it is something beyond words; it annihilates one." Then putting her lips close on my ear, she murmured, "Oh, if it were only something I was bearing for you; if it was only pain that I was suffering for your sake, then I should delight in it!"

I pressed her to me in silence, too far moved for words, and she clung to me.

"I can't bear to inflict the sight of my pain on you; but but if you were wit. h me if you stayed with me, I should not be so afraid."

"Do you think I could be anywhere but with you, knowing you were suffering?" I answered. " Dear little girl, of course I will stay with you all the time."

She put back her head and looked at me, and her lips opened to answer me; then they twisted suddenly into a half-smothered groan of pain. I had one glance of fleeting terror from her eyes, and then she fell forward against me unconscious.

I carried her upstairs and laid her on her bed and summoned her own attendants, the nurse and the doctor, whom I had staying in the house with us. Then I sat down by the bed, holding her hand in mine and realizing that that little, helpless hand held the whole globe of the world in it for me.

"I don't think we shall need you, sir," said the English nurse.

"My dear fellow, you had better not stay here," urged the doctor.

"I intend to remain," I answered; and they said no more.

Through the whole of that terrible night I stayed beside her; and whose was the greater suffering, it would be hard to say. The physical agony dominated her completely; but she was still blindly conscious of the touch of my hand and of my presence, and kept the teeth on her lip till the blood came, to hold back her screams for my sake.

The long hours stretched out their moments to infinite length over their heads, and it seemed to me impossible that any human frame could wrestle with agony and withstand it for so long. It seemed as if, in those wild struggles, the soul must get loose, free itself, and fly from me. In the last moments of terror, when my own heart was beating in my throat in dread, she tore open her eyes and fixed them on me. The fear in them was heart-rending, yet not only fear was there. There was a desperate appeal to me for that help and comfort she always turned to me to gain. She told me afterward my face had given her strength and courage for the supreme effort. Just as the lawn broke over the plains and the first soft light crept tranquilly into that room of agony, her child was born, and she herself fell back nerveless, it seemed lifeless. I bent over her and she told me later that she had felt my face close above hers; that she had longed to open her eyes, to smile, to speak, to reassure me, to thank me; but that her power was gone. Not even strength remained to raise the eyelids; they lay like lead upon her eyeballs; her hand would not obey her desire to close it on mine. And while I heard a voice telling me she was alive and safe, she lay, pallid and motionless, with closed eyes before me. 1 stooped and kissed her; and, for the only time, there was no response.

CHAPTER XI.

A SQUAKE landing with a door half-open into a room full of daylight. A bed with its white curtains looked back, and Anna lying there half-raised upon one elbow, and the white light of morning striking on her rapt, downward-gazing face. I was crossing the outside landing, and I paused and looked in and then remained there.

That look of rapture on her face held me motionless, and even my heart-beats seemed to grow still as I watched her. On her left arm lay Gaida's child, asleep; and, unconscious of my presence, unconscious of all else in the world but it, she was gazing down into its face.

"My darling, my sweet love," I heard her murmur. " You are all my own! How good God has been to give you to me!"

She was silent for a moment, lost in contemplation; and then, suddenly, in a passion of delight, she threw herself forward on the child, covering it with her warm kisses.

The child awoke, and a feeble cry went through the room. Anna raised herself and shook back her long, shining hair, raising the child on one arin so that it was brought distinctly into my view, and a shudder went over me. It was hideous with that curious hideousness of aspect that belongs usually to the fruit of Eurasian marriages. As it lay on Anna's arm now, the peculiar whiteness of her skin threw up its dusky tint. Anna bent over it again, pressing her lips to its head, just darkened by the coming hair.

"Did its mother wake it, then?" she murmured, laughing, and stopping its cries by kisses on its eyes.

The child cried violently, and thrust its tiny hand up to the silken masses of her hair, and she threw her head back, laughing, and I saw her face gleaming with happy light And her lips parted in smiles and her eyes full of joy. Then, as the child continued to cry, she bent over and kissed it again, as if her lips could never be satiated, on its finy, struggling hands and feet, on the little, red knees, that kept drawing up, on its heaving chest and open, crying mouth; and all her face expressed passionate adoration, and all the movements of her body joyous emotion; and I atood still, without the open door, watching her, transfixed.

It seemed some strange illusion of the senses that I stood outside watching my Anna or, at least, the Anna that had been mine absorbed in this worship of another life; and I realized that I was face to face with Nature and her laws. In that small, dark object on the bed, that I could; rush with one hand, was made manifest a force before which I and my life and my love and service were as nothing. Anna was now a mother, and with her maternity had come the insensate idolatry, the passionate absorption of maternity; and those feeble fingers of the child, beating the air, would sweep from her heart the record of our love the love that had withstood all the blows that shame and sin and sorrow could hurl against it.

I stood, gazing on the scene before me, realizing that I was helpless; that, strong as I had been and as my love had been, for her sake, I was now in the presence of a force to which I must yield; for Nature's own hand was uplifted against me, and Anna and the child were but helpless exponents of her eternal laws. That the child was hideous horrible in its suggestion of mixed blood; horrible as the evidence of a passion long since dead, and from which she had, in suffering, freed herself made no difference to her blinded eyes. It was her child; and, blindly following the instinct grown up in her, she loved it to the exclusion of all else as the jealous maternal instinct commands.

Within the room all sound had ceased; for the mother had gathered the child to her bosom and opened her breast to it, and the light fell now on her head drooping over it, and her face was rapt and dreaming, as the small, dark mouth drew life from her breast.

I turned silently and descended the stairs with noiseless feet, and gained a lower room and sat down with my head upon my hands. This, then, was my hour of liberation. This was the hour of my reward. This was what I had waited for through all these mouths.

I recalled her fevered words to me only a week ago, uttered in a voice almost smothered in distress and shame.

"I shall hate it, Gerald, so much; I never want my eyes to rest on it. You will have it taken away from me at once, won't you? Sent away from me where I can never see it; and then I shall be all your own, and nothing can come between us any more."

That is what she had thought and fancied; and I, why had I not foreseen the truth? But I had not; and quitff suddenly, after the suffering and hoping and longing for months for our emancipation and reunion, when it came, this iron law had risen between us; and she went forward blindly where it directed, and I fell backward, unnoticed and forgotten.

She was not to blame. As the child had been the consequence of her passion for Gaida, so this new maternal passion was the consequence of the birth of the child. Thus the chain of the past goes on, ever stretching into the future.

Some days passed, and I existed in Anna's life as somo shadow, undefined, that an artist puts in the background of a scene. She lived in the child. She was not the least unkind or ungentle to me. When I spoke to her, she answered me without looking at me; and when I kissed her, she kissed me back with absent lips. She was apparently unconscious of me and my presence, except when her own worship of the child failed to satisfy her and she wanted others to be charmed by it and render it homage with herself, and then she would call me to the bedside to admire it and rejoice with her over it.

The child, as the days passed, lost a little of its first re-pulsiveness; and to no eyes but those that knew the secret of its birth would it have seemed different from a Euro pean's. I myself being so dark, the child was supposed to " favor me " and " resemble me;" and these phrases fell upon my ears many times in those long, empty days from Anna's friends that came to congratulate us. But these small stabs affected me little.

The one great grief encom- passed and numbed me, and I felt only it: that she was no longer mine. Far less so now than when her body belonged to another, but her mind to me. Now her mind was closed against me. She was still too frail and delicate for me to trust myself to enter into any discussion of the position with her; and I let day follow day, acquiescing in all she said and wished, and watched the color and life flowing back to her, which it did with marvelous rapidity. So that, while she nursed the child and it drew its life from hers, it seemed also as if, in some subtle way, she received back from it more than she gave; and her face grew more brilliant and her laughter lighter and stronger each day.

And I watched her and waited and said nothing, asking mvself a thousand times a day, "What should I do?"

For herself, she seemed completely to have forgotten all that she had begged and entreated of me before the child was born. All the arrangements that had been made for its care and future home, far from Anna, 1 canceled without consulting her. She never alluded to them. All the frenzy of hate she had expressed to me in shamed whispers, seemed like something I must have heard in a dream. The child's actual presence had effaced, apparently, all those months and the feelings that belonged to them, as if they had never been.

One day, when a little over a month had passed since the birth of the child, I was sitting in my study at work, when she sent down for me and asked me to come to her. I went at once with my heart beating. It was possible, I thought, that the first abandonment of maternal love was past, and she wanted to take me back into her thoughts and life. Perhaps I had been unjust and impatient in my judgment of her. If, in the first blindness and intoxication of her love, she had passed me over and neglected me, it was wholly natural and to be forgiven; but now it was over, and she had remembered me.

With hope in my eyes and heart, I knocked gently at her closed door, and in answer to her gay " Come in " I entered, and all the hope died out. She had, apparently, been dressing the child, for the room was littered with lace and linen and veils, and the child itself was supported by cushions in its bassinette, and sat up like a doll in a yoluminous cloud of muslin. With her head half-turned backward to the cradle, she came to the door and took my hand and drew me over to it.

' Look, Gerald; doesn't he look lovely in his new clothes? Isn't he a darling?"

I stood silent and rigid by the cot. "What a bitter thing is jealousy! And that first deadly sip of it that we take from the cup, generally held to our lips by the hands we have loved and trusted till then that is the worst moment. That surpasses in pain the tragedies and open warfare that may come afterward. That first moment of tasting it, which we do with smiling lips because (re will not admit, we do not know, we are poisoned; that is the worst.

' Don't you like him in this new dress?" she pursued, not heeding me, but stooping over the cradle to tie a ribbon by the child's shoulder. " Gerald, I never was so utterly, so perfectly happy as I am now. I never could have believed 1 could be so happy." She finished tying the bow and rose from her knees. " Isn't he sweet?" she said, drawing off a little way and regarding him. " Don't you want to kiss him? You may, if you like," she added, laughing joyously.

Still I could not speak nor move. I seemed bound there and voiceless, and I suppose my silence penetrated at last even her self-absorption. She looked up suddenly in mj face. I do not know what she may have read there, but she gave a little cry and pushed me from the cradle.

"Gerald, you're jealous."

I turned away to the window and put my arms on the edge of the open j Until and said nothing. Words seemed so inadequate. The situation seemed so cruel beyond all hope.

"Gerald!"

There was astonishment, anger, reproach in her voice, and it stung me beyond endurance.

I turned and faced her.

Anna," I said, and the tone was the hardest and sternest she had ever heard from me, " there is no need to educate you in the emotions, surely, or has your maternity quite blinded and changed you and swept away your intellect entirely?"

Anna stood facing me with wide-opn eyes and a gradually blanching face. At first she did not seem to under- stand, and her eyes kept their usual expression now, of seeming to look at without seeing me. But'after a few minutes the expression grew more conscious, then keenly so, and at last sorrow, sympathy, and contrition rushed over it together.

"What have I done?" she said. " Have I been very selfish? Have I been unkind to you?"

She was awakened now, and her eyes no longer looked past me, but hard into mine. She stretched out her hands pleadingly, and her lips opened and quivered questioning-ly. I took her hands and drew them gently to my breast.

"Have you forgotten all we said a little over a month ago, and how we have both waited for our perfect union till now; and now, have we been nearer together or farther apart just lately? Have I been taken more into your life or less?"

There was a long silence. And it seemed to me that the old Anna, that had (belonged to me, was struggling to awake in this new Anna that belonged to her child. Then at last she said, brokenly and suddenly:

"I understand. Yes, Gerald, I remember; but when it came it was all so different. It seemed I never could have meant all I had said. And I thought you understood, too. And now, what can I do? I do love it so. Even il I tried, I could not conceal that love from you. The child is between us, I see it; but what can I do?"

"Nothing," I said, bitterly; " there is nothing to be done."

And I went away out of the room, leaving her standing in the center of the tumbled dolls' clothes, and the child in the bassinette at her side. I feared I might say something of which I should repent, and I went out and rode across the desert until it was late afternoon. When I returned, Anna's ayah was sitting on my library door-mat waiting for me.

"The Mem Sahib has been crying, crying all the afternoon," she said, " and told me to find the sahib and send him to her when he returned."

I went up the few short stairs without waiting for another word and entered the room alone. It seemed empty; but a little, glad cry guided me to the bed. Anna lay in it, white and exhausted. She stretched out her arms toward me as I approached and whispered as I bent over her:

"All this is so dreadful. We must do something."

I sat down beside the bed holding one of those very, very slim, delicate hands in mine, whiter almost than the embroidery of the sleeve above it. The child lay sleeping on the other side.

"It is another of those great, invisible, iron laws that we have stumbled against, that gird this life all round and make it what it is," I said, wearily. " It is natural for a mother to love her child; that is the law, and it is not our fault that this terrible position has grown up. We did not either of us foresee it, and it is simply the working out of all that has gone before."

She was looking at me intently. I sat facing the window, and the vivid glory of tawny light flung up from the desert came in upon my face. She seemed to see something there that arrested her eyes beyond removing.

"Gerald," she said at last, " in return for all you have done for me always, I am killing you."

I smiled a faint, weary smile. I could not contradict her. In truth, more than half of me seemed dead already.

"It is not your fault. These laws are greater than we we."

There was a long silence, and the tawny light died away autside and within, and then, out of the gray shadows, came her voice:

"I will be above the law for your sake."

I smiled again. When we are young, we all talk lightly Df the laws of life, even when we recognize their existence at all, which we generally do not do until we have stumbled against them in the dark and fallen back crushed and bleeding. As we grow older we know more and speak less lightly. I pressed her hand and rose.

"Go to sleep, dear child, and grow well and strong again, and do not try to arrange life. Life is stronger than you."

I was about to turn and leave her, but she called me back.

"Come here. Bend down and look at me." I did as she asked, and the fire of those eyes burned into mine. " Do you forget that I am Anna Lombard, and I love you, I love you, I have always loved you? I understand everything. You shall have the reward of your long, long service. The law shall break to give it to you."

I thought she was excited and light-headed. I stooped. ind kissed her.

"Try to sleep. Whatever happens, one law will always remain. I shall always love you."

And I left her and walked down to the lower room and then on to the veranda, where I sat gazing out over the desert with unseeing eyes.

"What should I do?" I asked myself. " How should I dispose of my life?" It seemed but a battered remnant that was left me. Take that in my hand and go with it whither? It was impossible to stay living on beside Anna, seeing her wholly devoted to and wrapped up in the child. I had tried a similar experiment that had left me dying at ipeshawur once before. And then there had been hope. Now there was none, I saw clearly, and refused to be deceived. This was a growing evil; one that would grow with the child's life, expand and blossom with its growth. It would absorb the whole of that passionate soul, once my own, that seemed to know no limit between affection and adoration. No, I would not undertake it. I would not allow it to enter my thoughts as a possible consideration. The only thing to be settled was to provide comfortably for Anna and her child and leave them both. Life stretched before me as dreary as the desert itself. Something of the old feeling I had had before I met her, was with me now; only then it had been mixed with the freshness and vigor of unsullied youth and the impatience and fever of overmuch strength. Now it was mixed with the dreadful languor of exhaustion. Life had caught me in its vise and wrung and twisted and bruised and battered me so, that I felt as an old, old man.

The next two or three days I noticed a change in Anna. She grew extremely grave and silent; never addressing me in any way, and starting visibly when spoken to. She seemed to have awakened from the ecstatic dream that the realization of her maternity had plunged her into. She gazed long and earnestly at my face whenever I was with ner, as if trying to read the solution of the problem she was studying there; and I noticed an effort to conceal the child from me, whenever I approached. She spoke no more to it nor of it in my presence, and her eyes were shaded and darkened with the shadow of heavy thought.

From all of this I drew a sad satisfaction. She was, at jeast, something more of my Anna again. She was no longer merely the absorbed mother, seeing and recognizing nothing but her child's face and hearing nothing but her child's voice. She was again allowing me some share in her thoughts; though what that share was and in what kind of thoughts, I had no idea, and she gave me no clew. I saw her look at me long and hungrily as I sat beside her, and then turn her eyes toward the little hump under the sheet where the child lay; but she would not answer me when I questioned her as to her thoughts, though once she burst into passionate tears and begged me to leave her room. I divined that she, like myself, was gazing into the dark mirror of the future and, like myself, shrinking from what it held for us we who had really loved. Perhaps I ought to have known what all this portended and Been where it was leading her. But not the faintest foreshadowing or premonition of the truth was vouchsafed to me. Nor should I have been able to influence her nor prevent what followed, had I been forewarned. In that singularly soft and gentle temperament there existed an underlying force and violence which, when aroused, dominated irresistibly everything opposed to it. During those few days I, too, was preoccupied with the problem my own future offered; but 1 saw in a dim way, that became clearer to me afterward, that she was wrestling in the throes of some terrible struggle with herself.

One evening, toward sunset, when the day's work was over, I was sitting alone, as usual now, in my library. A. nna and the child were upstairs. Since the day when,8he had looked into my face and read everything there, all her rapid convalescence, all that exuberant rebuilding of Nature had suddenly stopped. She had gone steadily backward, and lay now, day after day, pale and silent on her bed. I felt guilty and reproached myself. I should have withdrawn from her when I was no longer needed and left her to this new joy which had filled her life. Yet even that could not have been done without explanation and understanding. But I felt I had awakened her too roughly. Why does it seem fated, I asked myself, when one strives and strives to do well for another, that there should be always some moment of weakness, of selfishness that overtakes one and undoes all that one has done? I saw now clearly that the old love, reawakened in her heart, was battling there with the new and tearing her between them ii the struggle, just as in former times. Surely the best that I could do was to leave her to the fulfillment of the natural law and the natural destiny of women; to withdraw myself now, and so end the struggle for her. To that I must summon my strength. And yet, as I realized it realized that I was to finally renounce this thing that had teen my pleasure and my pain, my anguish and delighi and, through all, so entirely my own I shrunk back dis-Biayed. What should we be, one without the other; we, whose every thought even had been divided and shared? She was interwoven with me in such intimacy that to leave her, to lose her, seemed as impossible and absurd as if my right arm could drop from me and assume a life of its own. I looked up at her portrait on the wall and met the strangely powerful, gleaming eyes through the dusk, and iid to myself aloud in the silence:

"This impossible thing is to be!"

There was a step behind me, a movement in the room, fnd I turned and saw that Anna had entered. She came: lose up to me, and quickly, like some one who has a message to deliver. When she was directly in front of me she atopped and lifted her face. I bent forward, and a whisper I could hardly hear went through the room.

"I have expiated my sins to you, at last. I have killed it."

"Killed what?" I said in a vague horror.

Her words conveyed no sense to me.

"I have killed the child."

She said it very simply and naturally. I searched her Jface with terror. I thought she had lost her reason. But there was no insanity in that countenance, only a dreadful grief and sorrow, pathetic, tear-filled eyes and quivering ips that could hardly frame the words. Before I could peak, before I could collect my thoughts or realize it all, nhe went on:

"I saw all. It was all revealed to me in a sudden flash of light. I saw all your feelings these last weeks. I looked back through all the previous months; then I looked into the future and saw what that would be. One had to be sacrificed, either you or the child. And could it be you? Was this to be your reward for all yt u have done and suffered for my sake? Had it lived, it would have taken all my life. Now my grief will take me for a fe months. Spare me to it for that time; and then, after that, I am all your own, forever and ever. While you live, I will live for you and in you; and when you die, I will die with you."

She spoke in a trembling voice, and her face was wet with the streaming tears that welled inexhaustibly out of her eyes. She took one of my hands and kissed it witli cold lips, wet with tears. I stood still, dazed, horrified, frozen. What had she done? Was it all true and real or was she raving?

"What have you done?" I said, hoarsely. " I don't understand. Where is the child? Let me see it."

"Come upstairs," she said, simply, and turned to the staircase, and I followed as in a dream.

When we reached the landing at the head of the stairs I stopped still; a sort of numbness came over me. I felt I could not face what lay before me in the room. Then, as in a vision, I saw Anna turn back and take my hand and lead me into the room. It was only half-lighted; everything was dim, except the white charpoy in the center, and on it lay the child, as I had often seen it sleeping. Anna drew me forward, and lifting one of my hands when we stood beside the bed, laid it on the child's forehead. It was quite cold. I looked at it. The dusky, little form looked very, very small and helpless now. Yet what a terrible power it had possessed in life, a power before which our full lives had been as nothing, because Nature had invested it with the power of her law. Then I looked at the mother. Anna's eyes were fixed upon me with a devouring anxiety in them. In the dusk we looked at each other over the tiny, quiet form of the child. Then she stretched out her hands to me.

"Gerald, you do understand? I have done this foi you."

And I whispered back, "Yes, I understand."

And our hands touched each other's and there was silence. The room was very quiet and the dusk grew deeper and deeper round us. At last, in the darkness, Anna's voice broke out with a great cry, as she slipped to her knees beside the bed.

"Oh, how could I do it? It was my own, dear, little child, and I loved it so!"

JUST a week had passed over, a horrible week like a nightmare; but it had passed and left me and Anna if this frail, attenuated specter were really Anna alone in the bungalow, as in former times. There was no other presence; no call to summon her from my side; no duties to take her from me; no small, clinging vine running over the tree of our love and stifling it. Anna, or her sad shadow, was my own again. She was sitting opposite mo in the veranda, a thin, narrow figure in black, with all hei hair put back from her face, that was colorless and death like as a nun's.

She sat with her hands stiff and white in her lap and hen eyes looking out vacantly into the sunshine.

"I want you to go away for a time, Gerald," she wae saying. " I want to try and understand things. I want to lead the life of a penitent. I want to feel sure, before I can begin to be happy again, that G-od understands and forgives it all. It seemed right to me at the time; bui now now, I don't know." She paused a minute or two, and then went on, "You know, when the doctor came and questioned me about the child's death, and I said I must have suffocated it beneath me while I slept, then it came home to me. I felt I was guilty and I was. What a mist of lies grew up round me, and this grief great God 1 that is so real, it is killing me, even that seems all untrue and unholy, because every one believes it is grief for what I could not help, not for my own deed."

I was silent. What could I answer her?

"And I should like to be quite alone to pray and pray and pray and fast and think and get near again to God, as I have always felt I have been in my life; and whatever I have done, I have never done what thought wrong. I have never felt that God was angry with me. Now I foel so lost, so alone."

Her voice shook and dropped. I went over to her and stood by her.

"I am here," I said, gently.

"Yes, dear Gerald, I know; but the soul is a thing apart and has a life of its own, an utterly separate life that belongs to God, and no mortal can come into it. To my brain and heart and body you are all, but to my soul you are nothing. It does not know you nor recognize you. In the hour of my death, though your arms hold me and your love is all round me and your lips on mine, yet my soul will slip away from you into the darkness all alone." We were both silent, and the horror of this life and death seemed all round us, glaring at us from out of the gold sunlight. " And so," she went on, after a pause, with an effort, " if I have done wrong, I want to repent. I want to get back that peace of mind, that unity with God I always had before. Will you go and leave me for a time?"

"I will always do whatever you ask me, you know; but. why send me away now of all times? I ought to be witb you, surely."

Anna shook her head.

"No; I shall think too much of you, become too much drawn into your love, become too comforted and consoled. I must be alone, and suffer and work out eome sort of repentance for myself which will be accepted, and I shall be forgiven." She looked hard into iny face and then murmured, in her old, tender tones, "I know it is hard upon you, too. But it is only one little trial more, one sorrow to bear for a time, for I feel God means you to be happy. As for me, I deserve nothing; but he will forgive me, perhaps, for your sake, and let me be at last an instrumeul of happiness to you; but it can not be just yet. Leave me to suffer a little while. Be patient, just a little white longer."

I looked down at her; at the emaciation of the figure IL its close, black dress; at the fragility of the hand which 1 held in mine; at the white transparency of the face; at the eyes that were dry now, worn out with excessive weeping.

"Anna, I can't leave you like this!" I exclaimed. ' More suffering, more sorrow, and you will go from me altogether."

She shook her head, and a little smile that was full of power came into her face.

"No, I think not. I shall try to live, to 4o better than I have done. Only leave me to myself."

"But for how long?" I asked, desperately.

"I think it should be a year," she said in a low tone and with downcast eyes.

I groaned.

"A year! Exile for a year! But why Anna, it s absurd!"

"If I should feel I were forgiven sooner, I would write to you," she answered in a low voice. " But oh, Gerald! don't make it harder for me than it is!" she cried, suddenly, with a rush of tears. " Help me to do something which I think is right. Think what I am, what I have done."

"Dear child, your will is mine. It has always been, you know. Tell me when you wish me to go and when to return and it shall be so."

She was leaning back against me, exhausted.

"Go to-morrow," she whispered, faintly, " and come back when I send to you,"

"It will seem so strange," I murmured, mechanically. " What will every one say to see you alone, and I"

A ghost of a mocking smile came to her lips and eyes.

"Have we ever cared what they said?" she whispered.

And the following day I went into exile. These things are easy to arrange when one is in high places and money is at hand.

Anna's good-by to me was pitiful, pathetic as the young nun's to her parents when she has renounced the world; but it was as pure and unimpassioned.

Passion to her suddenly seemed revealed as a sin. It jarred with her grief, and she shrunk from the kiss of my lips and turned hers away.

After I had left her I recalled the parting with wonder; and it seemed as if the Anna Lombard I had known had vanished with the death of the child into the past.

For a whole year I stayed away in exile. I had plenty of work, for I only exchanged stations; and in one a thousand miles away I went through the same duties I had in my own. But my inner life seemed at a standstill. My own pleasure was dead. Anna had so long been the center of my thoughts that when that was cut away they seemed unable to rally round any other object. I saw other women and met them and danced with them and dined with them, but I felt as a deaf man at an opera. Some idle show is passing before his eyes which means nothing to him and can not reach him through his closed ears. I lived in the moment when I should return to her and in her let- ters. They were not very frequent, and they were subdued, even a little cold; but I felt in them a growing confidence in herself, a tone of increasing peace and calm, and I was satisfied. She was really working out her repentance, and when that was accomplished I knew she would summon me to her. Her past had been another's and her present was now her own; but her future belonged to me, I knew. And I waited and kept my patience. At last the summons came. It was very short.

"I believe I am forgiven, and that it is right to recall you. Come back to me. ANNA." j

And that same night I started to return. A heavy, sullen, orange sun was hanging low in the western sky over the rolling plains, as I rode from the station toward the bungalow on the third day. The light, parched dust rose in little whirls before me, as the hot desert wind ran over it and licked it up here and there. Otherwise there was no moving thing, and the silence was complete except for the thudding of my own heart as we rode forward. I wondered how she would receive me, and I remembered how I had left her. Was I coming back to that same black-robed penitent? Was the old, loving, impetuous, erring Anna shut away from me, forever, behind the invisible door of the past? It was fated, apparently, that I should love her through all time and metamorphoses; but my heart sunk as I thought of those firm, red lips faded to a nun-like paleness; and that curling, amorous hair, that held the changing lights, subdued beneath a veil, as I had seen it last; and all the buoyant passions of her nature tamed and put to sleep.

A chill seemed to surround me in the midst of the hot breath of the desert, and the huge burnished disk ahead of me sunk lower in the mist.

As the last long undulation of the sandy plain was surmounted, the roof of the white bungalow and the encircling palms rose into sight; and, drawing my breath almost still, I urged the horse forward.

There was no sign of life, as I approached. I descried the long windows of the upper story and the covered balcony where the child had slept. The garden beneath bloomed like one single rose in its wealth of blossom, and a cool air came from it and diffused its fragrance. I drew ny horse in at the compound gate; and at that instant there was a step upon the gravel, and I turned and saw her.

A figure in white with the sunlight in the eyes and hair. It was the same Anna Lombard I had left a maidea sleeping in the garden. Only now it was Anna awakened, with the look behind the eyes of one who has read all the secrets of life, and the look above the brows of one who has met life and conquered it.

She ran down toward me with feet that hardly touched the ground; then, when a few paces from me, she stopped, a, nd with one turn of her hand brought over her shoulder the bright, shining twist of hair that had captured my senses long ago, and she paused, gazing at me, expectantly.

"Do 1 please you?" she whispered.

Her eyes were shining, her wnole face was lighted from within, her body seemed expanding and dilating with the force of her nervous joy. She had in those moments a beauty beyond description. My eyes swam as I looked at her.

"Dearest Anna, you are beautiful; but it is not for these things that I love you, you know."

"I know, I know," she murmured, throwing herself into my arms, putting her own soft ones about my neck, a, nd pressing the rose of her mouth against my cheek. " But you are human and you like to have them, and I am human and I like to give them, and we have both suffered so much no one would grudge us our happiness now. Oh, I have so prayed for God to give me back my good looks to reward you with, and that he has done so is a sign of his forgiveness; don't you think so?"

And I answered, softly, "Yes, dear."

THE END.

A Sealed Book

By ALICE LIVINGSTONE 12mo. cloth, 8 full-page illustrations. 'Price 1.50

The story positively bristles with incident. The Academy. Miss Alice Livingstone shows a fertile imagination and remarkable ingenious constructive gift. The Gazette. A powerful story of crime and cruelty is Alice Livingstone's latest novel "A Sealed Book," which is one of the most striking tales of the year. The volume abounds with thrilling situations. It grips the interest and keeps it up until the end. 'Che Journal. We can thoroughly recommend "A Sealed Book".

'Cbc Qraphic.

This novel has what is called in theatrical posters " a strong heart interest". "Uhe Leader.

To read this novel is a pleasure, indeed. It is full of exciting incidents, and is powerfully written. Narrative succeeds narrative in such a way that the authoress retains hold of her reader until the last page is reached. "A Sealed Book" takes a front position in this season's fiction. Courier. Cleverly written, strong in plot and in character drawing. It is endowed with a measure of originality in con-truction and treatment that should win for it a wide public. The author, it seemes to us, has 'Hit her best work into this story. CVie JXCail.

It is an excellent tale of its kind highly exciting. The Globe. Deeply interesting. 'Post Crowded with incidents, crammed full of varying scenes.

The Sportsman.

Exceptionally powerful. One never tires of a single page.

Courier.

R. F. Fenno Company
Miscellaneous
THF WAHFS nf SIN to LUCAS MALET inej WAOILrtd OJ OHM (Mrs. M. K. Harrison) Special illustrated large type edition. Cloth, gold stamping
Size5Xx7 4: Price 1.50
Pipe Dreams and Twilight Tales by BIRDSALL JACKSON 12mo. Cloth Price 1.25
How to Succeed by AUSTIN BIERBROWER
Small 12mo. Cloth Price 1.00 " Small 12mo. Cloth Price30cto.
Fate Mastered ly W. J. COLVILLE
Universal Spiritualism by w j COL VILLE
Strong as Death ly GUY DE MAUPASSANT 12mo. doth Price 1.50 12mo. Cloth Price 1.00
The Santiago Campaign by MAJ. GEN. JOSEPH WHEELER,
Quarto, Cloth, with Maps Price 2.50,
BOOKS ly W R MALL 0 s
IS LIFE WORTH LIVING?. 1 2mo. Price 1.00 A ROMANCE OF THE 19th CENTURY I2rao. Price 1.00 PROPERTY AND PROGRESS. 12mo. Price 1.00
Miscellaneous
Anglo-Saxon Superiority ty EDMOND DEMOLINS
I2mo. Cloth.
Price SI. OO
Toor of His Soul by ZOE ANDERSEN NORRIS 12mo. cloth, in a box Price 1.00
Seven Smiles and
A Few Fibs
THOMAS J. VIVIAN 16mo. cloth. Price 75 cts.
Everything
Our New Possessions by VIVIAN and SMITH
Small 12mo. Cloth Price 60 cts.
John Jasper's Secret
SEQUEL TO EDWIN DROOD 12mo. cloth
Price 125
BOOKS fc
A. VAN DER NAILLEN
On the Heights of Himalay In the Sanctuary. Balthazar the Magus 12mo. Cloth. Price 1.25 12mo. Cloth. Price 1.25 12mo. Cloth. Price 1.50
Letters of a Business Woman to Her Niece
BY CAROLINE A. RULING
Editor of The BOOKSELLER and Latest Liter Mturt
These letters were published serially in an Eastern Magazine, attracting considerable attention and adding materially to its circulation. They embody suggestions in the preparation for business life, getting and keeping a position, ethics, dress, conduct, the investment of savings and the management of a business, getting and giving credit and other important matters of which young women are generally ignorant. There is nothing of this nature on the market, and a large sale is anticipated for the book. Miss

Huling has utilized the experiences of twenty years in business life, in these letters which are designed to be helpful to younger women.

Handsomely bound in doth, and neatly boxed for presentation purposes, iamo. in size, 1.00 net.

R. F. F E N N O CO., 18 East iyth Street New York

Lightning Source UK Ltd.
Milton Keynes UK
UKHW010855240419
341527UK00001B/292/P